# Sinful Revenge

## JANE BLYTHE

 Formatted with Vellum

# Acknowledgments

I'd like to thank everyone who played a part in bringing this story to life. Particularly my mom who is always there to share her thoughts and opinions with me. My wonderful cover designer Letitia who did an amazing job with this stunning cover. My fabulous editor Lisa for all the hard work she puts into polishing my work. My awesome team, Sophie, Robyn, and Clayr, without your help I'd never be able to run my street team. And my fantastic street team members who help share my books with every share, comment, and like!

And of course a big thank you to all of you, my readers! Without you I wouldn't be living my dreams of sharing the stories in my head with the world!

# CHAPTER

*One*

January 9th
10:13 P.M.

Blade ran through the forest, leaving his team behind.

The cold night air cooled his overheated skin, and he barely felt the pain in his body from the explosion.

They'd all been lucky to survive it, and while he was used to having his team at his back, they were where they needed to be right now.

Rose was still unconscious from whatever drugs the man Dragon had just killed had given her. Cassandra might have been conscious enough to fight back and run, but there were still drugs in her system as well. Plus, both women were injured from the explosion they'd all been caught up in.

Since they couldn't be positive that the mercenary who had tried to abduct Rose and Cassandra didn't have a partner, although it seemed unlikely because surely the partner would have stepped in when Cassandra ran, splitting up the two women, he wanted the remainder of his team with the women.

Not because they were women and therefore less capable, but because one was unconscious and the other had been seconds away from getting raped. They needed support, and the rest of his team needed to get them out of there and someplace safe, because the cops were on their way.

Besides, Steel wouldn't leave Rose right now, and Dragon was every bit as protective over Cassandra. With their focus on the women who had captured their hearts, they needed Thunder, Lion, and Voodoo to watch over all of them.

Which just left him to go after whoever he'd heard moving through the forest.

Not that he minded. Blade had a pretty good idea of who he was chasing. It was absolutely true that if the mercenary who wanted to collect the money for delivering Cassandra to Dr. Ridge Gardner was working with a partner, then that partner would have shown up before now. Cassandra running had left Rose alone in the van, a partner would have stood by and watched over one of their captives, while the now dead man had gone after the other.

Ruling that out left only two other options.

One was that the person running was the crazed scientist responsible for injecting him and the rest of his team with experimental drugs. While those drugs had given them enhanced skills, they'd also messed with their ability to feel and process emotions normally, stripping them of a conscience.

The only problem with that scenario was that they'd just laid a trap for Dr. Gardner a little over a week ago, using the man's sister as bait. They'd killed every single one of the armed guards the doctor had brought with him, and the only reason the doctor himself had escaped was because Steel had chosen to save Rose's life rather than go after the man they all wanted dead more than they wanted their next breath of air.

Only that wasn't quite true anymore.

Steel wanted Rose more than he wanted revenge.

Dragon wanted Cassandra more than he wanted revenge.

Where that left his team, Blade wasn't quite sure. But he was sure that if it was Dr. Gardner he could hear out in the forest, then the man would have come with a small army because he knew it was his only chance at getting them back alive.

And he wanted them alive.

According to a woman who had accosted Cassandra at the park a week ago, Dr. Gardner needed them back if he wanted to create more super soldiers. Blade and his team were the only ones who had survived the anger and suicidal thoughts that came as a result of the drugs. Apparently, the doctor had figured out a way to reverse what he'd done and intended to do it, then study them, then inject them all over again.

It was their worst nightmare.

Becoming lab rats all over again.

But if the woman was to be believed, that was what would happen if they got caught. Whether they believed her or not didn't really matter, Blade had no intention of once again becoming a test subject. Those three years he and his team had spent locked inside a glass cage, constantly observed and studied, had been a hell he'd rather die than endure again.

Since there was no army on his tail, none that had come searching for them in the rubble of the warehouse linked to the company that paid off the mercenaries after Cassandra, none that had accosted them as they searched the forests, he had to assume it wasn't Dr. Gardner he was following.

Nope.

It was *her*.

The mystery woman.

If Cassandra hadn't spoken to her, and there was no doubt she had since Cassandra had known things about what happened to him and the rest of Prey Security's Delta Team that she could only have learned from someone involved, then he'd be tempted to believe this woman didn't even exist. But not only had Cassandra spoken to her, but Dragon, stalker that he was, had watched the whole thing on his tablet after hacking into CCTV cameras.

Despite knowing this mystery woman was a real flesh-and-blood person, they hadn't been able to identify her. It was like she didn't exist, even though they knew she did. They had nothing to go on to figure out who she was and where to find her, despite searching every database they could get their hands on.

This woman was the key to unraveling everything. Blade knew she was. All he had to do was get his hands on her. Once he had her, he wouldn't hesitate to do whatever it took to get the answers he and his team needed to finally be free.

For ten years, they'd plotted revenge.

Three of those held as prisoners, another seven trying to rebuild their lives as they searched for the name of the man responsible for what had been done to them.

The only thing that had gotten him through this last decade was the men he considered his family. Not the one he'd long ago left behind, but the members of his team were every bit as much his brothers as the ones who shared his DNA.

Now that family was growing. Steel had fallen for Dr. Gardner's sister, a woman they'd abducted and intended to use as a lure to get to the crazy scientist. Dragon had fallen for Cassandra while she stayed with them as her family hunted for the people after them, and recently embraced his second chance.

With two more members of the Delta Team family, it felt even more imperative to finally find Dr. Gardner and end his life. Only then would they be free enough to embrace a future that could be anything they wanted it to be.

"Which is why you're not getting away, darlin'," he drawled to the quiet forest.

Quiet to others but not to him. His enhanced hearing meant he heard everything. *Everything*. Which wasn't always as great as it seemed. Hearing everything happening around him, the beating of hearts, the inhale of air into lungs, the flow of blood passing through veins and arteries, every word, whispered or not, was exhausting.

Utterly exhausting.

The only way he survived the day-to-day barrage of sounds was to use noise-cancelling headphones, and even those didn't always work.

Tonight, he'd gotten a taste of what it was like to live without his enhanced hearing, and the white noise generator in the warehouse had almost cost them their lives. No matter how much he hated dealing with his skill all the time, he was grateful for it.

"Yeah, I hear you. There's no escaping me," he whispered to the woman too far away to hear him.

But he heard her.

Heard each ragged breath as she ran, completely unaware she was being followed. Probably believing that her plan to blow them all up had worked and they were lying dead amongst the debris of the ruined warehouse.

"I'm coming for you," he promised as he picked up his pace. Just because he didn't have Thunder's enhanced speed didn't mean he wasn't easily gaining on his prey.

Everything inside him screamed that it was the mystery woman, that as soon as he caught her, he'd have everything they needed to destroy Dr. Gardner. There would be no remorse as he did whatever it took to get answers from this woman. She'd signed her own fate when she decided to work for a man who thought he could play God with other people's lives without suffering any consequences for it.

"Not happening. You picked your side, and whatever happens next is on you. Easy way or the hard way," he said as the sounds of feet pounding the ground grew louder.

Then, a minute later, he saw her.

A flash of black moving through the dark. Blade almost laughed out loud. Did the mystery woman really think wearing black would hide her from them? She knew what had happened to them, participated in it at least to some extent, and knew that they had skills that made them nearly impossible to beat opponents.

"Your world is about to come crashing down upon you, darlin', and I can't wait to see you fall and break."

~

January 9th
  10:37 P.M.

.  .  .

It was hard to believe she'd done it.

Free for the first time in ... too many years to count.

Maybe ever.

Even as a young child, Whitney Daley had had her every move mapped out for her. There had been no allowances for choice, no time allocated for fun. She had learned to do what she was told when she was told and not to ask questions.

Too bad she'd followed that rule.

Because of that, good men and women had suffered.

Died.

She might wind up dead, too.

What she was doing wasn't just dangerous, it was potentially deadly. If she got caught ... well let's just say she'd better not allow herself to get caught.

But despite the danger, the fear, it felt good to finally make her own decisions, to make the right ones for a change. As much as she wished she'd found her strength sooner, Whitney also knew that if she hadn't become the obedient little worker bee she'd been recruited to be, then she never would have been able to make this move now.

It was because he trusted her.

Trusted that after years of being manipulated and coerced, she was now so completely under his control that she would never think to move against him.

*Ha, take that, Dr. Gardner.*

*I'm not the weak and pathetic little girl you seem to think I am. I always hated what you were doing, you just had me too scared to do anything to stop it.*

*Not anymore.*

Now she was taking back her power and using the fact that Dr. Gardner trusted her against him. Every single piece of paper that had been in the lab was gone now. Destroyed. Long before the explosion.

As soon as she made up her mind that she was done going along with all of this, she claimed the lab's location was likely compromised now that the only surviving team had his name. Thankfully, Dr. Gardner had gone along with that theory without any real pushing on her side, and so he hadn't thought anything of it when she started removing all the files, reports, computers, vials, and everything that was stored there. Only she wasn't moving it to a new secure location, she was ensuring it was all destroyed.

Of course, there were other labs, but this one was the main one. It was where there were copies of everything stored. Or it had been. With all of that gone now, the only place where every single piece of carefully compiled notes on the drugs and their effects was held altogether was inside her own head, and she was done being a tool to be used.

The lab had been carefully cleaned down, erasing any signs of their presence there and what had taken place within those walls, and now it was blown to pieces.

That last step hadn't really been necessary. There had already been no traces of what had happened left behind, but she hated that building. Hated everything it represented. Blowing it all up had been her own personal way of getting petty revenge on the man who had controlled her life for far too long.

Only ... she was pretty sure she had messed up.

In the most major way possible.

The second she'd made the choice to turn on her boss, Whitney had known she was signing her own death warrant. There was no way Dr. Gardner would tolerate any dissent in his organization, not even from the person responsible for creating the drug that gave recipients enhanced skills.

So she'd gone into this with eyes wide open.

Finding a way to warn the team of survivors that the doctor had been searching for them for seven years had been the first thing she needed to do. Thankfully, the failed attempt to lure her boss into a trap had given her both the push she needed to finally break free and the means to do it.

Once she learned the missing team worked for the world-renowned Prey Security, it had been easy. Find a link, Cassandra Charleston had seemed like the best one, deliver her message, and then disappear. The lab was already cleaned down, the files already destroyed, so she'd contacted the woman and prayed that she had enough time to disappear for good before Dr. Gardner realized she'd betrayed him.

But he'd figured it out quicker than she'd realized.

Whitney had no idea how, but she'd kept watch over the woman to ensure that Cassandra delivered her message, and she'd seen the mercenary break into the woman's home the very next day. Watched as one of the men she'd created had saved the woman's life.

Knowing she was in danger, she hadn't returned to the place where she had lived and worked. It would be the first place Dr. Gardner looked for her, and so she'd watched from her hiding place as he'd sent in his men to capture her.

If she'd been there ...

She didn't even want to think about the horrors she would be enduring this very second.

One thing she'd learned about the doctor over the years she'd worked for him was that he wasn't a patient man. After finding the room where she lived in one of the back buildings behind the warehouse empty, he'd assumed she was already gone and so withdrew his guards.

But she hadn't gone.

Just hidden.

Then she'd slipped back in when it was safe. Calling in a couple of fellow scientists that she trusted, she'd given the warehouse a final clean, set the explosives, and then prepared to blow the place up and disappear for good.

Except she hadn't realized that anyone was in there until it was too late.

Had she killed the very men she'd been trying to save?

"I'm sorry," she whispered to the empty forest. "I didn't mean to. I didn't know you were in there. I should have checked before I blew it up, but I thought the team had left, and everything was ready to go."

Her voice was ragged from running, tears streaming down her cheeks, her heart breaking into a million pieces.

They were dead.

They had to be.

When she'd gathered her few belongings and carefully hidden a stash of money, she'd been sure the warehouse was empty. She'd waited until the clean-up team had gone before doing anything, and it wasn't until she was already back outside, ready to run through the forest to where she'd parked her getaway car, that she saw it.

A van.

Parked around the back of the main building.

It hadn't been there before, and it could mean only one thing. That someone else had been inside the warehouse. Someone she hadn't known about. Who else could it be but the team of men that had been created with her drugs? They must have linked this place to Dr. Gardner and come to check it out. It was the only explanation because if it were Dr. Gardner's men, they would have stormed the back building where she lived, not the main one.

Everything she'd risked had been for nothing.

If those men were dead, she was now on the run for no reason. She could have kept her mouth shut, kept doing what she'd been doing, and found a way to disappear when the time was right.

Now she might be free, but she would spend the rest of her life looking over her shoulder. Dr. Gardner would hunt her, she knew that. While he might not have much patience, he wasn't one to give up an investment without a fight, and she was the biggest investment he'd ever made.

Still, Whitney would gladly hand herself over to the doctor if it meant there was a way to undo what she'd done. Killing those men was the absolute last thing she wanted to do. She'd been trying to end what she'd started, and she had, except not the way she wanted.

More deaths on her shoulders.

As much as she'd love to say she'd lost count of how many dead men and women she quite literally carried on her back, she hadn't. She knew the exact number, and now there were likely six more to add to that.

There was only one thing she could hold onto right now.

One good thing she'd managed to do.

Without access to the research, most of which had been gathered through her, it would take Dr. Gardner years to catch back up to where he'd been before. Especially without her. He might take all the credit for the drugs, and she was happy for him to do it, but she was the one behind it all. Without her, and without everything in one place, regrouping would be almost impossible.

Not that it was enough to undo all she'd caused. It would save future lives, but it wouldn't bring back all those already lost.

Choking on a sob, Whitney paused, then crossed the road to the parking lot of a small shopping mall where she'd left her getaway vehicle. This mall had been her only link to the outside world for far too long, and now it was her gateway to freedom.

But was it real freedom when she would have to spend the rest of her life—however long that might be—carrying the consequences of her actions?

# CHAPTER

*Two*

January 9th
10:44 P.M.

*I'm sorry.*

The whispered words were loud enough for Blade to hear, and he chuckled to himself.

*Yeah, I bet you're sorry, darlin'. Sorry that you ever put your life on the line to try to warn us, if that's even what you were trying to do. Bet you realized you'd rather stick with your boss than help out a bunch of monsters.*

Monsters.

The word had been thrown around a lot by Dr. Gardner in those years they'd been held captive. It was no wonder the idea had stuck with all of them in the intervening years.

Back then, the scientist would calmly tell them that he was doing the only responsible thing he could after he'd created a bunch of monsters that were more animal than man. He'd used the anger raging inside all of them as proof that they would never be able to live safely around the general population.

Although the man had no problem turning them loose when it suited him, to take out some target he'd chosen for reasons he never shared with them.

After hearing it so much, of course they began to internalize the word, make it part of their self-image. But the facts were that the truth had always been staring them in the face. Lion had never been able to completely give up the woman from his past, even if he'd ruthlessly cut her out of his life. They'd all quickly grown attached to Beth Lindon, a woman Bravo Team had rescued who had lived through more darkness, pain, and suffering than they ever had. Dragon had developed feelings for Cassandra Charleston while the woman stayed with them for protection, and then Steel had fallen hard and fast for Rose Gardner.

None of them were monsters.

But maybe they weren't quite human either.

Something in between. An angry darkness had been planted inside them. Most days, they kept it on a short leash. Some days, it raged and howled and they let it out. Days when they struck down evil men and women, took out threats, and eliminated targets who put innocent lives at risk.

Days like today.

Today's target might be a personal one, it might be revenge for what had been done to them, but that didn't mean this was entirely self-serving. They knew from both what Dr. Gardner had told his sister, and what the mystery woman had told Cassandra that the scientist had never stopped with his experiments. Men and women had died after being given his drugs, either consumed by the anger ripping them apart from the inside out, or doomed by the suicidal thoughts that urged them to end it all.

Taking out this woman wasn't just about revenge, although Blade couldn't deny that it would satisfy him immensely to toy with someone who had so easily played with his life, it was about saving other lives.

No one else was going to suffer at the hands of Dr. Gardner and his staff.

There weren't enough apologies in the world to save this woman from the consequences of her actions.

As he followed close enough to watch her movements, the woman completely oblivious that not only was she being followed but that he was so close to her, he watched as she paused at the side of a road. They'd made their way through the forest and back down to the main road.

On the other side was a small shopping mall. At this time of night it was closed, the parking lot mostly empty other than for a handful of cars. Seemed like the woman was smart enough, at least, to have planned things through. Likely, she'd panicked when she saw them show up there, worried they would find something that would lead them to her, and decided that the plan had changed and it was better to take them out.

In her hands, she clutched a duffel bag, and he wondered if she'd perhaps been staying at the building. If they'd found the link to it sooner, they might have been able to catch her without the building exploding around them. She was lucky they'd all survived because if they hadn't, she would have been punished for stealing the lives of the people he cared about.

After dragging in a few breaths, the woman straightened, checked both ways, and then darted across the street. It was more than obvious that she had indeed planned this all out.

When the mystery woman headed for a small black car, Blade scanned the lot for one he could hijack. While he never liked doing things that would hurt an innocent, he needed to follow this woman, there was no other option. They couldn't allow this lead to slip away, so he was going to have to steal a car. He'd call Prey later and make sure that the vehicle was returned to the parking lot. Once he secured the woman, he could use her own vehicle to take her back to Delta Team's mansion, where she would remain until they finished dragging intel out of her, then they'd kill her and burn her body.

Setting his attention on a large black SUV that looked the same as most of the vehicles out there, he thought that was his best bet. It wouldn't look suspicious or draw attention if she happened to notice that she was being followed, but given that she hadn't so far, he guessed she wouldn't.

Her world was in the lab, but his was out here.

She didn't stand a chance. She was a dead woman walking and didn't even realize it yet.

Without even checking her surroundings, she scurried into the driver's seat of her vehicle and slammed the door. The sound echoed through the night, sounding much louder to his ears than it would to anyone else's, rising above the sounds of the forest.

Once she drove off, he darted out of the shadows, headed straight for the vehicle he'd chosen, and made quick work of gaining access to it. By the time he was driving out of the lot, he identified the sound of the woman's car, thankful for the quiet road that made it easy, and began to follow.

With his enhanced hearing, there was no need for him to keep the vehicle in his line of sight, all he had to do was let his ears guide him.

They drove for a while, close to two hours, deeper into the forest, away from the city, before the woman's vehicle slowed. Keeping his distance, he followed, noted the driveway she'd turned down, and pulled his vehicle to a stop.

Chances were, she would be keeping an eye on the driveway, believing that if anyone was going to come for her, that's how they'd approach. But he lived in the shadows, the darkness had become his friend, and he'd become accustomed to doing things the hard way. Blade drove his vehicle just into the trees enough to be hidden from both the road and the driveway.

Then he climbed out and melded into the forest. He could hear the woman opening doors and then closing them, he even heard the click of a light switch being turned on, which told him that she wasn't very far away.

The light was the first thing he saw as he crept through the trees. Another twenty yards or so, and a cute little farmhouse came into view. It had been freshly painted white, and the red trim around the windows glowed in the light streaming from inside. The car was parked out front, and he could hear the woman bustling about inside.

This was perfect.

Better than he could have hoped for.

While the woman had likely chosen this farmhouse as her hideout because it was remote and she thought it would decrease her chances of being found, it would now work against her.

Out here, no one would hear her screams—and she was going to be screaming until her throat was burning and her voice was hoarse—or come running to her rescue.

If he'd been choosing a location for his upcoming intel gathering session, he would have chosen one just like this. But as anxious as he was, he couldn't just go running in there immediately, grab the woman, tie her up, and make her bleed until her secrets oozed out of her.

Not yet.

This was too important to risk messing up. Right now, they knew that the mystery woman had flipped, but they didn't know if she'd flipped back. After all, she'd set off the explosions knowing he and his team were inside. While she had tried to save them before, he couldn't rely on the fact that when Dr. Gardner had figured out her betrayal, she hadn't gone crawling back to him, willing to offer anything to save her own skin.

So he had to wait, watch, and make sure the woman wasn't waiting on someone else to show up. Then once he was confident she was all alone out here, he was going to make his move, get the information his team needed to destroy Dr. Gardner, and then take this woman back to his team so they could kill her together.

January 10th
    11:00 P.M.

She was supposed to be less paranoid now that she'd made her move.

Wasn't she?

Whitney glanced around the small bedroom. It should feel safe, homey, a place where she was comfortable to finally be herself.

But it didn't.

Not at all.

This escape had been years in the planning. Far too many years, and when she thought about just how many, it made her feel sick and devastated. Dr. Gardner had been in control of her every move, but there had always been a teeny tiny little rebellious streak she'd nurtured even when she had no idea where it was going to end.

Finding a way out had seemed like a pipedream, but she'd worked toward it. She'd created herself a fake ID, a detailed one, with a history, bank accounts, credit cards, college degrees, a work history, everything she would need to start a whole new life. That included buying this farmhouse and fitting it out with all the things she would have chosen for herself if she didn't live in a single room in a warehouse that she was rarely allowed to leave.

When Dr. Gardner got an email from what had to be his team of surviving super soldiers, taunting him that they had his sister, and if he wanted to save her life, he'd have to hand himself over to them, she knew it was time.

The opening she needed to finally make her move.

So she had.

Getting to work, she used the hacking skills Dr. Gardner didn't even know she had, which had allowed her to siphon off money to buy her house and furnish it, as well as setting her up with enough money to live off until she could find a job, to try to find the team. But it wasn't until he learned that the team was now employed by Prey that everything had fallen into place, and she'd actually managed to escape.

Now she was here, and she should be celebrating, but instead, it felt like she was being watched.

Had Dr. Gardner followed her?

Found her already?

No.

He couldn't have. She'd been too careful. There was no way he could connect this farmhouse to her, and he likely thought that she was long gone. Even if he found out she'd done a second clean down of the warehouse and assumed she'd been hiding out close by, he would now think she'd made a dash out of the country.

It was why she'd chosen this place that was only a couple of hours from where she'd been living ever since Dr. Gardner acquired her. She was trying to do the opposite of what was expected of her.

"You're safe, so stop panicking," she ordered herself. "This is your dream bedroom. Everything in this house is what you've always wanted. You're free now. You have enough money to stay here for at least a year, and there are plenty of jobs you could work from home. Then, when it's safe, you can sell up and go anywhere in the world."

That was all true, but it didn't offer her any comfort.

Whitney had been so sure that once she was free, everything would be perfect, she'd be in control of her life, and she could live it however she wanted.

Only she felt the opposite.

She was so used to belonging to someone else that she didn't know how to be her own person. She had never learned.

Maybe it would have been smarter to ask Cassandra Charleston to take her to the super soldiers. They'd hate her, of course, punish her quite rightfully for her part in destroying their lives, but she could have helped them somehow. Because Dr. Gardner's death was the only thing that was really going to make her safe.

As long as he was out there, she would always be in danger.

The super soldiers might believe that they were the scientist's greatest asset, and she wasn't denying that Dr. Gardner wanted them back, but she trumped them. Without her, there was no future for his program.

"Too bad you don't know where he is, then you could just send them an address," she muttered as she rolled over for what had to be the thousandth time since she climbed into bed.

With a sigh, she tugged the blankets up and over her head. It was nice at least to sleep with as many blankets as she wanted. Nice ones, good quality ones, not the rough, scratchy blankets she had always been given.

Tears burned her eyes, and she hated everything she'd set in motion. Her good intentions had been used and twisted so many times that they no longer even resembled anything close to what she'd once tried to create.

If she could go back and do her life over, she would ...

What?

There was nothing she could change. She'd always been a pawn, and there was nothing she could have done to—

Whitney froze.

Was that a sound?

An inside-the-house sound?

Paranoia. Had to be. If Dr. Gardner had found her, he would have come rushing in with an army of his loyal guards. As much as he would have loved to kill her outright for her betrayal, he knew he couldn't do that. Not if he wanted to keep working on the drugs. While he liked to pretend he was the mastermind behind it all, unfortunately, it was all her. In fact, she was sure that if he stopped messing around with her formulas, they would work the way she'd intended, even if that wasn't the way Dr. Gardner wanted.

Forcing herself not to give in to the fear, Whitney rolled over again, so she was facing away from the door. No one was coming, and she wasn't going to let old fears tarnish her newfound freedom.

Hard fought for freedom.

Scrunching her eyes closed, she evened her breathing out, relaxing her muscles one by one in an attempt to push herself into sleep.

It should be easy, she hadn't had more than a couple of hours of sleep here and there since she made the decision to go to Cassandra with a warning. Despite the run through the forest the night before, she'd been too wired to sleep, so she was going on forty-eight hours without any sleep at all.

Yet it wouldn't come.

Too many emotions raged inside her, the most dominant was knowing that she had killed the six men she'd tried to save. Why hadn't she given the building one last check over before setting off those explosives? It was the smart thing to do, and yet she'd been ready to just get out of there, her nerves on edge, the prospect of freedom too heady.

Lost in her thoughts and her attempts to force her body to relax and go to sleep, when her covers were suddenly ripped away, she was caught completely off-guard.

A scream ripped from her throat as a hand tangled in her hair and yanked her upright.

Fear paralyzed her, and she stared up at a large figure standing beside her bed.

Guess she hadn't been imagining the sounds inside her house after all. Instead of writing it off as paranoia, she should have investigated. She didn't have a weapon, and she knew zero self-defense skills, but at least she wouldn't have been caught off-guard.

When the hand in her hair dragged her from the bed, it was automatic for her own hands to fly up and grab onto it, attempting to ease the stinging pain in her scalp.

It didn't help.

Scrambling to get her feet beneath her as the man began to walk with her, he didn't speak a word, just pulled her along with him out of her bedroom, down the stairs, and then out into the cold night.

Walking with purpose, it soon became apparent that the man had prepared for this before coming for her. Which meant it absolutely wasn't random. He was there for her.

*Run. Fight. You have to get away from him.*

The order echoed inside her mind, but she couldn't make her body cooperate. It was like she'd been turned to stone, all she could do was try to keep up with the man's much longer strides as he marched her toward a tree with a rope hanging from it.

At first, she thought it was a noose, and she was going to be dead in just a couple of minutes, but as he roughly released her hair to grab her hands, pinning them together with ease, she realized he wasn't going to kill her.

Worse.

Because the only other option was torture.

Pathetic.

That was the only way she could describe herself, because Whitney did absolutely nothing to fight back, to at least give herself a chance, and then she was bound by her wrists, the rope lifted until her feet no longer touched the ground, and she hung from a tree.

Helpless.

After all she'd done to save herself, she was a captive all over again.

# CHAPTER

*Three*

January 10<sup>th</sup>
11:23 P.M.

She was a timid little thing.

Her chest rose and fell harshly with each gasped breath she took, her heart hammered in her chest like it was looking for a way out, and her terrified eyes stared at him like he was the bogeyman.

Which he was.

This only played out one way, and it was with this woman bleeding, screaming, and then telling all.

Still, Blade had expected a little more fight from her. She hadn't put up a fight at all as he dragged her out of her bed, other than to grip his arm with her slender fingers in an attempt to ease the pain in her scalp. It was almost a disappointment. This woman was responsible for stealing a decade of his life from him, she had to pay for that, but he wanted at least a little fight from her. This felt like taking candy from a baby.

He'd take it, though.

In the end, whether this went easy or hard, he was getting the answers he needed. Every single thing this woman knew about the drugs and Dr. Gardner, he was going to learn. Then he'd offer her up like a sacrifice to his team, and they could all take the first step in their revenge.

Now that he had her strung up, hanging from the rope he'd prepared once he saw all the lights inside the house switch off, he was ready to get started. This place was remote enough he didn't expect any visitors, and he wanted her somewhere that he could do an easy clean up after he was done. How messy this got all depended on how cooperative the woman decided to be.

If she wanted to just offer up answers, then she could dramatically decrease the amount of pain she suffered. Not escape it entirely, though, she would pay for what she did, for all the pain he and his team had suffered at her and her colleagues' hands, it was only fair after all.

As he stood before his pretty little captive, there was no doubting that she was the woman who had accosted Cassandra. She matched the sketch Cassandra had given them, but what that sketch hadn't quite captured was how young she looked in person.

Not just young.

Sweet.

Innocent.

Like she didn't belong there.

But Blade had to remind himself that she did belong there. She had been at the warehouse, she was the one who set off the explosives, had to be, she was the only other person there besides them and the mercenary. She was the woman who had issued the warning to Cassandra, so she was up to her neck in this.

Maybe that was why she was pale and shaky with shock, hadn't fought back, she thought she'd killed them in the explosion, and now there he was standing before her. No wonder she looked like she'd seen a ghost.

"Surprised to see me, darlin'?" he drawled as he propped himself up against the tree beside the one his little captive was hanging from. Most people would be struggling, panicking, sending their body swinging wildly, but not her. She just hung there, limp and still. Not relaxed, though, not in control, just afraid.

Good.

She should be scared of him.

Not expecting an answer, Blade was pleasantly surprised when the woman slowly nodded. At least she wasn't so in shock that she was going to be of no use to him. While he wanted her terrified out of her mind, wanted her to get a taste of what it had been like for him and his team when they were held captive in a glass cell for three years, he wanted her cognizant enough to gather intel.

"Thought you could hide out here, Mary? Escape your fate?"

As he called her by the name he'd found on her ID when he searched her house after breaking in, she startled, as though unprepared to hear that name on his lips. She shouldn't be. She hadn't bothered to hide her purse with the identification inside it, it had been sitting out on the kitchen counter, and of course, he'd gone through it.

Before breaking into the farmhouse, he'd contacted his team to let them know that the woman he'd followed was still there, that no one else had arrived, and he was ready to break in and collect her. When he found the ID, he shot off a quick text with the name so that his team could finally do a deep dive on the woman.

Only now, at the sound of the name, he watched as she squirmed slightly. Was her reaction one of surprise because she hadn't realized he knew it, or because it wasn't really her name? Given that they had been unable to identify the woman from a sketch of her, it was no stretch to believe that she was using a fake name now.

"Hmm, or not Mary," he said as he pulled out his favorite knife and began to spin the handle between his fingers like one might a pen. This knife had been given to him by his dad on his thirteenth birthday. It was the only thing he'd allowed himself to keep from his life before, and that was only because he needed something to tie himself to the people he'd loved but given up for their own safety.

Now the knife was a good luck charm of sorts. It went with him on every single op, and he always preferred to kill with it rather than a gun whenever given the opportunity.

Not that he had any intention of killing the woman yet. Not unless she forced his hand.

When he'd called her on the name thing, her eyes had widened, and she sucked in a breath, all but confirming that Mary was not her real name.

No worries.

Blade knew the perfect way to finally identify this woman once and for all.

"You know it's rude to lie about your name," he murmured as he stepped closer, pressing his much larger body against hers and letting her feel the power rippling through it.

Intimidating women wasn't something he'd usually be comfortable with, but this wasn't just any woman. She had participated in creating the drug that forever changed him in ways he never could have guessed when he first signed up for the program. Her last-minute attempt to save him and his team went exactly zero ways toward making up for all the suffering she'd helped cause.

Especially when she'd then tried to blow them up.

"You've been a tricky little one to identify, you know that, darlin'? You think your buddy did a good enough job of scrubbing you from databases to pass this test?"

Crowding close enough against her that he could feel every shiver that rocked her slim frame, Blade slowly lifted his knife, allowing the thin moonlight to glint against the blade. If she didn't know which member of the team he was before, although he suspected that she did, then she certainly knew now.

There was no guessing at how he'd gotten his nickname.

Growing up on a cattle ranch, he spent most of his childhood outdoors. Cowboy blood ran through his veins, and he loved camping, hunting, fishing, and anything outdoorsy. It was why his dad had given him this knife for that long-ago birthday, and now it was all he had left of that carefree time of his life.

Now he moved his knife toward her, touching the tip against her temple at the corner of her eye. Filled with an irrational need to destroy the perfect beauty of the woman watching him from terrified blue eyes, he managed to control himself. Maybe he'd taunt her with that later, but for now, he wanted to get a fingerprint to his team so they could finally figure out who she was.

Although her ID said she was thirty, which still would have made her very young a decade ago when they were injected with the drugs, the still nameless woman looked so much younger. She must have been blessed with some magic genes, because if he had to guess, he'd put her at early twenties at most, likely younger than both Cassandra and Rose, who were twenty-four and twenty-three respectively.

But there was no way in hell that timeline worked, because then she would have been a mere pre-teen. Maybe the theory that she was the daughter of Ridge Gardner was correct. Rose had grown up mostly off-grid, although she did have a birth certificate, so it would make sense that the crazed scientist would keep his child off any database.

Regardless, they knew she was involved, and until he knew otherwise, based on the likelihood she set off the explosions to kill them, he was going to treat her like a threat, an accomplice in the horrors he and his team had suffered, and still battled on a daily basis.

Meeting those baby blues of hers, Blade pressed the tip of his knife into her skin just hard enough that a single drop of blood welled out. "No one is coming to save you, you're my plaything now."

~

January 10th
   11:32 P.M.

Whitney hadn't even known that terror at this level existed.

Most of her life, she'd been manipulated through fear. She'd thought she could handle mostly anything, but she'd never been in any situation that even remotely resembled this one.

There hadn't been a need for pain, and ropes, and knives to control her, she'd been so young, grooming was easy. Why close a door with a hammer when you could nudge it with a finger and get the same result?

Obviously, she couldn't handle fear.

At all.

Not only had she been paralyzed, trapped inside her own body as her system rejected both fight and flight and instead picked freeze, but at the sudden sharp sting of pain as the knife pierced her skin, she felt a sudden rush of warmth against her leg as she peed herself.

For one second, mortification overrode the terror, and she hoped that her assailant, who she had to believe was in fact one of the men she'd thought she killed, Blade, if the fact he was using a knife he'd held up rather proudly, didn't notice the fact she'd just wet herself.

No such luck.

Taking a step back, the man laughed as he looked down at her feet, where she was sure a puddle was forming even if she couldn't see it from this angle.

While it was quite obviously the least of her problems, it stung that he mocked her so easily. Of course, Whitney got that he hated her. He might not know all the details, but from her warning to Cassandra, he knew enough to know that she was involved in the program. But if he knew she was a scientist, he should assume she had no experience being dragged out of bed, strung up by her wrists, or experiencing pain like this. She used knives to cook, on the rare occasion she was allowed, that was all, and she'd never even touched a gun, only seen them because the guards at the facility wore them strapped to their bodies.

"It's okay, darlin', everybody makes a fool of themselves the first time around," the man—Blade—drawled.

The way he said darling made her skin crawl. It was so explicitly sexual, and she had never been given permission to indulge that side of her womanhood. Not only that, but this wasn't the kind of sex she'd even want to indulge in anyway. It was power and control, about taking advantage of her, about belittling her. It was pain, not pleasure.

"Don't worry, by the end you'll be a pro."

For some reason, she got the feeling he'd just winked at her, even though she couldn't see his eyes because he was wearing night vision goggles. Maybe it was because she understood what he was saying without saying it.

Torture.

He was talking about torturing her and letting her know that this was only the beginning of the horrors she was going to live through.

There was no denying that a huge part of her believed she deserved it. She was the one who had created the initial version of the drug, although at the time she had never conceived of the consequences of her discovery. How could she? She hadn't known enough about the world to think of anything outside her own little bubble.

But another part, a smaller part, a teeny, tiny little part knew how unfair it was for her to be punished for something that hadn't been her choice.

No way this man would believe that, though.

He knew she was part of it, he knew she was a liar because she hadn't done a believable job of acting like her name was Mary, and he knew as well as she did that she wasn't going to hold out under torture.

Thing was, though, she'd tell him anything he wanted to know without him having to stab her, or peel off her skin, or gouge out her eyes, or whatever other sick and twisted thing he dreamed about doing to her.

*Planned* on doing to her.

Because this wasn't really about intel gathering, if it was, he wouldn't have broken in the way he had, gone through her stuff, prepared this rope for her, and then brought her outside. He wanted to hurt her, to punish her, and was probably imagining Dr. Gardner's face in place of hers.

Too bad he would never think to ask if she hated the scientist, too.

Even knowing what had been done to this man and his team, to all the others who had been given the drugs as well, Whitney still knew that she had ample—possibly even more—reasons to hate the deranged doctor. Maybe she hadn't been given experimental drugs, but she had been imprisoned just the same, trapped in a situation she had no hope of getting out of.

Only she had.

She'd gotten out.

Found a way to escape.

Did she really plan to just hang there and give up? Give in to whatever this man had planned for her? Was she going to just sigh and accept her fate the way she had so many times before?

Where was that fire that had her working on her exit plan?

If she could do that, she could figure something out now.

Couldn't she?

Figuring out puzzles was what she did. If she just looked at this like a puzzle, maybe she could work on it and find a solution. It wasn't impossible, even if it wasn't particularly likely.

A tiny flicker of defiance lit inside her, and Whitney met Blade's gaze when it moved slowly back up her body. Well, she met where his gaze would be if he wasn't wearing those goggles, which gave him a creepy, otherworldly look.

Nothing had changed in that she was still utterly terrified of this man and what he had planned for her, but she was sick of being a pawn. She wasn't really who he wanted, he wanted Dr. Gardner, and she'd offer up the man on a platter if she could, but he'd punish her nonetheless for crimes she'd committed against her will.

Obviously picking up on her slight shift in demeanor, minuscule though it had been, he reached out and touched a fingertip to the spot at the corner of her eye where he'd dug the tip of his knife into her skin just enough to make her bleed. That finger pressed hard against the small wound, making her whimper, and he snickered and then pulled his finger back. Bringing it to his lips and letting her watch as his tongue darted out to lick off her blood.

Shivering, cold, fear, revulsion all merging together, she startled, her body swaying wildly as Blade moved closer again, his large body pressing up against hers, reminding her that he held all the power. Lifting his knife, he let it glint in the moonlight again before lifting it up above her head.

For a second, Whitney thought he was going to cut the ropes, let her down, and ... do something to her, although she had no idea about forms of torture or how you went about breaking someone.

But he didn't cut her down.

Instead, she felt something cold and smooth press against one of her fingers.

Heart rate spiking as she assumed he was going to slice the digit clean off her body, she was about to cry out a plea for mercy, beg him to understand she'd had no choice but to work for Dr. Gardner.

Only he didn't cut her at all.

Just held the blade of his knife firmly against one of her fingers and then took a step back. There was a smirk on his face, and he tipped back the goggles so she could finally see his eyes. She confirmed that he was indeed the man she knew only as Blade.

Holding up the knife, which she now realized had a pretty perfect fingerprint on it, his grin widened. "Think I'll be able to find out your real name with this, darlin'?"

Despite how smug he was, she knew he wasn't going to get what he wanted.

When he took her in, Dr. Gardner had wiped out every single sign that she'd ever existed at all. As far as the outside world was concerned, she didn't exist. There was no birth certificate, nothing to prove she'd gone to school and graduated, she had never had a driver's license, nor did she have any other form of identification. She was rarely even allowed outside the facility, so her face didn't appear in any CCTV footage either.

Her fingerprint wouldn't give him her name, and she wasn't sure if she should either.

What was she supposed to do? Was she supposed to beg for mercy and promise to tell him everything? Would he even believe her if she did? Would it change anything? Maybe it would only bring her more punishment and pain.

"You're a quiet little thing, aren't you, darlin'?" Blade asked, his head cocked to the side as his gaze examined her from head to toe. "Maybe a couple of hours hanging around might loosen your tongue a little."

With that, he turned and walked away, back toward the house, leaving her hanging where she was, staring after him, with no idea how she was supposed to get out of this alive, and the certainty that she likely couldn't weighing heavily on her.

# CHAPTER
## *Four*

January 11<sup>th</sup>
  7:01 A.M.

Hanging in the dawn light, the mystery woman, who he was no closer to identifying now than he had been when he broke into the farmhouse ten hours ago, looked like a sacrifice strung up ready to be offered.

Who exactly he was offering her to, Blade had no idea. To the universe, to fate, to Dr. Gardner, to his team, to himself, to the past, to the present, to the future, it didn't really matter, but she most definitely was a sacrifice of sorts.

In the hours since he'd taken her fingerprint and left her out there, she hadn't done anything more than cry quietly to herself. He'd expected her to beg and plead as he walked away, to offer him a deal, intel for her freedom, or at the very least to ask for mercy and her life to be spared.

But it seemed like his little hanging beauty had no idea what to do.

There was no doubt at all that she was afraid. While she might work for Dr. Gardner, it was more than evident from her lack of fight and pure, undiluted terror that she was a scientist and nothing more. She had no skills to attempt to fight for her life, and he didn't have to guess to know she had none for withstanding torture either.

Despite being a timid little thing, he'd felt the first spark of defiance in her. She had no fight-or-flight instincts, but she wasn't completely helpless. She was going to fight back, she just didn't know how yet.

Good.

Right now, he was itching for a reason to do more than string the woman up and scare her. The tiny taste of her blood wasn't enough, he wanted, needed, craved more. He wanted to hear her screams, allow them to soothe the rage that he kept on a tight leash but was always a single misstep away from flying loose.

Which was an unusual feeling for him. While he and his team were a family, there was zero doubt about that, they hadn't sat around and talked about their pasts, so he didn't know much about everyone's lives before they entered the program. But he had gathered enough to guess that of all of them, he'd come from the happiest family situation. His parents and extended family had been wonderful growing up. He'd had siblings, and cousins who were like siblings. He'd done well in school, had lots of friends, and played sport. Although he'd not been rich enough to have anything he wanted, he was well off enough to always have what he needed.

It wasn't until someone decided to play God with his body and his life without giving him all the information up front that he'd had his first real taste of rage.

When his phone rang, he stormed away from the window, annoyed with himself that he'd been standing there admiring the way the woman's soft blonde locks caught the rising sun and shimmered like lengths of spun gold.

This wasn't a dating game it was an intel gathering op, he was there to get everything he could out of her in case Dr. Gardner was somewhere nearby, and then he and his team were going to kill her. There was no sugarcoating things, no downplaying them. The woman was spending her last couple of days on earth hanging from a tree, and then suffering a slow, agonizing death.

"Did you get it?" Blade asked without preamble, snatching up his phone and accepting the call.

"Good morning to you too," Steel drawled, making him roll his eyes.

"Yeah, yeah, morning," he muttered. But then because he really did care and wanted to know, he asked, "How are Rose and Cassandra today?"

"They're both fine," Steel assured him.

"And you guys?"

"We're all fine too."

"Good. So ..." he prompted. After confirming that everyone was recovering from the injuries caused by the explosion, there was only one thing he wanted to know.

"No matches," Steel replied.

"None? At all? Surely her fingerprints were in a system somewhere. And I sent you a clear photo of her face, she has to be in some database somewhere." How could she not? The woman existed. Despite moving away from the window, he could still see her hanging out there. Her body was limp, although he could hear the sounds of her breathing and the beating of her heart so he knew she was still alive.

"She should be but she's not," Steel said.

"So she was scrubbed. Removed from everything so nobody could find her," he said. It was the only thing that made sense. "But why would Dr. Gardner do that? He didn't scrub himself from the systems, he just hid himself away so we couldn't find him. But now we have a name, he's searchable in several databases. Why isn't she?"

"I can't answer that," Steel replied.

"Her fake ID says she's thirty, but I'd bet my favorite knife that she's not. Even if she was, that would put her at twenty a decade ago, very young to be working on a program like this. Maybe Dr. Gardner was bringing in young college students because they were easier to control, but he would still need experienced scientists," he said, his gaze glued to the woman hanging in the tree.

"We keep assuming that just because she knew about the tests that she was in it from the beginning," Thunder spoke, and Blade realized he was on speaker.

"No way to know that's true," Voodoo added. "She might be new to the program. We know it's still going. We know that he never stopped the experiments and that the others all keep dying, which is why he wants us back. Maybe she just took a job for him, not realizing what it really entailed, and once she realized she knew she couldn't stay on and stand by while we're hunted like animals and decided to do something about it."

"That would make her another innocent," Cassandra said softly.

It would.

And Blade's stomach cramped at the thought.

Was the woman he had left hanging from a tree for almost eight hours now an innocent?

There was an innocent air about her, that was for sure. Those wide blue eyes screamed young and sweet, and the blonde waves and pouty lips added to the image. There was a softness to her he felt rather than saw, and he couldn't be sure whether it was real or a projection she wanted him to see.

The last thing he wanted was to be just another stupid guy to fall for a pretty face.

"You need to talk to her, get her to open up," Dragon growled, the implication clear even if he didn't want to say the words in front of Cassandra, who he'd almost lost once because of their need for vengeance.

He had to make her bleed, scream, and beg. It was the only way, and what he'd taken her to do.

So why did he suddenly feel uneasy about it?

"Keep looking for her real identity, just because she was scrubbed doesn't mean she's not still out there somewhere. I'll work on her and hopefully get her talking," he said before abruptly disconnecting the call.

As he walked to the kitchen and filled a glass with water, he realized what had him so unsettled. Dr. Gardner hadn't removed himself from databases, yet he'd made sure that this woman didn't exist anywhere outside his own facility. The only reason Blade could think of to do that was that this woman was important somehow. If she was important enough to erase, then it didn't make sense that she'd only been with him for a short time. But she was too young to have been there from the beginning, even if the birthdate on the fake ID was real.

Strolling out of the house, he felt the woman's eyes on him as he closed the distance between them. She still didn't say anything, but he could see the blood streaking the cuffs of her simple pink long-sleeve T-shirt, and the dried tear marks on her cheeks.

He still wasn't sure if her silence was a conscious choice or if she was just literally too scared to talk. But he did know she was freezing, the temperature had dropped further since he brought her out in the middle of the night, and she was wearing only the long-sleeve T-shirt and a pair of flannelette pajama bottoms. Her bare feet would be frozen and unusable even if she got free, which she wouldn't, and her hands must be numb, her shoulders screaming in pain.

But she didn't speak, just eyed the glass of water in his hands, and he knew she was thirsty, too, on top of everything else.

"Drink?" he asked conversationally, holding out the glass.

Surprise filled the blue eyes that snapped up to meet his, and the range of swirling emotions in them was like a punch to the gut. Some he expected, fear, uncertainty, confusion, guilt, remorse. But there was another one there. Gratefulness. Like she truly appreciated this seemingly genuine offer.

She really was so sweet and innocent that she thought he was going to give her water to drink. What the hell was up with her? Surely, she knew he had zero good intentions where she was concerned, yet she believed him.

Or she was playing him.

Annoyed that he kept feeling himself drift toward giving her the benefit of the doubt just because she had a pretty face and an attractive body, Blade stepped closer. He'd hung her just far enough off the ground that her feet couldn't take any of her weight, given their size difference, he was six three, she had to be around five two or three, their faces were about even.

Lifting the glass like he was going to bring it to her lips, she was already opening her mouth when he tangled a hand in her hair and yanked hard, tilting her face back so she was staring at the sky. Then he poured the water directly down her nose, making her choke and cry out as she attempted to jerk out of his hold.

Not that he let her.

He kept her there, the water pouring down her nose, enjoying knowing that it was causing her pain. If she thought her big innocent eyes were going to save her, she was stupid as well as evil.

When the glass was empty, he hurled it against the nearest tree, making the woman let out a shrill shriek even as she continued to choke on the water that he'd poured down her nose and had trickled down into her throat. Then he turned and stalked back toward the house. This woman wasn't an innocent, even if a part of him wanted her to be, and it was time to get his head on straight and into the game.

January 11<sup>th</sup>
    4:48 P.M.

Numb.

That's what Whitney felt.

Not just physically numb from the cold, it was only by some miracle that the man she was sure was Blade had come after her on a slightly milder day of weather, otherwise, she was pretty sure she would be dead from hypothermia already, but psychologically as well.

It had been stupid to think that she could escape the consequences of her actions.

Stupid to think that she deserved freedom after she'd inadvertently doomed dozens of men and women to death.

Just because she hadn't known what was going to happen when she first created that drug didn't absolve her of responsibility. If anything, she should be held more responsible because she should have known, should have seen, should have figured it out.

But she hadn't.

And people had died because of her negligence.

She deserved this. Deserved hanging by arms that had long ago lost all feeling, deserved the screaming pain in her shoulders that she could somewhat ignore if she stayed completely still. Deserved to be wearing her clothes, now stained with her own waste, because nobody could hold on indefinitely. Deserved the clawing hunger in her stomach and the need for water, even as her nose still stung from Blade's earlier game.

Deserved whatever was coming next as well.

There was no lingering hope that she could withstand whatever torture was coming. Not that there ever really had been any. She was an intellectual, she didn't have the skills to compartmentalize or withstand pain. She knew how to solve problems, look for mistakes and try to find solutions, and spend hours in a lab playing around with different formulas.

Not this.

Never this.

So, when the face in the farmhouse window disappeared, she didn't know whether to rejoice that Blade was no longer staring at her, something he'd spent most of the day doing, or despair because it likely meant he was coming out there to do … something awful to her.

How was she supposed to predict his behavior? Predicting patterns in scientific equations was one thing, it was what she loved doing, what had first drawn her to create the drug, or at least the original version of it, in the first place. But she knew nothing about the techniques used to break someone, not that Blade was going to have to work too hard when it came to breaking her.

Feeling like she was left hanging—and how she was able to make that joke, she had no idea—the seconds ticked by with an excruciating slowness, only to eventually reveal that she wasn't going to have to wait much longer to get another lesson in torture.

The front door to the farmhouse opened, and Blade came strolling out. He had something in his hand, well, two things, the knife he seemed to love, and something else. Something that only became clear when he crossed the small clearing to the tree where he'd strung her up.

As soon as she realized what he was carrying, her heart stuttered in her chest.

Not having any knowledge of torture didn't make her stupid.

Her nose was still stinging from the water poured down it earlier, and whatever pain the water had caused would be nothing if he shook up that can of soda in his hand and held it to her nose. That would be excruciating.

*Open your mouth and tell him what he wants to know.*

*Beg for mercy.*

*Ask him to understand that you didn't have a choice, you were dragged into this whole thing against your will.*

Despite her internal screaming, all that came out of her mouth was a small whimper as Blade stopped a couple of feet away from her and grinned when he saw she was staring in horror at the can.

Just like he wanted her to.

That stupid grin remained on his face as he began to shake the can.

Another whimper bubbled out, and she kept ordering herself to say something, but for some reason fear seemed to have stolen her voice, and for the life of her—and she was very aware that it was quite literally a matter of life and death for her—she couldn't make herself talk.

What was up with that?

Okay, she'd always been quiet, intellectual people could often be introverted, she got stuck in her head too much and understood equations better than people. But she'd never been so afraid that her words just got clogged inside her and couldn't come out.

Stepping closer, he lifted the can, gave it one final shake, and Whitney did her best to brace herself for pain she was ill equipped to deal with. But much like she couldn't brace her body, strung up as she was, she couldn't brace her mind either, and she wasn't prepared at all for the onslaught of agony that ...

Never came.

Instead, she got a spray of shaken-up soda all over her chest as Blade lowered the can at the very last second. The sticky liquid against her chest with the cool wind blowing was definitely unpleasant, but she knew she'd just dodged one major bullet.

Why?

Why had he changed his mind? It had been clear in his eyes as he watched her while he shook it up that he wanted to hurt her and yet he'd pulled back at the very last moment.

Why had he been watching her from the window most of the day? It wasn't like he'd tried to hide it from her, he had to know she could see him. Did he watch because he enjoyed seeing her suffer, knowing she was at his mercy, or for some other reason?

Taking a step away from her, for a moment, she would have sworn there was surprise in Blade's dark eyes, almost like he hadn't made a conscious decision not to shoot those bubbles right up her nose, his body had just acted without his brain being part of the decision-making. But the look passed quickly, and she assumed she'd just imagined it, her mind conjuring up what it wanted to see.

Was that part of torturing someone? Making them long for an ally, even if the only one around was their tormentor?

"Been a nice day, sunny," Blade said, his tone smooth and conversational, no indication in it at all that he was her captor and she was his helpless little victim. "Weather forecast says we're getting some snow tonight, though. Think you can handle a little snow, darlin'?"

Again, the way he said the word darling rankled. He already had her strung up, why did he have to mock her on top of it? Wasn't it enough that he could do anything he wanted to her? Was it necessary to humiliate her as well? If he knew the whole truth about what had happened, would he really be okay with everything he was doing to her?

Whitney badly wanted to say he wouldn't, but she knew better than anyone else what had been done to him and the rest of the test subjects. Their ability to access their consciences had been disrupted, and their emotions deadened. Not removed, both were still there, they knew right from wrong and they could feel guilt and remorse, and they could still feel the full range of emotions, but the drugs accentuated the anger and minimized everything else.

"Too bad it's not summer, long hot days out here in the sun would really suck. Then again, I've always preferred the cold to the heat," Blade continued to talk as he spun the handle of his knife between his fingers.

Hot or cold, with the modifications the drugs had done to his system, he could withstand both much better than she could.

"Maybe throw in a nice summer storm, love that smell after rain."

"Petrichor," she blurted out without conscious thought. Her brain was full of random facts, and she was prone to spouting them at random times because she just didn't do well in social settings and got nervous.

Eyebrows rising, obviously surprised by her suddenly talking, Whitney found her cheeks heating. She'd gotten her voice back it seemed, but she'd said something stupid that wasn't at all necessary right now.

"The name of the smell after rain," she added somewhat lamely.

"So she does talk," Blade said as he straightened and took a step toward her.

Her stomach chose that particular moment to grumble loudly. She hadn't just not eaten today because she'd been hanging from a tree, she hadn't eaten much for days, not since she made the decision to go to Cassandra Charleston and try to warn the guys of what was coming. Whenever she got too anxious, she got a ball of nausea sitting heavily in her stomach, and it stole her appetite.

"Hungry are we, darlin'?" Blade smirked, like he took pleasure in every little bit of discomfort she suffered. Which he probably did.

"Borborygmi," she murmured softly.

"What?"

"Borborygmi," she repeated. "That's the name for the sound your stomach makes when it rumbles."

Her useless fact was just that, useless, but for some reason Blade's calm veneer snapped, and a snarl marred his otherwise handsome features as he moved quicker than she'd ever seen anyone move, until he was standing right in front of her, the blade of his knife pressed against her neck.

"You mocking me, darlin'? Because I don't think that's a wise move. No more games, you're not going to make a fool out of me any longer. It's time to start screaming, darlin'."

# CHAPTER

*Five*

The control he was clinging tightly to snapped, and without conscious thought, Blade had his knife held to the woman's neck.

"You think cutesy comments are going to save you, darlin'?" he asked as he pressed the sharp blade into her skin enough to draw blood.

Instead of soothing him, the sight of her pale skin painted red stoked the fires of his rage.

All day, he'd been drawn to the window, unable to look away from the pretty blonde hanging helplessly. He should have been thrilled to have caught her, be excited about the screams that would soon be echoing through the forest, but he wasn't.

Anxiety sat like a heavy ball in his gut.

Each time he went to head outside and begin his interrogation, he found he couldn't make himself do it. This woman wouldn't be the first he'd killed, but she would be the first woman he'd ever tortured. Evil was not confined to a single gender, he knew that, and yet something about her soft curves and the gentle swell of her breasts was messing with his head. Add in those angelic blonde locks and the fact that he was a sucker for a pair of baby blue eyes, and in the end, he'd had to force himself out there.

But even then, he hadn't done what he intended.

When he was shaking up that can of soda, Blade had every intention of allowing the fizzy liquid to spray up her nose, but for some reason as soon as he popped the can open, he'd lowered it, spraying her clothes instead.

What the hell was wrong with him?

Why did this woman stir up protective urges when he knew who she was and what she'd done?

"Umm ... no ... I just ... when I'm nervous ... sometimes I say random things," she stammered, her cheeks red like she was embarrassed by spouting out random facts he couldn't care less about.

"Nervous, are we?" Blade pressed his knife a little deeper into her skin. More blood bubbled out, and he fought the urge to allow his tongue to dart out and lick it off her. He'd always had a bit of a blood kink, but he wasn't there to explore his sexual needs, he was there to get a job done.

"I ... I don't know ... am I supposed to answer you?"

There was genuine confusion in the woman's tone, and along with it a desire to please. Part of having enhanced hearing wasn't just the ability to hear things from a greater distance than the average person, or to hear them with better clarity. It was also the ability to detect all the intonations that allowed him to read more into the words someone chose and the way they spoke them than most people could.

Was the woman's desire to please him just because she wanted to spare her own life or did it run deeper than that? There was no denying she had an innocence to her that he hadn't been expecting, possibly because she looked so young, younger even than he'd expected based on Cassandra's sketch.

"You're supposed to scream, that's what you're supposed to do," he snarled. It didn't matter how innocent she looked, how young, she was involved in Dr. Gardner's experiments, and that made her an enemy.

Fear danced in her eyes, and he knew that he was hurting her. While he had to be careful not to cut her neck too deeply because he didn't want her bleeding out on him before he got a chance to question her, she still didn't scream. Just hung there, like a deer caught in the head-lights, trying to figure out how to live but unable to do anything at all.

"Your boss, he likes to make people scream, too, doesn't he?" Blade asked as he shifted his knife, moving it so the point was now pressed to her skin, right at the base of her slender neck, above the neckline of her long-sleeve sleep T-shirt.

While her breathing quickened, she didn't answer, and her gaze remained on his face, not bothering to look down at the line of blood on her skin and the knife that could end her life in a single heartbeat.

"Certainly liked to make us scream as rage assaulted our systems because of the drugs he gave us. Some days, it was all I could do not to pound into my teammates over and over again, just to get some relief from it. But they weren't really the ones I wanted to hurt."

As he spoke, Blade edged the knife down so it began to cut through the flimsy material, now soaked with soda. Because they were pajamas and he'd snatched her from her bed, there was no bra beneath it, and he bared inches of creamy soft skin with each drag of the knife.

"How many other people did your boss make scream? How many like me and my team? Only they weren't as lucky, were they? They didn't survive what your boss did to them. They gave their lives so he could enjoy playing God."

Her breath hitched, and tears swam in her eyes, making them seem bluer. Seemed the mystery woman didn't like being reminded of just what kind of man she worked for.

Good.

She needed the reminder.

Despite everything she was a part of, there was still a shred of humanity left in her. It was why she'd put her own life on the line to try to warn them. Which made no sense considering he was there now and she hadn't spoken a single word to him. She hadn't asked for mercy, offered intel in exchange for her life, or reminded him she'd turned on her boss. All she'd done was just spout out some random facts and then try to find out how she could please him.

With her top now split from top to bottom, gaping open to reveal a set of small but perfect breasts, he pressed the tip of his knife into her belly button. "He likes playing God, doesn't he? Creating life. Only he thinks his own creations are abominations. Monsters. Animals, I think he told his sister we were. But you know all of that, after all, you chose to work for him, right?"

A small whimper emanated from his pretty little captive. She didn't like being reminded that she worked for a man who had so little regard for human life. But at least he could take that as affirmation she was indeed one of Dr. Gardner's employees and not just the man's daughter, or some other innocent caught up in the whole mess.

Not that he'd ever really thought that was the case. If she weren't involved, she would have come clean with him about how she was connected to the man as soon as he dragged her from her bed.

It was her own guilt that kept her silent.

Moving to stand behind her, Blade reached up and grabbed the end of the left sleeve of her ruined T-shirt, dragged his knife through the thin material, and then repeated the process with the right sleeve.

Ripping the clothing from her body, he was about to start cutting through her pajama bottoms, about to taunt her about other ways to create life, possibly imply he might be down with raping her—not something that was on the table, he had his limits and that was one he wouldn't cross, not that she knew that—when he froze.

Hell ... her back.

The entire thing looked like someone had branded it, not just once but over and over again. Starting up near her left shoulder blade, there were those little bundles of five lines people did when marking things off, four lines side by side, then one crossing over them, tally marks. There were five lots of those marks in a row, and then five rows beneath, for a total of six rows, then beneath the sixth was a seventh that had two complete bundles of five and one with two lines.

Those last two marks were bright red as though they had been recently inflicted.

Someone had used this woman's back as some sort of sick tally board.

Who the hell would do that to her?

Running the pad of a finger over the bumpy marks, he knew enough about different ways to torture people to know that these were brands. Someone had seared this woman's flesh repeatedly. But why? What did the marks mean? And why the hell hadn't she told him that she hadn't just worked for Dr. Gardner, she'd been tortured by him?

"What do they mean?" he growled as his finger circled the newer, redder lines, but didn't brush over them since he wasn't sure if they were still painful.

Instead of answering, she just whimpered, and once again Blade felt his control snap.

Closing a hand around her throat, he pressed up against her until her back was plastered across his chest. "You better tell me what the hell is going on, who burned your back like you're some kind of scorecard, why you broke rank to try to warn me and my team, and what your involvement is, or I'm going to make what was done to your back feel like a massage in comparison to what I'm going to do to you."

January 11<sup>th</sup>
    5:17 P.M.

"I'm the one who created the drug, so I have to bear the marks of each person who didn't survive the treatment," Whitney shrieked, terrified of what this man would do to her if she didn't tell him what he wanted to hear.

She barely survived the burning pain in her back each time one of the test subjects didn't live through the process. The smell of burning flesh as she was branded, knowing it was her own burning flesh, made her throw up every single time.

There was no chance she could survive worse than that.

Like she'd destroyed whatever control Blade had left with a single sentence, the hand around her neck tightened until she could no longer draw in any air. The knife, which had tormented her and then cut her top from her body, was suddenly poised on her chest above her heart. While he didn't push it into her flesh deep enough to cause her any serious injury, he did allow it to dig into her skin, and she felt the trickle of blood trail down her stomach, the liquid icy cold in stark contrast to her suddenly overheated skin.

"You? You did this to us?" He snarled, his breath hot against her ear.

Was she supposed to reconfirm what she'd just said?

Backtrack and pretend he'd misheard her?

He hadn't given her a clear indication of what he expected of her, so she wasn't sure what to do. Whitney didn't know how to exist in any scenario that didn't have explicit guidelines. She'd been groomed and trained to be the perfect little scientist, she lived in order, under the strict control of others. There was no room for her to make her own choices or have her own opinion, which was why Blade would never understand the courage it had taken her to plan herself an out.

An out that had failed pretty spectacularly, given her current situation.

"It's all because of you." That hand tightened further, and on instinct her body began to buck as her lungs screamed for air.

Only there was no air for them.

Just a rough hand slowly killing her as the knife dug deeper into her skin.

*Just do it.*

The words whispered through her mind, and Whitney realized that she meant them. She was tired of being forced to do things against her will, tired of living as a prisoner, tired of never being free to be in charge of her own life.

Maybe it would be better if Blade just killed her here and now without any more suffering. Strangled or stabbed through her heart, she didn't really care, either worked and in the end the result would be the same.

Instead of fighting against the encroaching darkness, Whitney allowed herself to fall toward it.

Soon.

It would all be over soon.

Right as she was about to slip into unconsciousness, the pressure around her neck was suddenly gone.

For a second, her lungs couldn't quite figure out what to do.

Should they inhale a lifesaving breath, or should they do what they'd been prepared to and just give in to the peacefulness of death?

A sharp slap on her back took the decision out of her hands, and she gasped and choked on the oxygen that flooded her system.

"Breathe," a voice ordered. The harsh command seemed to seep inside her body, and she was powerless to do anything other than obey.

Another breath followed the first, then a third, and a fourth. Gradually, the choking ceased as her breathing evened out and became more natural.

Slowly, her vision cleared, and the forest, bathed in the soft glow of twilight, came back into view. Standing right before her was a man with dark hair and eyes as black as the darkest night. He was staring at her with an expression she wasn't sure she'd be able to read even if she hadn't just nearly died.

"Breathe," he ordered again, and this time a hand lifted to settle on her head, sweeping gently down her hair. If she didn't know without a shadow of a doubt that the man hated her, she would have described the gesture as tender.

But he did hate her.

With good reason.

She was the one who had created the drug that had stolen a decade of his life from him. Forever changed him. Forced him to leave everything behind and hide away from the rest of the world.

"S-sorry," she stammered. If only a simple apology was enough to undo the mess she'd created.

Instead of accepting her apology—which she hadn't expected him to do—or to yell at her some more, maybe slice her open again, tell her he only didn't want her to die because she deserved to suffer a much longer, more agonizing death, he merely shook his head.

"I don't believe you," Blade said. Once again, he circled her neck with his long fingers, only this time he didn't squeeze, if anything, he almost caressed the bruises she was sure were already beginning to form.

He didn't believe her?

Why wouldn't he? After all, he knew who she worked for. Was it that much of a stretch to believe this had all started because of her?

"You're too young. I don't know how old you are, but you're not thirty like your fake ID says. Even if you were, that would make you only twenty a decade ago when my team and I were injected with the drugs. You wouldn't even have been old enough to graduate college, let alone create a drug like that."

Oh dear.

If he thought twenty was too young to have graduated from college and created the drug, he certainly wasn't going to believe her if she told him he was a decade off.

But what else could she do?

She'd come this far, she had to follow through, had to tell him the truth. Even if he tortured and killed her afterward, she'd give him every bit of information she had on Dr. Gardner, although granted it wasn't a lot.

"I was ten," she whispered, letting her head drop, unable to look at him while she bared her greatest sins to one of her victims.

"Uh-uh." The hand on her neck shifted slightly, cupping her jaw and tilting her head back up so she had no choice but to meet his gaze. That or close her eyes to block him out, and that seemed too childish.

Seemed impossible too.

There was something magnetic about those midnight eyes of his that she couldn't break away from.

"Tell me. Everything," he commanded, and once again she felt powerless to disobey.

"Ten. I was ten when I graduated from college. My name is Whitney Daley, and I was a child genius. I graduated from high school at seven. At ten, I had four college degrees. I didn't have friends, no little kid wants to be friends with another little kid who doesn't actually know how to be a kid, and no adult wants to be friends with a ten-year-old smarter than they'll ever be. The drug was something I'd been thinking about since I was five."

"You wanted to create an army of super soldiers when you were five years old?" Blade sounded incredulous at the idea.

"No. That's not ... the drug wasn't supposed to .... When I graduated, my parents were approached by a man. One who had connections to the military and was a scientist just like me. He told them if they let him take me, I'd help him change the world, and since they never really knew what to do with a child like me anyway, they agreed."

"Your mom was a scientist, too. Worked for From Nature."

Shocked that he knew that, she nodded. "Her family owned the company, but she was the only one left still working there. He bought the company, but really what he was buying was ..." Whitney trailed off, unable to say it out loud.

"You," Blade finished for her. "Dr. Gardner bought you when you were ten years old. That's why your mom retired so early."

"I don't know how you know that, but yeah, she did. Win-win, she got enough money to live the rest of her life however she wanted, and she got rid of the problem that was me. I went to live with Dr. Gardner, at the warehouse, in one of the buildings out the back. He scrubbed my existence from every database, making it like I don't even exist. I don't think you'll find me with the fingerprints, he was thorough. If I didn't exist, then I couldn't run. I had nowhere to go, and I was just a little girl, barely in double digits. What else was I supposed to do but whatever he ordered me to?"

The image of Blade standing before her blurred as tears filled her eyes. It had been a long time since Whitney cried for the little girl she'd been back then. Alone and scared. Locked away from the rest of the world, no ally who put her needs first, no one to care what happened to her.

"All of what happened to you was my fault. I created that drug, but, Blade, please, you have to believe me. I never wanted that to happen, never intended it to. My drug was supposed to help children living in poverty have a better chance at survival. Make them strong, more immune to illness, better able to withstand temperature extremes, and their bodies better able to tolerate not having enough food. My drug was supposed to save lives. Instead, Dr. Gardner turned it into something that ended lives, and now I carry each and every one of those deaths on my back, where they belong."

# CHAPTER Six

January 11th
5:29 P.M.

"No."

The word burst from him with a ferocity that caught him by surprise. Whitney, as well, if the way her mouth dropped open and her eyes widened was anything to go by.

If what she'd said was true, then ...

Hell, he and his team were batting two for two when it went for going after people connected to Dr. Gardner and winding up with innocents.

*If* it were true.

And right or wrong, Blade was inclined to believe her.

Sure, it was one hell of a story, but they'd always worried from the beginning when Cassandra first gave them the sketch of the woman who had accosted her at the park with a warning for them that she looked far too young to be involved. There was every chance the woman was lying about her age, but then again, he would have put her around early twenties, which was exactly how old she claimed to be.

What she'd said about From Nature also linked to what they knew. That the woman Cassandra thought looked similar to the one she'd met, just several decades older, had taken a huge payout and retired early. That was around twelve years ago, which would again put Whitney at twenty-two if she'd been ten back then when she graduated from college.

Graduating from college at ten with four degrees, that had to be a lie, right?

There was no way, and yet was it really any less believable than everything else the woman had just told him?

"Yes," Whitney countered, although her bottom lip wobbled and tears shimmered in her eyes. It was abundantly clear that she wholeheartedly blamed herself for each and every mark on her skin that she said counted for a person who didn't survive the anger and suicidal thoughts that came with the drugs.

There was a hint of defiance back in those big blue eyes of hers, and he found it somewhat amusing that she was prepared to argue with him over blame for the deaths of those who took her drug, but not to spare her own life.

"If what you just told me is true, then it would make none of what happened your fault. Little girls can't make their own choices about their futures, and your parents, damn, darlin', they sold you."

"If," she repeated, and it was like her entire body sagged at that one small word. "So you don't believe me. Of course you don't," she muttered, although that seemed to be more to herself than him, a reminder that she was on her own, she didn't have a single ally or a team member to have her back.

What he and his team had suffered at the hands of Dr. Gardner was horrific. The tests, the loss of freedom, being treated like test subjects and not humans, and spending three years locked in a cage, the pain, the anger, but through it all, he had never once been alone. There had been plenty of times during those three years of captivity that he'd wished for privacy, that his every move wasn't watched, and he could have just a moment to himself, but the truth was, he might not have survived it without knowing he had a team at his back. Without them, he might have fallen victim to the same rage and suicidal thoughts that had claimed the rest of the test subjects.

"According to your own story, there's nothing to verify it because your very existence has been wiped away."

How the hell were he and his team going to know whether Whitney could be trusted or not? He couldn't even prove it was her real name. There were definite indications that what she'd said was true, she was young enough for her story, and it did link into the sale of the building, but was that enough?

Trusting her could lead to their destruction. What if the whole setup was a ploy? She goes to Cassandra, offers a warning, and Dr. Gardner would know they'd search for the woman. Then she magically appears after the explosion that nearly killed them, and she has a whole house rented out a couple of hours away where she's just waiting for him to show up.

Just because he couldn't hear anyone out there in the forest didn't mean they weren't being watched. This whole place could be under surveillance, and Dr. Gardner was just waiting for the rest of his team to show up to get their vengeance before springing the trap and coming in to try to abduct them.

"Because I'm just a tool to be used," Whitney whispered wearily, and despite the fact that he still held her neck in his hand, her face angled so it was looking right at him, her gaze dropped, and a single tear rolled free.

Something about that lone tear called out to him. He wanted to catch it with his tongue, absorb it, carry the heavy weight that had been placed on this woman's shoulder, a woman young enough that she was barely able to drink legally.

But what if it was all a lie?

A game?

A trap?

There was no way he could allow himself to fall for it without some sort of verification, but if there was none, then despite her possible innocence, killing this woman might be the only way to keep his team safe.

Abruptly releasing his hold on Whitney, the thought of ending her life making him nauseous even though that had literally been the plan when he followed her, Blade took in a deep breath. He couldn't allow emotion to cloud his judgment. Who the hell would have guessed that after spending a decade believing he was barely capable of feeling any emotion that wasn't anger, that he would now be concerned that he'd make a mistake because he felt something?

Leaving her hanging right where she was, the safest place to keep her, even as Blade fought guilt because his gut screamed at him that she was indeed an innocent, he headed back for the farmhouse. He needed to call his team, tell them what he'd learned, and allow clearer heads to decide what came next.

Slamming the door behind him, Blade went straight to the kitchen counter, scooped up his phone, and brought up Steel's number. His team leader answered on the first ring.

"Nothing on the fingerprint yet," Steel informed him.

"Don't think there's going to be anything on it," he said.

"You got her talking?" Thunder asked.

"Yeah." And he wasn't proud of what he'd done to make it happen. For a moment there, he was positive he'd killed her. By the time the haze of fury had cleared enough that he was able to process the fact that she was too young to have done what she claimed, Whitney had barely been breathing. Now knowing that he might have placed blame on a ten-year-old's shoulders left him ... shaken.

"What did she say?" Lion asked.

"That her name is Whitney Daley. That Cassandra was right, and that woman who ended up connecting us to From Nature is her mother. That she's the one who created the initial version of the drug when she was ten years old."

"Ten?" Voodoo repeated, incredulous.

"So she's what, twenty odd?" Dragon asked.

"Twenty-two, according to my calculations," he confirmed.

"She created it?" Steel asked, again clearly incredulous.

"She created *a* drug that she wanted to use to save children living in poverty, but then her parents sold her to Dr. Gardner, who must have found out about it, and decided to buy her so he could keep her as his own personal little scientist slave," he replied.

"If that's true ..." Lion trailed off, but they all knew what he meant.

If this woman was innocent, then once again, they might have burned a bridge that could have potentially helped them.

"Is she okay?" Cassandra asked softly.

Dragging a hand through his hair, Blade hesitated. How did he answer that? Whitney was alive, breathing, none of her injuries were serious, but she could hardly be described as being anywhere close to okay.

But he didn't want to say that. Cassandra had walked away from all of them, from Dragon in particular, when she found out they had plans to go after Dr. Gardner's sister. The two of them had only just gotten together, and it was mostly because of the woman hanging in the tree outside. While Cassandra now understood the stakes, he still knew she wasn't okay with torturing people, even if they'd believed them to be an enemy.

"She's as okay as she can be," he replied.

"Maybe I could talk to her," Rose offered. "I know my brother better than anyone else because he raised me. If he kind of raised her, too, I can probably figure it out by asking some questions."

"If she's lying, though, and we bring her here, that makes for one hell of a security risk," Steel said, and he knew that now the man had Rose, he took their safety even more seriously than he always had before. "Do you believe her?"

Therein lay the problem. As much as he hated to answer that, admitting his weaknesses to his team, keeping them alive and safe was his only priority so he had to be honest. "I don't know. I think when it comes to reading her, I'm compromised."

∿

January 11<sup>th</sup>
6:05 P.M.

He'd been gone a really long time.

At least it felt like it.

Maybe it wasn't ... Whitney wasn't sure anymore.

Everything felt hazy ... distant ... numb.

Other than an overall throbbing throughout her body, and a cold that seemed to have seeped deep inside her and would never be able to be removed, she didn't feel anything else, even though she knew she had several cuts from the knife, bruising around her neck from Blade's hand, and her wrists and shoulders were a mess from hanging for so long.

"Doesn't matter that you'll never feel warm again," she reminded herself aloud because she needed something to break the oppressive silence, and now that she'd started talking again that block of fear seemed to have disappeared.

What was the point of being afraid?

It wouldn't change the outcome of her situation.

Blade didn't believe her, and of course, he was right, there was nothing to verify anything she'd said, because for all intents and purposes, she didn't exist anymore.

"You exist for the purposes of revenge, though."

That was absolutely true. And she deserved whatever Blade and his team had planned for her. After all, whether it turned out the way she had intended or not, it was her drug that had forever changed his life. It was because of her drug that he'd been kept captive for three years and then had to live the last seven in hiding because Dr. Gardner would never stop looking for them.

Never stop looking for her, either.

Although she guessed that since Blade and his team were going to end her life anyway, she didn't have to worry about her former boss getting his hands on her. She might be a commodity he didn't want to lose, but he could still punish her for turning on him and escaping. Guess there was a silver lining to every cloud.

Was there really?

No.

But it sounded nice.

Sounded hopeful.

Sounded ...

"Hey."

A slap to her cheek accompanied the harsh word, and Whitney realized with a weird sort of detachment she hoped stuck around for her upcoming torture, that she must have passed out.

Oh well.

What could he expect? She hadn't slept properly in over a week, none at all in the last couple of days. She hadn't eaten or had anything to drink in twenty-four hours, and she'd been hanging from a tree in the cold for almost a day.

"Sorry, won't be much fun to torture, can't stay awake," she mumbled, some distant part of her mind telling her she didn't need to apologize for that, but she didn't care.

Didn't care much about anything anymore.

Just wanted to rest.

That would be nice.

When had she ever really been allowed to rest? She had to always be working. Brain too big, too smart, had to work.

But not now.

Now she got to rest.

At least until the torture started.

"Not torturing you," Blade snapped, like he was offended by the idea.

Which was stupid. That's why he'd followed her there. It was what he'd been doing for almost a day now.

"Although this is going to suck. Big time," he muttered as he wrapped an arm around her waist.

He felt nice. Warm. But then he lifted her body, and agony unlike anything she'd felt before tore through her shoulders, and she screamed, long and loud.

Hadn't he just said he wasn't going to torture her?

Moving her was torturing her.

"Leave me," she begged as the pain worsened when he shifted her position a little. She'd rather hang there in her numb state and die than be moved and live. Messed up maybe, but honestly, she had nothing to live for other than the sake of being alive. And being alive was seriously overrated.

"No. It'll get better in a moment," Blade said, his voice tight, and she'd felt him flinch at her scream because he was holding her weight. "Tell me something."

"Tell you something?"

"One of your random facts that you say when you're nervous."

"Oh ..." For once, her mind was blank. Nothing in it. That never happened, her brain was like a machine always running on overdrive. It was nice to have a break from that.

"Come on, Whitney. Tell me something," Blade insisted. "This is going to be hell, but it's going to be over soon."

"You're going to kill me?" she asked, noticing the note of hopefulness in her tone. Right now, death seemed like a blessing if it stopped her from hurting like this.

"No," he snarled the word at her. "Now start talking. I'm going to cut you down, then carry you inside. Your shoulders have dislocated from holding your weight for so long, but they'll feel better when I put them back in. Inside, I'm going to clean you up, get you pain meds, and something to eat and drink. Warm you up as well. But this will all be easier if you distract yourself."

Easier?

For her or for him?

Because from where she was standing—hanging—nothing about this was easy for her.

"Please, Whitney." That whispered plea held more emotion than she would have guessed, given that she was his enemy and he wanted her dead.

Or didn't?

She wasn't sure whether that had changed despite the change in his attitude.

"The space between your eyebrows is called your glabella," she started reciting meaningless facts. Maybe he was right. Maybe it would help with the torture. Because he could call it whatever he wanted, but being moved more would be torture.

"Good girl," he murmured, and then she felt the nick of a knife, and the next thing she knew, her arms were dropping down.

Another scream was torn from her lips at the excruciating agony.

The world shimmered again, and she didn't hesitate to let it tug at her consciousness.

"Talk," Blade ordered, and the word seemed to have some sort of magical power over her, because she did.

As he carried her toward the house, she kept spouting off facts.

"That little bit at the end of your shoelaces, the plastic or metal bit, it's called an aglet. When a newborn baby cries, it's called a vagitus. The prongs of a fork are called tines."

Another cry of pain derailed her speech when Blade stepped inside, and the warmth against her frozen skin felt like thousands of fire ants dancing all over her.

The tension in Blade's body seemed to ramp up several notches, but his steps didn't falter as he carried her toward a couch. At the edges of her blurry vision, tears streamed down her cheeks in a steady flood. She noted he'd put a towel down on the couch to make it an easier clean up after he killed her?

"Make it quick, please," she whimpered as he set her down on the towel, and a fresh wave of pain rolled over her.

"I'll have them back in place in a moment," he assured her.

"No, I meant killing me, the towel, to clean up after, quick, please," she rambled, not sure if she was making sense in her effort to get the words out.

A large hand grabbed her face. The pressure was enough to clear her vision a little, and she found Blade's face mere inches from her own. "Towel is there because you're dirty, I told you I'm not killing you."

Had he?

Implied it maybe, but not outright stated it.

Was that a good thing or a bad thing? Did it mean he was keeping her alive to torture her indefinitely or that he believed her despite there being zero evidence?

"Not made to survive torture," she whispered. She wasn't strong or tough, wasn't a warrior, she was a brain and nothing more, and she hadn't trained her brain to handle those levels of pain.

"I think you're made to survive a whole lot more than you give yourself credit for, darlin'."

For once, the way Blade said the word darling didn't sound like an insult. It sounded almost affectionate, even as she knew that couldn't be true. Even if he believed she hadn't been a willing participant in creating the drug as it had been developed, she was still an enemy. Still the one responsible for everything he'd been through.

This close, he was very handsome.

Had nice eyes ... so dark.

Nice lips ... might be nice to kiss them.

Totally inappropriate thoughts ... but she couldn't seem to help them. Must be delirious from the pain.

A hand ghosted over her cheek. "Keep talking, Whitney, this is going to be the worst part."

Keep talking.

Okay.

She could do that.

Following orders was kind of her thing.

"When you close your eyes, press your hands to them, and you see that flare of light, that's called phosphenes."

Hands braced just above one of her shoulders, and just below, and her entire body tensed, bracing for the pain.

"Will go a whole lot easier if you relax," Blade told her, but that was impossible. No way she could relax.

"The day after tomorrow is called overmorrow. And when you put an exclamation mark together with a question mark, it's called a—"

Whitney never finished that sentence, because Blade popped her shoulder back into place, and the shaft of indescribable pain that stabbed through her was the final strike her brain needed before it checked out.

# CHAPTER

## Seven

January 11th
6:16 P.M.

At least putting her other shoulder back in had been a whole lot easier after Whitney passed out.

Blade had also been able to strip her out of her ruined clothes, quickly wiped her down with as much professional detachment as possible, although she would need a real shower when she was stronger, and got her dressed into another pair of pajamas he'd found in her closet, while she was out. All of that was easier to do while she wasn't awake and in pain, but it still left him feeling like he'd violated her, even if all he'd done was the same thing a nurse would do if he'd dropped her off at a hospital.

Maybe he should drop her off at a hospital.

Being around her, knowing what he'd put her through and that she was likely another of Dr. Gardner's victims, made him feel like the monster the scientist had tried to turn him into. Knowing that he'd made the right move with the information he'd had at the time didn't help.

Ten.

Hell, he couldn't get over that.

Whitney had only been ten years old when she was sold to Dr. Gardner. She'd been groomed and trained to be the perfect little scientist slave, and yet, she wasn't. Not really. Despite over a decade of conditioning and brainwashing, she'd broken away from her captor and made the choice to warn him and his team, knowing it was going to put her life on the line.

Which was why he couldn't take her to a hospital, even as the rage inside him howled at himself, wanting to punish him for hurting an innocent. Dr. Gardner wouldn't allow Whitney's betrayal to go unpunished, he'd send people after her if he found out where she was.

So his options were to believe Whitney, which meant she was in danger and leaving her would put her back in the doctor's clutches, or not believe her, which meant she was an enemy and he needed to get her back to his team for interrogation.

Because one thing he did know was that he was compromised when it came to this pretty blonde.

A moan tumbled from her lips when he began to massage her right arm to get blood flowing again, and her lashes fluttered against paper-pale cheeks. Seemed like Whitney was waking up. Honestly, all of this would be easier if she stayed unconscious. He could just bundle her up, stick her in her vehicle, and drive her to the airport.

"Hurts," she whimpered as she woke further.

"Got to get blood circulating again," he said, somewhat gruffly, trying to gentle his tone a little to keep her calm, even as his anger grew.

At her?

At him?

Blade wasn't even sure, but he knew that it was mostly directed at the man truly responsible for all of this, Dr. Ridge Gardner.

"Finish what you were telling me," he ordered, needing the distraction as much as she did.

"Telling you?" Her eyes had opened now, those pretty blue orbs locked onto him. He could still see fear in them, she didn't trust him, and she was wise not to.

"When you put an exclamation mark together with a question

mark, it's called a ..." he prompted, reminding her of what she'd been saying when the pain got to be too much for her and she passed out. Actually, he knew the answer to that one, but he wanted to hear her say it. Maybe even needed to hear her say it, needed to know he hadn't completely broken what more than likely was an innocent woman who had been used and abused.

"An interrobang," she finished softly. Then she coughed a little, choking on her words, the red marks on her neck, caused by his own hand, darkening almost before his very eyes.

Knowing he'd almost killed her, that he'd lost control like that ...

Was there any other way to describe himself than as a monster?

He stood abruptly. Her limbs would need more work before full blood flow returned, but right now she needed water for her throat. Leaving her on the couch, there was no way she was in any condition to escape, he went to the kitchen, grabbed a bottle of water from the fridge, and poured it into a glass.

It wasn't until he walked back toward the couch, saw her eyes grow wide, and her body begin to tremble that he realized what she was thinking about.

Hanging from the tree, him pouring water down her nose, choking and spluttering as she probably felt for a moment like she was drowning.

"Just for you to drink," he assured her, holding up his free hand, palm up, in an attempt to calm her already racing heart.

That heart rate jumped again when he kept moving until he was standing over her, her terrified gaze now locked on the glass in his hands. There was no way for him to avoid this, short of depriving her of water when she was already dehydrated.

"You can't hold the glass on your own," Blade told her, doing his best to infuse as much gentleness into his tone as possible, even as it didn't seem to do any good. "Your shoulders, and the lack of blood flow, you need help. I swear, Whitney, I'm not going to hurt you, just hold the glass to your lips and let you drink."

Forcing himself to stand completely still, he waited until she got herself under control. He'd already stolen enough of her autonomy, and now, knowing how she'd spent most of her life, he needed to give her this choice.

After a tense sixty seconds, Whitney gave a tight nod.

Permission granted, he knelt beside the couch and curled his free hand behind her neck to steady her, very aware of the spike in her pulse at the contact. But his other hand was steady as he brought the glass to her lips, even as his own heart rate accelerated.

Whitney's body trembled, but she parted her lips and swallowed a tentative sip. It was like that first mouthful cleared away her fears, because she then began to drink greedily, and whimpered a protest when he pulled the glass away after she'd downed half of it.

"You're dehydrated, don't want you vomiting this right back up again," he told her as he set the glass on the coffee table. "I'm going to clean and bandage your wrists, then you can have some more."

She didn't say anything, just tracked his every move as he reached for the first aid kit he'd found earlier, and began to tend to her torn wrists. Hanging for so long had ruined the skin beyond repair. It would heal, but not well, and she'd be left with nasty-looking scars. If she'd been guilty, she would deserve every second of the pain dangling from her wrists would have caused her, but the more he watched her, saw how timid she was, how scared, he didn't believe she was guilty of anything.

Once her wrists were bandaged, he brought the glass to her lips again. This time, she didn't hesitate to drink, and although she jumped when the glass was empty and he began to massage her arms again, she didn't try to pull away.

"What happens now?" she asked several minutes later. There was a weariness in her gaze he wanted to erase, and the guilt from being told she was responsible for the deaths of those who hadn't survived being injected with the drugs seemed to cling to her.

If he hadn't already wanted Dr. Gardner dead, he would now that he knew the man had literally branded a young girl and told her she was responsible for people's deaths. If the ages were correct, Whitney would have only been twelve when he and his team signed up for the program. They were the first, but there had been others in the facility with them. At most, Whitney would have been thirteen when the first men died, barely a teenager, nothing more than a child.

But it was clear she believed what she'd been told. She carried the weight of each death on her slim shoulders, just like it was clear she still believed he was going to punish her for sins she had been forced to commit.

"Now you get some sleep," he told her simply. She needed food, but she needed rest more. He'd get her some more water and some painkillers, and then she needed a good night's sleep. In the morning, he'd break the news that he was taking her back home with him, and he was only reasonably certain the rest of his team believed she was telling them the truth.

"Sleep?" she echoed like it was the last thing she expected him to say, and it was obvious she was waiting for the catch.

Which was smart, because there was one.

"We both need sleep," he said firmly as he set her arm down and moved to grab something he knew was going to freak her out.

"Both of us?"

"Both," he agreed as he turned around and snapped the metal cuff around her wrist before she registered what he was doing, the other end of the handcuff went around his own wrist. "Hope you don't snore because I hate that sound."

~

January 12th
6:38 A.M.

Whitney had to pee, but she wasn't sure what the rules were.

She was a prisoner, she knew that much. The very fact that she was still chained up, even if it was now a handcuff attached to a huge man instead of ropes around her wrists and hanging from a tree, was proof of that.

At least she'd been allowed to sleep in the bed. After cuffing her to him, Blade had scooped her up, carried her to the bedroom, and tucked them both under the covers. Hard as it was, she'd managed to fall asleep in a position where her body didn't touch his, but when she'd woken up a moment ago, she could see she'd shifted during the night.

Not just shifted, but rolled onto her side, pressed herself right up against Blade, and used his rock-hard chest as a pillow. A surprisingly comfortable pillow. She wasn't the only one who had moved, though. Blade had shifted, too, angled himself so that he brought her closer, their joined hands sandwiched between them, and his other hand resting on her hip.

The position was ... intimate.

Exactly how she would imagine happy couples sleeping together. Only they weren't a happy couple. They weren't a happy anything. Or at least she wasn't. No doubt her take on the situation as the captive and Blade's as the captor of someone responsible for altering his life were entirely different.

"How long do you plan on lying there before you say something?"

Totally unprepared for his voice, especially since she'd thought Blade was still asleep, Whitney let out a startled yelp and jerked herself backward, temporarily forgetting that she was cuffed to the man. Pain screamed through her shoulder at the movement, and she cried out before she even realized it. The sound startled her again, and she would have fallen off the bed if Blade hadn't caught her.

Not just snapped his hand into the one cuffed right beside his, which would have done the job, although caused her more pain in the process. Nope, he somehow moved his entire body in the same second she was falling, and wrapped an arm around her waist, pulling her against him.

"Didn't mean to scare you," he said, his voice rumbling through the chest she was now once again pressed against.

It really was a very nice chest. All hard planes and perfect definition. Of course, she got that she was still in danger from this man, even if he had been gentle with her just then, gentle with her last night as well as he cleaned the wounds on her wrists and massaged feeling back into her arms.

But that didn't change anything, and she would do well to remember that.

"It's okay," she whispered, her gaze darting about, settling anywhere other than on the face far too close to hers. Not just because she was afraid of what she might see in his eyes, but also because she was afraid to let him see what was in hers. He would expect the pain and fear, but he'd think she was stupid if he noted the attraction.

She just couldn't help it, she'd never been this close to a man so full of raw power. Usually, she was around scientists, people who spent more time sitting in front of a computer or working in a lab than they did in a gym, their bodies were soft and gooey not hard and toned. Sure, there were always guards about, but they kept their distance, mostly patrolling outside the lab not inside it.

"What were you thinking about?" Blade asked as he lifted her with him as he climbed off the bed and stood.

Slowly ... oh so slowly ... he let her body glide down his as he set her on her feet. There was not a single chance she could have missed his morning erection as she brushed past it, and her cheeks flamed as she cleared her throat uncomfortably.

"Sorry," he said, not sounding the least bit sorry. "Can't help it. Side effect of sleeping with a beautiful woman plastered against me."

Shock had her gaze finally darting up to meet his, her mouth hanging open. There was no way a man who looked like Blade thought she was pretty. Absolutely no way. He was messing with her, he had to be, trying to ... disarm her? Make her trust him so he could use it against her? Make it easier on her if he raped her because she'd think it meant something?

"Relax, you know you're beautiful, don't pretend otherwise."

Uh, she absolutely did *not* know that she was beautiful. Why would she? She worked with middle-aged men and women all day, all under the same boss, one who was cruel and harsh. They worked, they didn't talk, and no one ever implied in any way that they thought she was attractive.

So, no, she didn't know that.

"I need to pee," she squeaked out in answer to his earlier question about what she'd been thinking about, and pretended the whole he thought she was pretty thing had never happened.

Wait.

Was she even allowed to go to the bathroom?

She was cuffed to Blade, and she didn't know how permanent it would be. Would he follow her to the bathroom and watch her do her business? If he tried, she'd likely freeze up, even as she was a little desperate after the water she'd been given last night. Blade had brought a bottle up with them and told her to sip her way through it before they lay down to sleep, and now she really did need to go, even if she did have an audience.

Eyeing her carefully, she half expected something mocking to come out of his mouth because surely, he still hated her and would enjoy taunting her, but instead, all she read in his gaze was thoughtful consideration.

"Take a shower while you're in there and get dressed."

"On my own?" It was almost too much to hope for.

Blade nodded. "I'll go downstairs and make us some breakfast. We should eat before we head out."

"Head out?" They were leaving? Of course they were, it would make sense, although she assumed leaving meant taking her to his team so they could all join in the fun of punishing her for choices she'd no other option but to make.

"I'm hoping you'll agree to come back home with me."

Whitney scoffed before she realized antagonizing her captor was a stupid thing to do. "As if it matters if I agree. You hold all the power here, and we both know it. If you want me to go back with you then I'm going, I don't have a choice." Never had a choice. Her life had been in someone else's hands for as long as she could remember.

Nodding slowly, Blade continued to examine her. "I'd like for you to agree. You have information we can use to bring down Dr. Gardner, and I think that's something you want to do as well."

That was still being used, but for an infinitely better purpose than what Dr. Gardner had been using her for the last twelve years. And Blade was right, she wanted the man destroyed for everyone he had made her hurt.

But she wasn't stupid, she did not need to have one of the highest recorded IQs to know that it wasn't all these men wanted from her. They wanted someone to punish, someone to hurt in return for all the hurt they themselves had suffered. They might use her knowledge, but when they had gotten everything out of her that they could, Whitney had no doubt that what came next was the same torture and death they had originally planned for her.

Still, she owed them that.

Owed them her pain, her screams, her blood.

Whether it had been her choice or not, she was still the one who created the drug, still the one responsible not only for the suffering of Blade and his team, but for all the others who had lost their lives.

This wasn't really a choice, just the illusion of one, but since she had no other options, she gave a weary nod. Maybe if she played along, it would take the edge off a little of the torture they had planned for her.

"Okay," she agreed. "I'll come with you." Why fight against something that was happening anyway?

With slow, deliberate motions, Blade removed the key from the pocket of the sweatpants he had slept in and unlocked the handcuff from around her wrist. Before releasing her hand, he lifted it carefully and rotated it, examining the white bandage he'd secured around her wrist. Only when he must have seen that there was no blood did he lower her arm until it hung by her side.

"Take as long as you want. When you're done, I'll rebandage your wounds, then we can eat and leave. Oh, and, Whitney. Don't bother trying to run, I'll hear it if you open a window. I don't want to have to tie you up again."

After delivering his warning, he turned and left the bedroom, leaving her staring after him, tears welling in her eyes. So much for he would like her to agree to come with him. There had been no choice, never was.

It seemed she was destined to live her entire life trapped in a cage.

# CHAPTER

*Eight*

January 12th
  8:11 A.M.

It was crazy, but Blade was fairly certain that he actually trusted Whitney more right now than she trusted him.

They should probably both distrust each other equally. He had no way to prove that she had been nothing more than a ten-year-old girl when she created the drug and was sold to Dr. Gardner, and she had no way of knowing that he didn't have any more plans to torture her.

Maybe he should. Little girl or not, she was still the person who had created the drug that stole his life from him, but what kind of monster would he be to punish a literal child for something she'd had zero control over?

Whitney's drug was intended to save lives, not create super soldiers, and certainly not end lives. Blaming her for the fact that her parents, the people who were supposed to love and protect her, sold her to a mad scientist who exploited her was wrong. Plain and simple.

The thing was, he did believe what she'd told him.

All of it.

The timeline and what she'd said about her mom aligned with what they already knew, and she very clearly looked like she was in her early twenties. Sure, she could just have really good genes, but he didn't think that was the case.

Then there was this ... "Whitney."

Without any hesitation, she turned her head to look at him, the sound of her own name so ingrained in her that even though she'd clearly been lost in thought, staring out the car window at the farmhouse they were about to leave behind, she'd registered her name being called.

More proof she'd been telling him the truth.

"Hmm?" she asked, like she wasn't quite sure she was supposed to talk. He'd noticed that about her. She seemed unsettled whenever he didn't give her explicit instructions about what he expected. Floundering. It was no wonder. He knew enough about Ridge Gardner and how the man treated others from what Rose had told them about her childhood to know that the man would have micromanaged every aspect of Whitney's life for the last twelve years.

"You ready to go?"

"If you're ready," she answered, like she believed what she wanted had no bearing on the situation.

In some regards, she wasn't wrong. It wasn't safe to leave her there alone, she was too close to the warehouse, and he wouldn't put it past Dr. Gardner to have people combing the area for her, after all, she'd betrayed him and he wouldn't accept that. He'd cuffed her last night because he needed sleep as much as she did, and neither one of them would get it if Whitney escaping was on the table.

But he didn't consider her a captive.

A tool to be used, sure, she had valuable intel about Dr. Gardner that Rose could never provide because the crazed scientist's little sister wasn't part of his military plans to turn regular soldiers into super soldiers. But Blade was making sure he didn't stop seeing Whitney as a real person, a living, breathing human being with her own thoughts, needs, and emotions. She'd been used more than enough in her young life.

And damn, was she young.

Twelve years younger than he was. Twelve years, the entire time she'd been living as Dr. Gardner's prisoner. And what had her life been like before that? Graduating from high school at seven, and college with four degrees by ten, hadn't left her with much time to just be a child. Likely her entire life had been doing what others expected of her.

"Let's get out of here then," he said as he turned on the engine.

"Yeah," she whispered, and she sounded exceedingly sad to be leaving a house he knew she'd only been at for a handful of days. He knew that because she'd told him that she was made to live on site, so she didn't waste valuable working time traveling. This place was in the same name as the fake ID he'd found, so she must have set herself up with a new identity, hoping it would be enough.

If he hadn't heard her in the forest the night of the explosion, it might have been.

Neither of them spoke as he drove in the car she'd obviously also set up for her getaway. It was in the same name as everything else, so it was clear it had been a piece of her plan. She'd done well, getting herself set up so she could escape, finally be free to live her life the way she chose, and Blade couldn't deny he felt bad about ruining that for her, even if he was selfish enough to keep her close and use her.

Use but not torture.

Before leaving this morning, he'd talked to his team, and they knew he was on the way. They trusted his judgment that Whitney appeared to be telling the truth. Torture was off the table for all of them, they weren't going to make the same mistakes they'd made with Rose.

Besides, he'd already tortured Whitney, and he couldn't let go of the heavy weight of guilt he felt because of it.

Should have been smarter and done more research before assuming the worst. Although he knew they couldn't possibly have guessed that a mere child had created the drug. The logical assumption was that she was running because she was involved, but still, he wished he'd simply locked her up and then figured things out.

No going back though.

All he could do was move forward. Get Whitney home, find out everything she knew, use it to destroy Dr. Gardner, and then ...

Blade wasn't sure what came next.

Let Whitney go and allow her to finally find her own way in a world that had controlled her every step so far seemed like the fair thing to do, especially if she helped them get their revenge. So why did the idea of letting her go leave him feeling like—

Abruptly, he lost his train of thought when he noticed something he didn't like.

Three cars, all black SUVs with tinted windows, were driving slower than necessary along the winding mountain roads. There wasn't a doubt in his mind that those were Dr. Gardner's people. The vehicles were the same ones that the scientist had used when they'd set the trap for him with Rose.

"We might have a problem," he warned Whitney. While he was ninety-nine percent positive that she wouldn't try to get away from him, she had to know that she was safer with him than she was with Dr. Gardner, there was that tiny sliver of doubt that she might try to escape while he was dealing with these people.

"What?" Whitney turned away from the window she was still staring out of to meet his gaze.

"Three SUVs up ahead of us."

"Those look like ..." she paused, swallowed audibly, "like the vehicles Dr. Gardner's guards use."

"Thought the same thing, darlin'."

"Can we just drive around them?"

"If we do, we're only going to draw their attention."

"Then we just keep going, follow along behind them, sooner or later they'll turn off somewhere, and we can drive past them and then go on to the airport."

That was a possibility, but he was pretty sure that as soon as they registered their presence, they would try to pull them over.

What they had on their side was that he doubted Dr. Gardner and his men knew that he was there. They were looking for Whitney, not him, and not two people. Even if he got Whitney down low, had her hide, if they saw him, they'd recognize him. There was no way every person on Dr. Gardner's staff didn't know what he and the rest of his team looked like and had orders to take them into custody if spotted.

Before he even had a chance to figure out what he wanted to do, the cars suddenly did U-turns and picked up speed as they headed toward them.

"They're coming," Whitney squeaked, shaking in her seat.

"Hold on." That was the only warning he gave before he did the same thing. Swinging the car around and heading back up the way they'd just come. All he needed was to put a tiny bit of distance between them so he could kill these men before they could get to Whitney.

"What are you doing?" Whitney cried when he suddenly yanked on the steering wheel, so they were now heading toward the trees.

"Crashing the car."

"Killing us?"

Blade chuckled despite his fear for the woman beside him. "No, darlin'. Just going to make them think we crashed, then I'm going to get you to hide while I take them out."

Because he knew Whitney was only going to panic more the longer this took, Blade aimed them at a large tree just up ahead, drove right for it, then slammed on the brake at the last minute, so their impact was minimal.

Barely feeling it, he was moving the second the car hit the tree. Grabbing his weapon, he flung open his door, closed it behind him, then rounded the car to get Whitney.

It was time to do a little hunting.

~

January 12th
   8:40 A.M.

"You're really just going to leave me here?" Whitney asked as Blade physically picked her up and set her in one of the branches of the tree he'd just crashed the car into.

He said that he was making her hide so he could take out the men in the cars that had suddenly U-turned and come after them, but she didn't believe him.

How could she?

She was his prisoner, and he had zero reason to care whether she lived or died. Okay, that wasn't entirely true. He wanted information from her, but that was it. She still absolutely believed that once he had that information, he and his team were planning on torturing her and killing her. Or maybe just killing her if they believed she'd been just a child when she was forced into this world. But in the end, dead was dead, and what else would they do?

Let her go?

Not likely.

Why let go of a perfectly good target for revenge when you could just kill them and be done with it?

Even if they let her go, she had no job, no identity, no money, no home, no family, she had nothing and nowhere to go. It wasn't like she could set herself up with a fake identity the way she had before, because then she'd been using Dr. Gardner's funds to set everything up.

"Not sure your high IQ is going to help us with this one, darlin'," Blade replied.

There wasn't really an argument she could give him to that. What good was a high IQ in a gun fight? She didn't know how to shoot, didn't want to know how to shoot, and didn't want to shoot anyone.

"But they'll see me here, I'm right above the car," she protested as the roar of engines grew closer.

"Which is exactly why they won't see you. They'll check the car, and when they see it's empty, they'll start fanning out to search for you. Now go, Whitney. Climb. Now."

The order made her whimper, but it also got her moving, and she did her best to grab hold of the branches and get up out of sight. Her arms were aching and trembling with exhaustion, and she'd never climbed a tree before in her life. Outdoor play hadn't been on her childhood schedule, and once Dr. Gardner got his hands on her, no type of play was permissible. She was a tool to be used, not a living, breathing child who might be a genius intellectually but was still a little girl emotionally and psychologically.

When she heard car doors slamming and voices shouting, Whitney froze. Looking down, she saw that Blade was no longer down there by the car, he'd disappeared somewhere and she couldn't shake the feeling that he was gone for good.

There really wasn't any reason for him to stick around. Chances were, the men searching for her had no idea that he was even with her. They were looking for her not him, and while if they spotted him, they would try to capture him alive to deliver to their boss, Blade was more than likely able to take them.

Briefly, she wondered if he might make a deal to save himself, tell them she was there, and he wouldn't kill them all if they let him go, but he wouldn't really even need to do that. Even if they didn't look up this tree right away, they would sooner or later. She had zero skills to survive out there in the woods, and while she might be able to make it back to the farmhouse, eventually the guards would find it.

Her gamble to stick close to the lab, thinking Dr. Gardner would assume she fled the country has obviously failed. She should have run when she got the chance, as fast and as far away as she could get.

Beneath her, she saw half a dozen men dressed all in black, carrying huge weapons, approach the crashed vehicle. They had those weapons pointed at the driver's seat.

Right at where they thought she was.

If they got their hands on her, she was as good as dead.

Not literally. Dr. Gardner needed her too much to kill her, but he'd double down on security for her. Keep her locked up permanently, refuse to let her have any access to the outside world, and restrict even more the little freedoms she was allowed. There would be a physical punishment as well, Whitney didn't doubt that. Something horrible, maybe even something that would leave her permanently disabled. Breaking her back and paralyzing her, confining her to a wheelchair would be something she could see him doing. Being unable to walk would make escaping nearly impossible.

"She's not there," a voice spoke, one she recognized as belonging to one of the guards who worked at the lab. He'd always been one who leered at her, talked to her like she was a child, and watched her a little too closely. He'd given her the creeps, and she didn't doubt that he'd want to join in on delivering whatever punishment Dr. Gardner issued her.

"Can't have gotten far away," another spoke, she recognized him too.

Holding her breath, Whitney kept expecting them to just look up and spot her. It was probably easier for her to see them than it was for them to see her, but still, she was dressed in jeans and a soft yellow sweater, she stood out in the tree, and these men were trained guards.

If they looked up, they would see her, it was as simple as that.

But for some reason, they didn't look up.

Instead, they started discussing how they would find her.

"We should split up," one suggested.

"In pairs," another added.

"Shouldn't take us long, after all, how far can the baby genius go on her own?" someone else asked with a snicker.

She hated that nickname. Abhorred it. The youngest of the guards were in their late twenties, which wasn't all that much older than her. Twenty-two was hardly a baby, even if she'd basically been one when Dr. Gardner first acquired her.

It was no wonder nobody knew anything else about her, though, that her intellect was the only thing that existed as far as the outside world was concerned. She herself wasn't sure who she was outside of her high IQ, she'd never been given a chance to find out. More than half her life she'd been kept locked up, forced to work long hours creating a drug she didn't believe in, especially with the side effects Dr. Gardner's meddling kept causing.

"Yeah, there are enough of us to cover each direction if we go off in pairs," said a voice that made her shiver and almost lose her grip on the tree branch she was perched on.

That voice ... it was the stuff of nightmares. That guard was her personal handler. He went everywhere she did, and he liked to hurt her. A bruising grip on her arm, a shove that sent her sprawling to the ground, taunting her as he branded her flesh and enjoying her screams of pain.

By escaping, she'd made him look like a fool, and she knew the consequences if that man in particular were to get his hands on her.

But right now, he was the least of her problems.

Where was Blade?

When he left her, he claimed she was useless in a firefight, and he had to go so he could take out the men after them, except ... nothing.

No shots.

No dead bodies falling.

No anything at all.

It was getting harder to believe that he'd left her there so he could take the guards out more easily, and more likely that he'd lied and just wanted to get himself to safety while he still had a chance.

After all, what did she know? This could be the first place they looked for her. Well, not the first since no one had looked up yet, and they seemed to believe she'd crashed and run, but they would find her there eventually.

So she had to figure out a plan to save herself. She had no intention of becoming a sacrificial lamb so Blade could escape. Of course, part of her believed she owed him her life after her drug had destroyed his, but she was fairly certain he'd just abandoned her, so maybe that debt was paid now.

All she had to do was wait until the men left, climb down the tree, check to see if her car was still drivable, and if it was then she was getting out of there.

If it wasn't ... well, she'd cross that bridge when she came to it.

# CHAPTER

*Nine*

January 12th
8:56 A.M.

Watching from the road, where he'd circled around to get behind the twelve men who had been in those cars, Blade saw them split off into pairs and start trekking into the forest.

Perfect.

Time to make his move.

If all he wanted to do was kill them, he could have just started shooting as soon as they got out of their vehicles. One to twelve didn't make for great odds when it came to a firefight, because as soon as he fired that first shot, they'd have his position, and he'd be unlikely to take out more than three or four before they rallied and started firing back. Chances were, he'd still get the other eight, but it would be a lot riskier, especially when he had someone with zero training to protect.

But he didn't want to just kill them.

He was taking Whitney into a potentially volatile situation when he got home. While his team had all agreed to trust his gut that she was telling the truth, especially with the small things they could verify, that didn't mean there still wasn't wild distrust on all sides. If he could have some concrete facts to back up what Whitney had told him, it would help immensely.

And he wanted his team to trust her.

Accept her.

It seemed more important than it should.

So he needed to get at least one of these men alive.

From what he'd heard so far, he did know that these men knew who Whitney was, and they wanted her back. They'd called her baby genius, which again backed up what she'd told him about her age and her intellect. But he wanted more. Enough to put any doubt to rest and convince all of them that they weren't enemies and would achieve more if they worked together.

Assuming the men were wearing comms units, given that they'd been split up between three SUVs, Blade knew he'd have to kill them silently. His plan was to take out five of the six pairs first, and then one from that final pair, so he could interrogate the final man. Might even take the man with him. Who knew what other interesting and helpful intel they could get from him?

Picking one of the pairs as all twelve men disappeared amongst the trees, he followed after them. It was clear that these men were trained, likely former military, they were moving mostly silently through the forest, and if he were anyone else, he probably wouldn't have been able to hear them.

But since he wasn't anyone else, he could hear every step they took, and easily kept track of their distance and the direction they were moving in.

That wasn't the only thing he could hear easily.

Each ragged breath Whitney took echoed through his head. She was afraid, he knew that, but he'd made the right call in having her hide in that tree. It was a gamble, but everything was a gamble, and the men would be expecting her to run, not hide, because they believed her to be alone.

The first pair never saw death coming.

Blade merely crept up behind them, sliced the blade of his favorite knife through first one man's neck and then the other. Carotid arteries slashed wide open, all they could do was fall to the ground, blood gushing out everywhere. Knowing these weren't survivable injuries he'd inflicted, he didn't bother to stay and watch until the life drained out of them. That was two down, but there were still ten to go.

Thankfully, both the second and third pairs also went down without a hitch.

With six dead bodies behind him, half the men taken from the equation, Blade began to breathe a little easier.

Tracking the fourth pair, he was glad that so far, not only had nobody heard the muted thuds of dead bodies hitting the ground, but nobody had spoken anything into the comms units either. There was no need for him to take one of the sets to monitor it, he knew no one had spoken because he would have heard it if they did. They might not think much of Whitney's abilities to evade them, but at least they knew she would hear them if they spoke, so they kept quiet.

Unfortunately, when he went to make his move on pair number four, the second man turned right as he was slicing through the neck of his partner. Letting go of the dying man, Blade threw himself at the other guy. The last thing he wanted to do was use his gun. He would if he had to, but it would alert the others, and there were still four other men hunting Whitney.

Four other threats to go after the little genius if he didn't eliminate them.

Colliding with the other man, who had raised his weapon, but the moment of surprise had given Blade the upper hand he needed. While these men had likely served, they were no match for a former special forces soldier, who had been injected with a drug that enhanced all of his natural abilities and who trained with his team virtually every single day.

Using his body to pin the man in place, Blade placed his hands on his wriggling opponent, who was trying desperately to buck him off while simultaneously trying to get his weapon up. Blade had a knee on the man's shooting hand, there was no way he was getting a shot off, and one jerk of his hands had the man's neck snapped, his now lifeless body joining the others littering the forest floor.

Eight down, four to go.

Wiping off his knife, Blade was just pushing to his feet when he heard the last thing he wanted to hear.

Whitney was panicking, and it was messing with her ability to think logically because she was climbing down from the tree.

*No, darlin'.*

*Trust me.*

*I'm not leaving you hanging.*

*Almost there. Four to go, just stay put, go back up there, please.*

Of course, there was no way she could hear the thoughts screaming through his mind, even if they seemed inordinately loud.

The moment of distraction by his fear for Whitney almost cost him his life.

Realizing a split second before he was a dead man that he'd been spotted, Blade raised his gun, knowing he wouldn't have time to use his knife to kill both of the men before one of them could get off a shot.

Even distracted as he'd been, something he knew better than to be in the field, especially when he had an innocent in his care, he fired two shots, dropping both men before they could fire at him. They were dead, but there were still two other men out there, and now they knew that someone was shooting at them.

Would they think that Whitney had been armed and was now trying to defend herself, or would they assume that someone had been with her when the car crashed?

Deciding the next man he found would be interrogated, Blade listened, figured the distance between himself and the nearest man, and took off at a dead run in that direction. Enhanced hearing helped in the field, even if he wished it had an off switch so he could get some peace and quiet. He quickly climbed a tree just before where the man he was hunting would soon come running.

Then all he had to do was wait.

When the man was directly below him, Blade dropped, taking the guard to the ground. There was no hesitation, he snapped the man's weapon arm, causing him to howl, but he was no longer worried about being heard. That ship had sailed when he'd had to fire two shots to kill the last pair.

Besides, there was only one other man out there, and he'd hear his approach before the man was within shooting range.

"Hi," Blade said with a grin when the man's now pain-filled eyes locked on him. "I take it you know who I am?"

"One of them," the man whispered, and Blade was pleased that he'd managed to end up with one of the guards who was going to be easy to get talking.

"You know who she is, too. Tell me her name."

The man hesitated, and Blade slammed his fist down on the man's broken arm, making him howl.

"Whitney," he screamed. "Whitney Daley."

Checked with what she'd told him, so she wasn't lying about that. "How long has she been working for Dr. Gardner?"

"Don't know, man, I swear. I've only been there a year. But she's been with them a long time. Please don't hurt me."

Begging.

Pathetic.

"Why did Dr. Gardner send so many men after her?"

"Needs her. She's the center of everything. Baby genius is what they call her because she's so young, but without her, Dr. Gardner wouldn't be able to do what he does. Talk is if he stopped butting in, the drugs would work the way he wants, but he's a control freak, has to stick his nose into everything, even things someone else is better at."

Blade opened his mouth to ask another question, but a scream echoed through the night, one he didn't need enhanced hearing to hear.

Whitney.

"Don't kill me, man, please." His victim moaned beneath him, but there was no chance he was leaving anyone alive today.

A single swipe of his knife through the man's neck took care of him, and then Blade was up and running, wishing he had Thunder's enhanced speed, because the last man left alive must have found Whitney, and he wasn't sure he could get to her in time.

~

January 12th

9:19 A.M.


Climbing down the tree, Whitney almost lost her grip and fell several times.

Her hands were shaking too badly, and she wasn't coordinated enough to climb trees. She was the kind of person who bumped into walls and crashed into furniture. There was always some bruise or other dotting her skin, and she was usually lost in her own mind enough that she never even remembered where she got the bruises from. They just seemed to appear out of nowhere.

Not today, though.

Today, if she fell, she would know exactly where the bruises had come from, and they wouldn't be the last to mar her skin today.

Blade was long gone. He wasn't killing any of the men who had chased them, he'd just left her there and disappeared. If he were out there somewhere, she would have heard gunshots by now.

There had been none.

It definitely shouldn't, but it absolutely stung that he'd just left her high and dry. He hated her, she knew that, but she thought that she at least held enough value that he would save her from these men.

Well, not really save.

Did it count as saving someone when you only wanted the person to live so you got to kill them before someone else did?

Not really.

In the end, it didn't matter who ended her life, but the thing was, at least if she went with Blade, she knew the end was coming quickly. As soon as she told him everything she knew about her boss, she was dead, there was no reason for him and his team to keep her alive. But Dr. Gardner would keep her alive indefinitely. Force her to keep working on the drugs while he sabotaged them himself with his incompetence.

She didn't want any more deaths on her conscience.

Enough, there was already more than enough.

So she kept climbing down the tree and made it to some of the last branches before she'd have to jump to the ground when her luck ran out. Whitney reached for a branch, her hand slipped, and she was falling, landing with a bone-jarring thud that had her groaning, tears stinging the backs of her eyes.

*No time for tears, if you want to survive you have to get out of here.*

Scanning the area, when she didn't see anyone, she quickly pushed herself off the ground and scrambled for the driver's door of her car. If Blade had taken the keys with him, then this would all be over pretty quickly. She'd run of course, but there were twelve men out there all hunting her, and she had zero survival skills.

All the men appeared to still be off searching for her, and nobody stopped her as she yanked open the door and pretty much threw herself inside. Not bothering with her seatbelt, Whitney searched for the keys so she could start the engine, but they weren't there.

Why weren't they there?

Why did Blade have to think of everything?

He hated her, she knew that, but ... but ... there had been something in his eyes when he'd been so gentle with her the day before as he tended her wounds, and this morning when he made them both breakfast that made her think ... that he cared a teeny, tiny, little bit about what happened to her.

That maybe he didn't hate her.

But of course he did. What more evidence did she need? His abandonment was proof enough. Why wouldn't he hate her? She was a bad person, the evidence of that was quite literally seared into her skin.

A loud bang caught her attention.

That sounded like ...

No it couldn't be ... could it?

Gunshots?

Had Blade not left after all? Had he been out there all along? Killing the men after them silently so he could take them all out without them even knowing he was there?

Hope soared inside her, and even though she resumed her search for the keys, in case they'd just fallen somewhere in the crash and Blade hadn't taken them with him, she prayed that those shots had come from Blade and he hadn't abandoned her.

"Looking for something, baby genius?"

At the sound of the taunting voice, her gaze snapped to the side where she saw Mark Lucas standing there, grinning at her. Her personal babysitter, the man who loved tormenting her, of course, it had to be him who found her.

With a terrified squeak, she launched herself across the seat, heading for the passenger door.

Of course, she couldn't escape him, but she had to try.

She wasn't going back to her old life without a fight.

Honestly, she'd rather die out there right now than either of her other options. Torture and death at Blade's hands, or torture and forced imprisonment at Dr. Gardner's hands. Both of those choices were awful, and if she could make Mark angry enough, maybe he'd just kill her now and it would all be over.

"Uh, uh, uh," he tutted as he reached into the car just as her fingers grazed the doorhandle.

So close and yet so very far away.

Fingers tangled in her hair, and she was yanked back hard enough that it made her feel like her scalp was on fire. Screaming was a bad idea, she knew that, knew that Mark liked it when she screamed, and yet she couldn't seem to help it.

Terrified didn't even begin to describe how she felt.

Plus, she hurt. All over. Her wrists, her shoulders, the thin scratches from the knife that Blade had left behind on her skin. It was all just too much.

Too much.

"Did you really think you could escape?" Mark taunted her as he shook her and then threw her down onto the ground.

Some long-buried instinct seemed to kick in, because instead of cowering like she usually would, Whitney immediately shot back up to her feet and tried to run.

Not that she got anywhere. Mark was on her in an instant. Large hands hit her shoulder blades, shoving her forward. Tripping over her own feet, Whitney went down hard, sending arrows of pain spearing up her forearms all the way to her aching shoulders.

"Made a mockery out of me, didn't you, baby genius?" he taunted as he stood above her. "Look at me when I'm talking to you." Leaning down, his hand circled her already bruised throat as he physically spun her around so she was sitting on her backside staring up into his angry face.

If she thought she'd seen this man angry before, that was nothing.

The way he looked at her now ... that was pure evil. It reminded her of the look in Blade's eyes as she hung in that tree, only maybe it was worse. Blade had every right to hate her, to blame her, to want to punish her for her sins, but she'd never done anything to Mark to earn his fury.

"Did you think about the consequences to other people when you decided to try to play hero? Did you think it would turn those monsters into pets if you tried to warn them? You're just a brain, you should learn to know your place. That's your only worth. Did you think Dr. Gardner would let you go without a fight? You belong to him, baby genius. He bought you fair and square, and if you think you're just going to return to your cushy little lab unharmed, you've got another thing coming. I found you, which means I get to decide your punishment, and I can assure you it's going to—"

Mark never finished that sentence.

One second, he was leaning down over her, his hand still around her neck, the next, blood sprayed all over her as somebody cut his neck wide open.

The hand on her neck loosened. Mark's dying body fell, and behind him stood Blade. Like an avenging angel, dressed all in black, his dark hair mussed, the bloody knife gripped in his hand tight enough that she could see his knuckles had blanched.

"Did he hurt you?" Blade growled, his glare fixed on the man lying at his feet but then softened as he looked to her.

Slowly, she shook her head, hardly able to believe he was there. That he'd saved her. That he hadn't abandoned her.

"You didn't leave," she whispered.

Confusion filled his dark eyes. "Of course not. I told you I was going to kill them."

"You saved me," she said in awe. Nobody had ever done anything like that for her before. Without any conscious thought on her part, she scrambled to her feet and threw herself at Blade, who easily caught her. Wrapping herself around him, she clung to him as she buried her face against his neck, all her emotions crescendoing inside her until they had no choice but to burst out into noisy sobs.

He hadn't left.

He'd stayed.

Killed for her.

Saved her.

And now she was more confused than ever about how he felt about her, and about how she felt about him.

# CHAPTER

*Ten*

January 12th
  10:01 P.M.

As Whitney explained, still somewhat hesitantly, like she didn't really believe he was interested, about some theory she had on how to use plants to boost the immune system in a way that hadn't been tried before, Blade still couldn't get over her reaction to him when he'd killed the man hurting her.

She'd thought he'd left her.

Truly believed that he'd abandoned her and she was on her own.

The look on her face when that last body fell, and she saw him standing there, would forever be etched into Blade's mind.

There should be no reason that he cared one way or the other how she felt about him. As long as he secured whatever intel she could offer them that would lead them to the man they sought, that was all that mattered.

It should be all that mattered anyway.

But it wasn't.

For whatever reason, he didn't like Whitney's immediate reaction to just assume that no one was on her side. He got why she thought that way, she'd been sold by her parents to a man who had basically imprisoned her, twisted something she'd intended for good, and then blamed her for its failure by literally putting the deaths of others on her back.

Only that wasn't her cross to bear.

From everything the man he'd questioned told him, and what he'd heard from the man Whitney had told him after the fact was her personal babysitter who enjoyed tormenting her, what she'd told him was true. She had been with Dr. Gardner for a long time, she was the creator of the drug, and Dr. Gardner himself kept messing it up by insisting that he fiddle with it. She was nicknamed baby genius because she was so young, and she'd been bought by the scientist. And she was going to be punished for her brave attempt to warn him and his team of the dangers facing them if they were caught again.

Through every hellish thing he had endured at Dr. Gardner's hands, Blade had always had his team at his back. But Whitney had no one, and she'd been just a child. A little ten-year-old girl, thrust into a situation that wasn't meant for children even if they did have one of the highest IQs ever recorded.

Knowing how lonely her life must be, had likely always been even before she was sold, filled him with a desire he couldn't explain to change that. Fix it. Give her a place to belong where she'd have people who cared about her, fought for her, protected her, and accepted her. A family, even if it wasn't born from DNA.

"B-Blade?"

Tearing himself out of his thoughts at the sound of her timidly saying his name, he turned to look at her even though she couldn't see him. Protocol was that anyone they brought to their remote Gothic mansion came blindfolded. They'd done it with Cassandra when she first came to stay with them, with the entire Charleston Holloway family when they also came to hide out there as they hunted the people after them. It was for safety reasons, they didn't want anyone outside of their team and Eagle Oswald, founder and CEO of Prey Security and the man who saved them by giving them a job and a home, knowing where they were, but for some reason, it felt wrong to do it to Whitney. She was a part of this, and he no longer had doubts about her loyalty.

"Yeah, darlin'?"

"You ... seem distracted," she continued hesitantly, and he was filled with loathing for both her parents and Dr. Gardner. They'd kept her stuck in an almost childlike state emotionally. She knew she was an adult, but she also knew she had no freedom. She'd never learned the way the rest of them did how to exist in the real world.

When this was all over, and Dr. Gardner was dead, he wanted that for her. For her to find her way, find herself. Be free.

"Not distracted, darlin'," he lied through his teeth. He was, but he didn't know how to explain to her that he felt something for her that he shouldn't. Not only was the twelve-year age gap a stumbling block, especially considering he would bet his lucky knife that she was a virgin with zero experience when it came to the opposite sex, but he'd also hurt her.

Tortured her.

While she might have been grateful he'd saved her, and she'd definitely relaxed a little on their drive to the airport and then the flight, she was still way too wary of him for his liking. Probably always would be.

The bruises on her neck might heal, the scratches on her body would likely leave behind no scars, although the ones on her wrists would, but there would be permanent scars on her psyche. He was just another person to use and abuse her, to not see the real Whitney Daley, to treat her as nothing more than a mind, a tool.

Gratefulness that he'd saved her life only earned him so many points, and not nearly enough to earn him any sort of permanent spot in her life, not even as a friend.

Did he want to be her friend?

Crazy though it was, yeah, he did.

Did he want to be more than a friend?

Totally inappropriate, but it was hard to look at Whitney without imagining what it would be like to kiss her, touch her, taste her, sink inside her, and feel her tight heat close around him, squeezing until he lost control and showed her how it felt to be treasured as they both came hard enough to steal their breaths.

"Blade?"

Once again, the timid voice tugged him from his thoughts, and he glanced over to see that Whitney had her hands twisted together in her lap. She was gripping them so tightly, he was concerned she was going to pop the joints right out of their sockets.

Reaching over, he placed his hand over hers. She jumped at the contact, and he hated the implication that she never felt safe, judged everything as a potential threat, and knew she didn't have a single ally. Gently pulling apart her hands, he then grabbed the blindfold and tugged it free. They were almost at the house, and anything she saw from here on out wasn't going to give her a location.

Blinking rapidly, Whitney cleared her vision before turning to him. It might be dark inside the car, outside it as well, with no streetlights on this remote country road, but he didn't need to see her properly to know she was worried.

Anxious.

Afraid.

"Is this ... going to be okay?" she asked. Although he'd kept her talking on the flight, as much because he enjoyed hearing her lose herself in talking about things she was obviously passionate about, as to try to ease her nerves, she'd gotten tenser the closer they got to landing.

When he'd gotten her settled in one of the SUVs they kept at the small private airfield, she'd all but regressed to the silent woman he'd first strung up in that tree. Now he knew she retreated inside herself when she was scared, became almost paralyzed with fear, and couldn't speak even if she wanted to. It had taken a lot of prodding to get her talking again in the car, but now he was pretty sure the only thing that was going to put her at ease was meeting his team and seeing for herself that none of them were going to hurt her.

Which they weren't.

At least he was ninety-nine percent sure of that.

"It's going to be fine," he assured her.

Doubt cloaked her, but he saw her nod, at least accepting his words on the outside even if he knew she was coming up with a million reasons inside her head to negate them.

"They know what I heard from the men hunting for you. You told the truth about your name, you told the truth about being sold, you told the truth about your age, you told the truth about creating the drug, but Dr. Gardner kept messing with it."

"You ... really believe me?" she asked, like she was sure that couldn't be true.

"Yes," he answered simply. No words would convince her of that, only actions. He'd have to show her that he was on her side, but he was going to have to do it by figuring out a way to keep his hands off her delectable body. It was her vulnerability that called out to his protective side, drawing him in like a moth to the flame, but that was exactly why he couldn't indulge himself.

She was sweet, innocent, naïve, there was no way he could corrupt her, and that was exactly what he'd do. Whitney had lived enough of her life in the darkness, it was time to rid it from her life and then set her free to fly toward the light.

"Here we are," he said as he pulled up to a driveway, punched in a code, allowed the retinal scanner to scan his eye, and then drove through the gate as it opened.

There was a long, tree-lined driveway, and when they finally got close enough to the house for it to come into view, he heard Whitney gasp.

"It's stunning," she whispered, the same reaction everyone had upon laying eyes on the Gothic mansion.

"It's home," he said simply, a very different one than where he'd grown up, but a home nonetheless.

Lights were on inside the mansion, and he had expected his team to be waiting for them to arrive. They'd want to speak to Whitney themselves, and while he'd allow it, it would just be a cursory introduction. She needed sleep, they could start the real interrogations tomorrow when she was well rested.

Turning off the engine and climbing out, Blade was just opening Whitney's door and offering her his hand when the front door of the mansion suddenly flung open, and Dragon came flying down the steps, yanking Whitney from the car and slamming her up against it as his hand circled her neck.

～

January 12th

10:22 P.M.


Blade lied.

He said it would be okay.

She'd believed him.

Stupid.

All he'd done was lull her into a false sense of security and then lead her right on into a trap.

Why didn't she have an ounce of self-preservation in her?

What was the point of being smart if you couldn't use that outside of a lab or a classroom?

Perfect scores and college degrees didn't keep you alive.

The hand around her neck tightened. Her throat had already been sore from Blade's hands wrapped around it, but she'd been able to somewhat ignore it along with all the other aches and pains littering her body because she'd been so scared about this.

Coming here and being tortured all over again.

Should have run when she had the chance, risked it at least. Maybe she wouldn't have gotten away, but she might have Blade angry enough to kill her outright.

No.

Wouldn't have happened.

They wanted her intel.

Which meant this man—she hadn't gotten a good look at him as he flew down the mansion steps toward her because she hadn't been expecting a welcome quite like this one—wasn't going to kill her now.

Just torture her some more.

Maybe she deserved it after all the lives she'd destroyed.

How could one drug, intended to save lives and make the world a better place, end up causing this much damage and death?

Seconds seemed like an eternity.

A growl rumbled through the chest of the man pinning her between the car and his huge body. When he leaned in close, she got a glimpse of his eyes through the light spilling out of the windows and open front door. Violet eyes. Dragon.

His nostrils flared, and she didn't know what he was scenting, but whatever it was seemed to enrage him further.

How long had it been since he grabbed her? Not even long enough for her to struggle to draw in air yet, although that was coming within the next couple of seconds. Whitney wanted to embrace that darkness, find it and cling to it, and refuse to let them drag her back.

Whatever lay beyond this life had to be better than the one she'd been living.

"What the hell?" Blade bellowed from beside them, and Whitney assumed he was yelling at her for some reason.

After all, why would he be yelling at his friend and teammate?

He'd brought her here, he'd lied to her, said that his team believed him, and since someone else had corroborated her story, she knew that Blade now believed her. He had to have known one of his friends would pounce on her the second she got out of the car.

Didn't even make it out of the car before Dragon had her.

Then all of a sudden, Dragon was ... gone.

Blade's body must have collided with the other man because now they were both on the ground, wrestling, swinging fists at one another, fighting.

Fighting?

Why?

Over her?

Legs shaking too badly to hold her up any longer, Whitney sank to the ground, pressing her back against the side of the car, and pulling her knees to her chest, attempting to make herself as small a target as possible. She had no idea what was going on, but her heart hammered so hard in her chest it hurt.

Other people spilled out the front door, walking toward them, shouts and exclamations filling the air, but she was having a hard time differentiating the words. They all melded into one, and really, it didn't matter what they were saying anyway.

Maybe Blade had been led into a trap, too, maybe the others didn't believe him. Maybe they were going to kill him, too.

All because of her.

People always died because of her.

Someone was close to her, she didn't know who, didn't care, but she kept her gaze locked on the two fighting men as she called out, "Please don't hurt him."

They wouldn't listen, but she had to try. Blade had saved her life, and now he was going to lose his, and it was all her fault.

"Steel, break them up, they're being ridiculous," a female voice called out.

There was a woman here?

She hadn't known that. Blade might have asked her questions about herself, encouraged her to talk on their journey here, but he'd been tight-lipped about his team and what she'd find when she got there.

"They're fine, they're just fighting for the honor of their women," a voice—she assumed Steel's—replied.

Only that made no sense. Fighting for the honor of their women? She didn't know who Dragon's supposed woman was, and she didn't know if Blade had a wife or girlfriend, but she did know he wasn't fighting for her.

Or was he?

"I can't believe three of you have now fallen," someone else muttered.

She didn't care about who had fallen for whom, all she cared about was that Dragon was going to kill Blade, and it was all because of her. Why did death always follow her wherever she went?

"Please," she whispered, her voice ragged, the word felt like it was being torn from her aching throat.

"Stop them, Steel, they're scaring her," the woman said again.

Steel must have been the one who sighed, because she saw another man approach the wrestling pair right as someone else knelt in front of her. Close enough to touch her, but thankfully, they refrained. Right now, she was wound so tight that the smallest thing, the smallest touch, might cause her to snap.

To break.

"Hey, it's going to be all right," a woman—a different one—said gently, and Whitney blinked because she recognized the voice, and tore her gaze away from the fight.

"Cassandra Charleston?" she murmured as she saw the familiar face.

This was the woman she'd linked to Prey Security and decided would be the perfect one to deliver her message to. The woman wasn't a Prey employee, and she wasn't married to or involved with a Prey employee, so Whitney had guessed that the woman wouldn't just kill her or abduct her to take in for interrogation.

She hadn't wanted to be caught, she just hadn't wanted anyone else to suffer or die.

"It's going to be all right," Cassandra repeated, and Whitney so badly wanted to believe that.

"Break it up, children," Steel called out, and she looked over to see that the man with the enhanced strength had physically grabbed hold of both Blade and Dragon and dragged them apart, although both men were still trying to swing at one another. "A little help?"

Two of the other men moved to hold Dragon. She wasn't sure which without seeing their faces properly, and Steel and the other man held onto Blade. She could see blood dripping from his nose and a cut under his eye, and her heart clenched as she whimpered.

"It's okay," Cassandra whispered, giving her knee a gentle squeeze before standing and moving to plant herself right in front of Dragon.

Whitney almost yelled a warning, not wanting the huge man to attack the small woman the same way he had her, but something stopped the words from escaping. Cassandra approached with confidence, and instead of cowering, lifted a hand and palmed Dragon's cheek. The huge man was still breathing heavily, but he softened somehow at the light touch.

"You scared her," Cassandra said, not a hint or a tremor of timidity in her tone.

"She smells of explosives," he snarled, and Whitney realized he must still be able to scent it on her days later, after she'd showered, even over the blood she'd shed when Blade played with his knife on her skin.

All eyes seemed to turn to her, and she was too afraid to even try to figure out the energy pouring off them. Instead, she just whimpered, pressed her face to her knees, and tried to make herself smaller. If she could make herself small enough to disappear, she'd do it in a heartbeat.

"Get off me," Blade snarled.

"Not if you're going to go after him again," Steel said.

"Children indeed," another voice muttered, making Blade growl.

"He put his hands around her neck, Thunder," Blade snapped.

"He's not going to do it again," Cassandra said like she knew that for a fact, however Whitney was not convinced. "No, Dragon, at least give her a chance to explain herself. You know Blade got confirmation that everything she told him was true, which means she was just a baby manipulated by a man old enough to be her father. He erased her entire identity so he could own her, treat her like a possession instead of a real person. We are not going to do that."

That the woman she had approached, put in danger by doing so, seemed to be on her side confused the life out of her.

"Cassandra is right," the other woman piped up, and now that she wasn't afraid Dragon was going to kill Blade, she could place the voice as belonging to Dr. Gardner's sister Rose.

Which made sense, she guessed, since she knew about Rose winding up with Delta Team, and how they'd tried to lure her brother into a trap. The woman also seemed confident with the guys, and she'd spoken to Steel specifically. Was there a reason for that, or was it just because Steel had been the leader of the team?

"Would you let go of me?" Blade growled, and they must have because a moment later she felt him kneel before her. "Look at me, darlin'."

No way was she lifting her head.

She wanted to squeeze her eyes closed and pretend that could make all of this go away.

"Please, Whitney," he coaxed, and his hand nudged between her face and her knees, his thumb and forefinger grasping her chin as he firmly but gently tilted her head up.

"You're hurt," she whimpered, getting a close-up look at the damage.

Something in his dark eyes softened. "I'm fine. Are you?"

As he asked, the fingers of his other hand stroked gently across her neck. It hurt, sure, but she was pretty positive it was the least of her worries right now, so she just nodded.

"How about we go inside, and you can tell us why you smell like explosives."

Blade said the words softly, almost phrased like a question, but she knew they weren't. It was an order. And as she glanced around at the five other men and two women gathered behind him, she knew it was one she had no choice but to follow.

Even if it led to her death.

# CHAPTER
## *Eleven*

January 12<sup>th</sup>
  10:28 P.M.


Tension hung heavily in the air as Whitney gave a weary nod.

If he'd had any inkling whatsoever that Dragon was going to do that the second they arrived, he would have handled things differently.

Honestly, he'd forgotten all about the explosives. He'd been too busy trying to decide if Whitney was telling him the truth about her past and how it connected to Dr. Gardner's. But they'd assumed when he originally went after the person in the woods immediately after the explosion and saving Cassandra and Rose from the bounty hunters, that they were the one to set the explosives.

Knowing that the place had been cleared out before they got there, Blade could make a guess at why Whitney had set them, assumed everyone else other than Dragon, who wasn't thinking clearly right now, could, but Whitney would have to explain for herself.

It was important to him that the others learn to trust her simply because they did and not because he said they should. It shouldn't be important. Once they had intel from her and her former boss was no longer a threat, Whitney would leave, finally free to forge her own path in life. But it was important. More than it should be.

Because he wasn't entirely confident that Whitney could stand on her own two feet, she looked like a gentle breeze could knock her over, Blade released his hold on her chin, let his fingers once again brush over the darkening marks on her neck, bruises layered upon bruises, and took hold of her elbow, pulling her up with him.

When she swayed, he tightened his hold, doing his best to make it feel supportive instead of restrictive. But from the way Whitney's bottom lip trembled, he was pretty sure she felt like she was trapped and being led to the slaughter.

Dr. Gardner viewed them as monsters, beasts, one step away from animals that he could train to be his pets. Blade was pretty sure that Whitney didn't view them the same way, but she was terrified of them, and so far she had good reason to be. He'd almost killed her the exact same way that Dragon almost had tonight.

Guiding her up the steps and inside, he noticed how her trembling increased the second the front door closed behind him. He had no idea how to convince her that she would be okay. As far as she was concerned, he'd already lied to her when he told her things would be fine when they arrived.

Damn Dragon acting before he thought.

"You want something to eat?" Rose asked when they all entered the living room.

Shooting her a grateful smile, he gently squeezed Whitney's arm until she looked up from where she'd been staring at the floor, her blue eyes confused, and it was clear she hadn't expected the question to be aimed at her.

"Not hungry," she murmured her response, but he frowned at her.

"You haven't eaten since breakfast. She'll have something, whatever you make is fine," he told Rose.

"No, I can't ... I can't eat," Whitney protested, her free hand pressing to her stomach.

Offering her an encouraging smile, Rose indicated to one of the couches. "Maybe after we talk you'll realize no one here is a threat to you. Dragon is just ... he has anger issues. Trust me, I know. Some days I'm still not sure if he's going to try to kill me."

"Told you a million times I'm not a threat to you, Rose," Dragon grumbled, making Rose laugh, breaking some of the tension.

It was barely noticeable, but Whitney relaxed ever so slightly. "It's okay," she whispered. "I know why he wants to kill me. Why you all do. I'm the one who created the drug. I'm the one responsible for what happened to you. I deserve your anger and whatever you decide to do with me after I tell you what you want to know."

She spoke the words so bravely, her spine straightening as she gained momentum, and he knew she meant every single word. Whitney absolutely believed that once she told them everything she knew about Dr. Gardner, they were going to torture and kill her.

Yet she'd come here anyway.

Because she felt like she owed them, that all the deaths from the drugs rested squarely on her shoulders.

"You don't deserve to pay for someone else's sins," he said firmly as he maneuvered her onto one of the couches and then sat beside her. "Dragon is an idiot. He acts without thinking, but he won't hurt you again. Right?" Shooting a glare at his teammate, Blade dared him to disagree.

Stubborn man that he was, Dragon didn't answer. "You set the explosions, there's no point in pretending otherwise. I can smell it all over you. Tell us why," he demanded.

"It was the only way," Whitney said, the shaking in her slim body increasing until he could hear her teeth chattering together.

"Only way to what?" Blade asked, keeping his voice soft when what he wanted to do was yell at Dragon to tone it down. He was scaring Whitney, and she'd been through enough these last few days. Enough in her entire young lifetime.

"To make sure he couldn't keep using my equations," Whitney replied. Her gaze darted to Rose, and he could tell that she knew who the woman was. "I'm sorry, but your brother, he's not as good at chemistry and biology as he thinks he is."

Rose laughed, long and loud and free. To the point where Steel actually stepped up to her, placed a hand on her back, and guided her into his arms.

"You okay, little ladybug?" Steel asked.

"I'm perfect. She just made my day. My life really." Rose ghosted a hand down Steel's back when he huffed. "You know what I mean. All my life, I had to hear from Ridge how smart he thought he was, and how stupid he thought I was because I deliberately played dumb when it came to his pet subjects. Knowing that a literal genius is telling me that my brother is basically an idiot, I love it."

"He ... he kept messing with my drug. It wasn't supposed to do this. It was supposed to save lives, but instead, it keeps taking them. Dr. Gardner, he keeps insisting on fiddling with things. Making it worse. I ... I always wanted an out, but how is a little girl supposed to survive on her own? When I was fifteen, I started putting away money, sneaking it into a secret account. I created a whole new identity, and after Dr. Gardner came back after being lured into your trap, I knew it was time."

"You were responsible for clearing out the lab," Lion said, and Whitney nodded.

"I convinced him it was likely compromised, then destroyed every shred of paper, every computer drive, every vial inside the place. After I went to warn Cassandra, I intended to disappear. I waited until I knew he would have checked the labs, then I hid out there. I waited a few days, then brought in a team to completely disinfect the entire building. I wanted to erase everything, all of it. But it wasn't enough. The whole building, my prison, it had to go," Whitney whispered.

"Why set up the white noise generator?" Blade asked her.

Surprise rounded her eyes. "It was always there. Always on. I forgot about it. I didn't know you were in there." Tears trickled down her cheeks. "I swear, I wouldn't have tried to warn you if I wanted you dead. I waited until the clean-up team was gone, and then I grabbed my stuff, and I was leaving. I never wanted to hurt anyone. I just needed it to all be gone." Imploring eyes met his, begging him to believe her.

Thing was, he did.

But did everyone else?

It wasn't until his gaze roamed the room, waiting until each of the other people in it had nodded at him, even Dragon giving a reluctant agreement mostly at Cassandra's prodding, that he hooked a finger under Whitney's chin and made sure she was looking at him.

"You didn't do anything wrong," he assured her. "You did what you thought you had to do, and if you'd known we were in there, I'm positive you would have left without setting off the explosives."

"I would have," she quickly agreed. "I never meant to hurt anyone. All I ever wanted to do was help people. I wanted to save lives, and all I've done is take them time and time again."

"That's not on you," Cassandra rushed to assure her.

"That's on my evil brother," Rose added.

Seemingly surprised by the support, Whitney looked around the room to see that everyone was offering her encouraging smiles. It seemed to bolster her a little bit, but honestly, she was dead on her feet. She needed food and rest, everything else could wait until tomorrow, and now he was satisfied, Dragon wasn't going to try to kill her in her sleep.

Blade got that his friend was reacting out of fear, he'd almost lost the woman he loved in that explosion, but that couldn't be laid at Whitney's feet. Not only had she not known they were in there, but she hadn't known about the bounty on Cassandra's head.

"Food and bed for you," he announced, nodding to Rose who quickly moved toward the couch.

"How about we go raid the fridge, see what looks good," Rose suggested.

"I could go for an almost midnight snack," Cassandra added.

"Are you coming, too?" Whitney asked nervously, her blue eyes begging him not to abandon her.

"Right behind you, darlin'," he assured her, giving her a little nudge toward the women, and Whitney somewhat reluctantly followed after them as they both chattered away at her as they led her to the kitchen.

Before he followed, Blade had one thing he needed to do. Walking up to Dragon, he slammed his fist into the other man's cheek without preamble. "You ever lay a hand on her again, and I will kill you," he warned before striding out of the room to go catch up to his little genius.

❧

January 13<sup>th</sup>
   7:35 A.M.


Jerking off the bed, Whitney was shocked to realize she'd actually fallen asleep.

After forcing down a grilled cheese sandwich last night, Blade had led her up to a beautiful bedroom on the second floor. It was like the set of a movie in there, the antique furniture perfectly fitting the Gothic mansion, and despite the trepidation still flooding her system, she'd been in awe of the pretty room.

At least until she was on her own in it.

Blade had told her there was an attached bathroom, and he'd set the bag of clothes she'd packed and brought with her when they left the farmhouse on top of the dresser. Then he'd wished her goodnight, told her to call out if she needed anything and he'd hear her, and then left.

If asked, she would have sworn that alone, away from the raw power of the men who lived there, she would feel infinitely safer. But she hadn't. Didn't. All she'd felt was the same crushing loneliness she should be used to by now.

When you were two years old and reading proficiently, you didn't have friends. When you were seven and completing your final year of high school, you didn't have friends, and when you were ten and completing four degrees simultaneously, you didn't have friends. And when you were kept locked away in a lab, forced to work basically around the clock, you didn't have friends.

So why did it matter now that she was alone again?

It wasn't like any of these men wanted to be friends with her. Maybe they weren't going to kill her, and that was still a maybe as far as she was concerned, but that didn't mean they liked her. They wanted to use her, and the fact that Rose and Cassandra had been so nice to her last night was probably just a ploy to make sure she didn't refuse to cooperate after Dragon had almost killed her.

Crawling to the edge of the huge bed, she wondered when she'd actually passed out. She'd tossed and turned for hours after putting on some pajamas, brushing her teeth, and climbing into bed. At some point, exhaustion must have come for her, although she felt no better for whatever sleep she'd gotten.

Wearily, she grabbed a change of clothes, jeans and a sweater, and headed into the bathroom. She'd set up her toiletries last night, and now she stepped into the huge walk-in glass-enclosed shower and did her best to wash away the horrors of the day before.

The horrors of her life.

Once she was clean, she shut it off, towel-dried her hair, and pulled on her clothes, then she headed for the door, intending to go downstairs to the kitchen. Just because she still didn't feel like eating didn't mean she didn't have to. An interrogation was coming today. Maybe it was coming with words instead of fists, but it would be terrifying all the same, and she needed to be fueled for it.

Only when she grasped the door handle and turned it, she found it didn't open.

Locked in.

That shouldn't surprise her, but it did. These people weren't her friends, and they didn't care about her, she'd known all of that, but more than that, they didn't even trust her enough to not keep her locked in like a prisoner.

Because she *was* a prisoner.

All that chatting the girls had done was to make her feel safer than she was, and Blade wishing her sweet dreams was again nothing but a ploy. Why did she keep falling for it?

"Why can't you ever understand that nobody cares about you unless they want something from you?" she muttered as she crossed the room and dropped down into a large rocking chair by the window. Whitney didn't bother to try to look out it, she didn't care what was out there. Were they going to starve her? Leave her there until she was so weak that it would be easy to get information from her?

It wasn't necessary, she'd gladly tell them everything she knew and then plead for mercy.

Maybe they wouldn't give it to her, but she truly had nothing left to lose.

If they said no, then this house would be the last place she ever saw before she took her final breath.

A knock on her door startled her, but given that she was locked in, she doubted whoever was out there was truly asking for permission to enter. Nobody needed permission from the captive to enter their cell.

When she said nothing, the person out there waited a moment and then opened the door just like she knew they would. She'd been expecting to see Blade on the other side, but it wasn't, it was Rose and Cassandra, and both women were smiling at her as they carried in plates filled with all sorts of breakfast food.

"We don't know what you like," Rose said by way of explanation as she set down a tray of waffles, pancakes, and French toast on the bed. Beside it, Cassandra put down her tray with toast, fruit, and an assortment of toppings, jams, jellies, and peanut butter.

The food looked good, but she wasn't hungry.

Too nauseous to even consider putting anything into her stomach.

"Thanks," she said, because it would be impolite to say anything else. She'd nibble at the food, because again, manners, but she wasn't going to be able to get much of it down.

"Don't be too upset about being locked in," Rose said, not bothering to beat around the bush, and Whitney appreciated that. This woman might look similar to her brother, but it was clear they were nothing alike.

"It's fine, I get it," she mumbled, not wanting to make a big deal out of it. She was a prisoner, it was what it was.

"I don't think you do," Rose countered gently. "Do you know how I ended up here?"

"I assume they kidnapped you? That's what Dr. Gardner said anyway, but then you lured him into a trap, so I assumed you switched sides?"

"They did kidnap me," Rose confirmed. "Wanted to make me break. But they didn't know my brother had been torturing me all my life. Handling what they gave me was child's play. After I got hurt trying to escape, they brought me to one of these gorgeous bedrooms. Beautiful but still a cell. They kept me locked in until they realized I had more reason to hate my brother than they ever could. One thing you should know about them, and I say this as someone who they have hurt, they aren't monsters."

"I know they're not," she rushed to assure them. From what she had seen last night, Rose was dating Steel, and Cassandra was with Dragon. The last thing she wanted was for them to think she thought badly of the men they loved.

"Do you?" Cassandra asked, but there was no judgment in her tone. "Do you really get that they aren't monsters? I know Dr. Gardner thinks they are, and you've been with him for a long time. And Blade ... he hurt you."

"He thought I was one of them," Whitney hurried to defend him. "I don't blame him for hating me, and I don't blame him for hurting me. If I'd been put through what he had and thought I'd caught one of the people responsible for it, I would have reacted the same way."

Well, that wasn't really true, she was way too weak and cowardly to fight back against someone who had hurt her, but she really did understand that it wasn't personal. Blade was treating her the way she would expect him to, given what he thought he knew about her. What he *did* know about her.

Both Rose and Cassandra's smiles warmed further, and they shared a secret look that she had no idea how to interpret.

"He and the guys are doing their morning workout, but he wanted to make sure that we were here with you, that you weren't alone," Rose told her.

"He was worried about you," Cassandra added. "He's very protective of you."

"I have information he needs," she reminded them.

"Don't do that," Rose ordered. "Don't pretend. Not with us. We understand these men better than anybody else does. Better than my brother thinks he does. They're good men, but they were taught to believe they were nothing but monsters. That they couldn't feel normal human emotion, that they had no consciences."

"The drugs can't do that, can't eliminate that, only dull it a little," she said softly.

"That's right. They feel. They drive to kill threats, to protect what's theirs," Rose said, raising her eyebrows suggestively.

Only Whitney wasn't sure what she was suggesting.

That she was somehow Blade's?

That was crazy.

Wasn't it?

Why would Blade think of her as his? He had attacked Dragon last night when the man put his hands around her neck, but that was just protecting an investment, wasn't it? She had value to offer in what she knew about Dr. Gardner, but that was it. It had to be, because she didn't understand the implications of it being more.

# CHAPTER
## Twelve

January 13<sup>th</sup>
11:13 A.M.

"Going up to see her?" Steel asked as Blade crossed the foyer, heading for the stairs. They'd finished their morning workout and training session a couple of hours ago, but he hadn't been ready to come inside yet to face Whitney and the mess of emotions she stirred up in him, so he'd run the perimeter of the property a few times.

He couldn't avoid her forever, though.

She was there, in his home, locked in a bedroom, and she wasn't going anywhere for the foreseeable future.

While she was at the mansion, there was no way to keep his distance, so he was going to have to figure out a way to be in the same room as her and not drag her into his arms and kiss her senseless. She was so damn beautiful, and that innocence made him delirious with a need to corrupt her, taint her, drag her down to his level.

Made him a terrible person, but he was nothing more than a monster after all.

"Don't do that," Steel ordered, and Blade cocked his head, wondering what his friend was talking about.

"Do what?"

"Well, do that as well. Playing dumb is ridiculous."

"Not playing dumb. I'm not sure what you think I'm doing that I shouldn't be doing."

"Idiot," Steel muttered. "Whitney. You. Don't let what he told us ruin things between you."

Ah, so that's where this conversation was headed. It wasn't that Blade didn't appreciate Steel's attempt at helping, because he did, they were a family, and ever since Rose had come there a few weeks ago, they felt like more of one than they had in the entire previous six years they'd lived there.

But Steel's situation with Rose wasn't the same as his with Whitney.

"How many times did he call us monsters?" Blade asked, not really needing an answer, just wanting to make a point.

"More than I can remember," Steel replied.

"Whitney was there, from the beginning, from before we were, she was a part of this. How many times do you think she's heard us called monsters? Hundreds? Thousands? She's been with Dr. Gardner for twelve years, since she was just a little girl. You really think how he views us hasn't rubbed off on her?"

There was no way it hadn't.

And all he'd done since she met him was prove what her former boss had said about him was true. He'd dragged her from her bed, hung her from a tree, poured water down her nose, cut her skin, and wrapped his hands around her throat. The truth was, he had acted like a monster, and hoping Whitney might see him as anything else was ridiculous.

"I think she's a whole lot smarter than you give her credit for," Steel answered.

"She's a genius, I fully accept that."

"Then act like it. Maybe she's a timid little thing, but that doesn't make her weak. She just needs to find her strength and tap into it."

"Not arguing with you there."

"If you weren't, you wouldn't have spent the last couple of hours hiding from her. You heard her this morning. You're the one who told Rose and Cassandra to hurry up and get up to her room because you heard her say that people only care about her when they want something from her. She needs to know that you don't want anything from her."

"But I do," he whispered, more to himself than Steel.

"Not what she thinks you want," Steel said, then turned and walked away.

How the hell did Steel know what he wanted from the sweet little genius sitting upstairs in her room, feeling all alone in the world, even as Rose and Cassandra kept her company?

Was he that obvious?

That he craved her more than he craved his next breath of air?

That she was the oxygen his soul had been needing for so long that he hadn't even realized he was missing out on anything?

Things had changed around there when Cassandra first came to stay with them. It soon became clear to all of them that there was something between her and Dragon, regardless of whether he admitted it. Then Steel fell for Rose, and Cassandra returned, and now Whitney was there, and she felt like ... life.

The life he'd been living for the last decade was all about survival. About getting through each day in the glass cage they were trapped in, about evading capture as they remained constantly on the move, about joining Prey and proving they could do good instead of the evil they'd been created for.

There had been no time to just be.

To figure out who he was beneath enhanced skills and superhuman hearing ability. To figure out what he wanted his future to look like. But there was no way not to think about those things now as he'd watched two of the men he considered brothers fall hard and fast.

Now a confused, terrified woman sat upstairs, pretending she wasn't confused and terrified, and feeling alone and abandoned.

The look in her eyes as he killed the last of the men after her and she'd thrown herself at him, utterly in wonder that he was still there, that he hadn't left her, was front and center in his mind as he took the stairs two at a time. Drawn to the pretty little genius by a pull he didn't even understand. It seemed to transcend everything else, it went beyond logical thought, beyond emotion even, it just pulled him to her, and he was helpless to fight against it.

It was no wonder Whitney had abandonment issues after she'd been sold by her parents. If he had to guess, she'd never had their love and support, they'd likely always viewed her as something that could potentially make them rich. And it had, but at the expense of their child's freedom. How could they pay such a steep price?

At the door to her room, he paused. He could hear them talking in there, Whitney and Rose discussing the latter's brother, while Cassandra interjected her thoughts on what a despicable person Ridge Gardner was. There was still a timidity to Whitney's tone, but it had grown more confident over the last couple of hours as the girls kept her company.

When he finally pulled up his big boy boxers and opened the door, her gaze immediately flew to his, and he would have sworn there was relief in those pretty baby blues of hers. But he could be imagining it.

The truth was, he wanted her to need him.

Wanted her to want him.

Wanted her to crave him.

"Hey, Blade," Rose said, waving him into the room. "You have perfect timing."

"I do?" he asked

"He does?" Whitney asked at the exact same second, making Rose and Cassandra laugh.

"Of course he does, we were just going to go and start on lunch, and now we don't have to leave you alone," Rose explained.

"You don't have to worry about that anyway," he said, making up his mind and hoping the guys weren't angry he'd made this unilateral decision. "I'm not locking her in anymore. I didn't even need to last night, it was stupid, I don't want Whitney to feel like she's a prisoner here."

"But I am," Whitney tentatively said, although it came out sounding more like a question.

"No, you're not," he contradicted firmly. "You're a part of this, as much a victim of Dr. Gardner and his plans as the rest of us. If we work together, we have a better chance of destroying him, and nobody deserves to be destroyed more than that man."

If Whitney didn't trust them, it was because of him, of how he'd treated her when he first followed her, what he'd done to her, and how he'd hurt her. But he also knew that even without trust, she would give them everything she could, because that was all she saw herself as, her value was dependent on the knowledge she could share. So she'd share it, even if it cost her, and even if she still believed they'd kill her when it was all done.

"Told you it wouldn't last long," Rose said as she climbed off the bed where she'd been sitting cross-legged.

"Come down to the kitchen when you're finished here," Cassandra added as she too stood.

"Finished here?" Whitney asked.

"Finished with Blade," Rose explained, and then winked, which made Whitney's pale cheeks flame red, and he suddenly wished he'd been paying better attention to their conversations instead of trying to block them out.

The other two women left the room, and Whitney began to fidget with the hem of her sweater. It was a pretty shade of mint green, and looked velvety soft, although not as soft as her skin. Skin he was dying to mark up as his own. Blade liked the idea of knowing that Whitney had zero experience, that he could be her one and only.

But then he noticed the small scab at the corner of her eye from where he'd cut her. The bruises on her neck were darker today, Dragon's fingerprints layered on top of his own. There were more cuts on her skin where he'd dragged his knife as he was cutting her clothes off her.

And those were just the physical marks his torture had left behind. It spoke nothing of the psychological damage he'd inflicted on a woman who had already been used and abused since she was just a child.

"You should go help the others with lunch," he said, turning abruptly.

"Blade, wait."

He heard her jump up and cross the floor, hovering just behind him, but he didn't turn around to look at her.

Couldn't.

Or he'd have her in that bed, naked and spread out before him, quicker than she could offer a protest.

He heard, or felt, her hand lift to reach for him. Part of him prayed she didn't touch him, the other part prayed she did. When her small hand lightly, uncertainly, touched his, he turned and found her staring up at him.

"I ... I have ... I need ... a favor." She licked her lip as though unsure whether she could ask him for anything, having no idea she could ask for anything at all and he'd find a way to make it happen for her. Anything to banish the shadows that lurked in the depths of her eyes and show her what it was like to have a team, to have people who cared.

"What's the favor you need, darlin'?"

"Would you ... could you ... I need you to teach me how to defend myself. How to fight. How to be like you."

∾

January 13th
  11:31 A.M.

He was going to say no, and Whitney had zero idea how she was supposed to convince him otherwise.

But she had to.

This was something she needed desperately.

Once she gave the guys her intel, and they used it to finally find Dr. Gardner and kill him, something she was utterly confident that they could and would do, then she'd be leaving there. She'd be all alone in the world, and she didn't have the skills to keep herself safe.

With Dr. Gardner dead, it would eliminate the direct threat to her. Dead men couldn't own other people, but he wasn't the only evil person that existed in the world. There was a whole world full of them. She'd met plenty. The guards who worked for Dr. Gardner and her fellow scientists. They might not outright hurt, maim, and kill the way the guards did, but they were evil in a different way. Their indifference to the suffering of the people enduring the trials of the drugs showed their true colors.

Maybe she would never truly feel safe again, but if she at least knew some self-defense maybe it would help her confidence and make her feel like she wasn't completely helpless.

"Please," she whispered, as though that would make any difference.

After another few tense seconds, Blade gave a sharp nod. "We'll start now."

"Now?" she squeaked. That wasn't the response she'd been expecting.

"You really want to do this?"

"I have to," she answered honestly. "If I don't, I'm always going to be vulnerable. I know I'll always be smaller than most assailants, but I want to at least know I stand a chance. I don't want to be helpless ever again."

Whitney couldn't help but shudder as all the moments people bigger and stronger than her had used that to their advantage. Blade was amongst them, but like she'd told Rose and Cassandra, she knew he wasn't a monster and understood why he'd done what he did to her.

What she felt for him was ... too complicated for her to consider.

Her body responded to his with a womanly hum that she'd never experienced before. Her head knew that he was a potential threat because of who she was and what she'd done, and her heart yearned to have a man like him look at her the way Steel looked at Rose, and the way Dragon looked at Cassandra.

Wishful thinking was what it was. Not only was he never going to look at her with fiery, passionate affection, he certainly didn't want to have sex with someone like her who was so inexperienced she'd never even been kissed.

But he could give her this, and it would have to be enough.

"Okay, now," she agreed.

"Change into something comfortable that you can move easily in, and we'll head down to the gym."

Instead of leaving the room to let her change, he merely turned his back, and her cheeks flamed as she scrambled through her bag and settled on a pair of leggings and a T-shirt. That should work, and without her even telling him she was done, he seemed to know, because he headed out of the room so sure she would follow.

Which she did.

They headed through the house, her gaze constantly roaming, worrying they would run into one of the others. Although they'd all been in the kitchen last night while she ate, she wasn't comfortable around them. They were too big, too strong, too powerful, and they had every reason to want to use that on her.

Thankfully, they didn't see anyone, and they ended up in a huge basement gym with equipment everywhere and a large mat in the center. Blade headed right there. He moved so confidently, aware of his strength and his skills, and prepared to use them any time they were necessary.

Unlike her.

She was never confident, and while she knew she had skills, they weren't the ones she wanted. Her high IQ helped in some situations, but all it had ever gotten her was locked away as someone's lab slave.

"We're going to start by working on how you break out of some common holds," Blade started. "We'll need to build up your strength and stamina, so I'll write up a daily workout plan that will include some self-defense training. But today, let's work on some basics. Come over here," he prompted when she stayed right where she was.

Tentatively, she stepped onto the mat, closing the distance between them. This close, she could all but feel the power rolling off him in waves, and for a second, she doubted herself. This had to be a bad idea, didn't it?

Crazy though it was, she was attracted to this man. He terrified her, there was no doubt about that, but he hadn't left her, he'd saved her life, and last night he'd fought his own teammate to protect her from Dragon's wrath. Maybe he wasn't a genuine ally, but he was the closest she'd ever had.

"First thing to know is, given your small size, you are never going to be able to beat down any attacker, so that's not your goal. Your goal is to just get away. That's it. You do what is needed to get free, and then you run. And you always, *always*, scream for help. You would be surprised at the number of attackers who'll abandon a target if that person screams, because screams draw unwanted attention."

"Always scream, I can do that," she squeaked, already intimidated by this large man, and he hadn't even touched her yet.

"Second thing to know, is this isn't about brute forcing your way free. That won't work. Again, you're too small. This is about using your head and outsmarting anyone stupid enough to come after you. You should be good at that, shouldn't you, darlin'? With that big brain of yours."

His fingers swept across her temples, their touch featherlight, but still she shivered, warmth pooling low in her belly, tingles between her legs.

This man made her feel all sorts of out of control, and usually she hated that, but something about this kind of out of control felt good, empowering even.

"How do I do that?" she asked, a little breathily as he moved behind her.

"You want to catch him by surprise," he answered. "Throw your center of gravity in a direction he'd not expect, make him have to adjust his grip to keep his hold on you, and then you fight dirty."

Why did that word have her conjuring up sweaty bodies, claiming kisses, and all-consuming pleasure?

Pushing those thoughts away, Whitney gasped when Blade suddenly banded an arm around her chest, pinning her against him. For a second, she panicked. Her limbs flailed, or tried to, as she attempted to wriggle her way out of his hold.

"Smart, darlin', not strong," he reminded her, and she forced herself to still, to take deep breaths and control the fear.

If she didn't learn to control it, it would consume her.

"How do I do the gravity thing?" she asked, her breathing still coming much too fast, but slightly under control.

"Drop, like you passed out, just let it all go, it will force me to shift how I'm holding you even if I try to stop it."

Trusting his word on that, Whitney forced every cell in her body to obey and then allowed all her weight to sink into Blade's hold, as though she really had fainted. Just like he said, the arm around her chest moved, because it was either that or drop her.

"This is when you'd play dirty," Blade coached. "Groin, neck, eyes, you go for something vulnerable. If I were holding you like this, with your arms pinned at your sides, you'd go for my groin."

Right.

His groin.

His penis.

She'd never seen a real one before, but she could guess what Blade's would look like. Long and thick, almost too big to take, but she was sure once it was buried deep inside you, he would know how to use it. How to work a woman's body until she was writhing in pleasure, lost to the moment, unable to think because she was too busy feeling. How nice that must be, to just turn your brain off, rid it of all conscious thought, and just ... feel.

"Whitney."

His large hands closed on her shoulders, and he turned her around to face him. There was concern on his face, his mind obviously taking a very different turn than hers had.

"You okay? I lost you there for a moment."

Electricity seemed to hum through her system, and for once, Whitney acted without thinking. Curling her hands around the back of his neck, she tugged him down at the same time she pushed up onto her tiptoes and crushed her mouth to his.

It was her first kiss.

Or half kiss.

Did it count if the other person didn't kiss you back?

If they just stood there like they were made of stone, their grip on your shoulders disappearing as their arms dropped to hang loosely at their sides?

He didn't kiss her back.

Of course, he didn't kiss her back.

Mortified, tears burned the backs of her eyes, as her arms dropped to hang limply by her sides. She took a step back, more embarrassed than she'd ever been before in her life.

What had she done?

"Sorry," she mumbled before she took off at a dead run for the stairs, needing to get away from him. If only she could outrun herself and her own stupidity so easily.

What was she thinking?

Why had she done that?

What was wrong with her?

# CHAPTER

January 13th
   3:44 P.M.

She kissed him.

Whitney had kissed him.

Kissed *him*.

A woman like her, so sweet and innocent, had made the choice to press her plump lips to his.

Or had she made a choice?

Had she been caught up in the moment and reacted without thinking?

Did she regret it now?

*Of course, she regrets it now, you idiot. You didn't kiss her back. You just stood there like a moron while an attractive woman kissed you. Didn't even go after her when she ran because you're a coward.*

There was absolutely no defense he could offer to his own internal ream out. That was all true. He'd been too shocked to react when she suddenly surged up on tiptoe and kissed him. When he'd talked about her next move being going for her attacker's groin, he'd thought he might have triggered something. They hadn't talked about her time being held prisoner by the doctor, but she'd been with him for many years, and it was possible she'd been sexually assaulted either by him or one of his employees. She'd seemed particularly afraid of the man who had found her when they'd been in the woods.

But before he could check in with her, make sure she was okay, ask her to give him a list of any triggers so they could work around them, and then through them at a later date, she was kissing him.

Even though she had been the one to kiss him, Blade couldn't help but feel like he had somehow taken advantage of her. He had been as close to flirting with her as he was willing to permit himself to get when he'd brushed his fingertips across her temples. She was so damn innocent that a simple touch was probably enough to confuse her.

Because she had to be confused.

It was the only way to explain why she would kiss him.

There was no logical reason why a pretty girl like Whitney, who was smart as can be, would choose to kiss a man like him. One who had taken pleasure in her pain, who had tortured her, made her bleed, and been prepared to end her life and not feel a second of remorse for it.

"For someone who has enhanced hearing, you sure don't seem to use that particular skill very wisely," Lion said, and Blade blinked to find all five of his teammates watching him with varying degrees of concern.

After fleeing from their impromptu training session, Whitney must have gone back up to her room, gotten paper and pens from somewhere on her way, and written out a very detailed list of everything she knew about Dr. Gardner. Like he would have expected her to be, she'd been very thorough, started at the beginning, and logically worked her way through the years. She'd included names of people, guards and scientists, descriptions of them, including how she thought they might respond if caught, and how loyal she thought they were to their boss.

Some of the information was too technical for him to figure out without looking up the names of drugs, but she'd given a brief rundown on the composition of the drug and how she made it, noting that the changes Dr. Gardner made weren't usually passed on to her. There were some locations in there that they would check out, but she wasn't sure if they were still active labs, claiming that other than the main building, which she had cleared out and destroyed, the other labs popped up, remaining there only for a short time before being dismantled and moved on.

Everything was written out in a neat script, and she'd passed the notes along to Rose and Cassandra to give to them, still hiding out in her room the last he'd heard, although he'd been too much of a coward to go and see her.

What was he supposed to say?

Thanks for kissing me, but are you out of your mind? Why would you do that?

"What happened in the gym?" Voodoo asked, and Blade wondered how much they already knew.

"She wanted to learn self-defense," he replied.

"And?" Lion prompted.

"And what?"

"Playing dumb again," Steel tutted.

"And she went running out of there like the room was on fire and then went to her room and didn't come back out," Thunder added.

Blade just shrugged. Was he supposed to tell them that she'd kissed him, and he hadn't kissed her back? They'd think he was an idiot for sure. It wasn't that he cared what his team thought, only ... he did care what his team thought. Because they weren't just his team, they were his family now, and they had fought and lived side by side for the last decade.

"I messed up," he finally said.

"Rose will be mad," Steel said with a smirk. "She's taken quite a liking to your little genius."

"Cassandra too," Dragon said, although he didn't smirk, if anything, he was pouting. "She said she won't have sex with me again until I apologize to Whitney for trying to kill her. Only I wasn't really trying to kill her, I just smelled the explosives, knew she set them, that Cassandra had been in that building when she blew it up, and I ... lost myself to the anger for a moment."

It was clear the man felt bad about it, and honestly, they'd all been there. Just because they had survived the anger and suicidal thoughts that came with the drugs didn't mean they didn't battle against them every single day.

"I'm sorry," Dragon said, sincerity shining from his unusual violet eyes.

"Why are you apologizing to me?" Blade asked.

"I think we all know why," Dragon said with more gentleness than he was used to seeing from the other man. "I should have thought before I acted."

Dragging his hands through his short hair, Blade shook his head. "I get it. We all do. Sometimes the monster in us takes over, and we lose control. Cassandra could have died in the explosion, we all could have. We were lucky to walk away with minor injuries. Trust is still shaky when it comes to Whitney, even though we all know that she was just a child and was not responsible for being forced into the position she was in."

"There's no monster in us, Blade," Steel said, serious now.

"You know what I mean," he said with a shrug that was meant to be nonchalant but likely failed.

"No, I don't," Steel pushed. "We all thought we were monsters, and over these last few weeks we've begun to accept that we aren't. Dr. Gardner tried to control everything about us, including our thoughts, but he failed. Rose is proof of that, Cassandra is proof of that, Whitney is proof of that. Even though we know Whitney is technically responsible for changing the course of our entire lives, we're also still capable of accepting that the circumstances surrounding that were outside of her control. Do you know why that is?"

"Why?" he asked, petulantly refusing to give the answer that they all knew.

"Because we aren't monsters. We were never monsters," Steel said firmly, his gaze including all of them.

"I still remember the talk you gave me about Cassandra," Dragon said. "You pushed me to go to her, to make things right."

"That was different," Blade protested.

"How?" Thunder asked.

"Because it's easier to admit that the rest of you aren't monsters than it is to admit that I'm not. I feel like I am when it comes to her.

The things I did to her ... honestly, I don't even know how she can stand to be in the same room as me, let alone look at me in a panic and ask me if I'm coming with her because she feels safer with me close by."

"Dragon and I have both been there," Steel said. "I made the final decision to go after Rose. I ordered her torture. I still don't understand how she can love me back and have my bite mark tattooed on her skin. I know Dragon feels the same way when it comes to Cassandra. But I had to accept that I'm not a monster, Dragon had to accept it. I mean really accept it, not just pay lip service to it. Until you can accept it, too, you're never going to be happy."

There was so much wisdom in those words, but how was he supposed to take them and internalize them? Make them his reality?

They didn't change the fact that he'd left permanent marks on Whitney's body and soul, that he could never love her the way she deserved, that he would never in a thousand lifetimes be good enough for her.

Maybe he wasn't a monster, but he was a rough and tumble cowboy turned special forces operator, and she was a sweet and innocent genius virgin. How was he supposed to give her what she needed when all he wanted to do was corrupt her mind and body and make her like him?

~

January 13th
8:08 P.M.

So far so good.

Whitney had successfully avoided everyone for the remainder of the day.

After fleeing Blade after that mortifying non-kiss kiss, she'd found paper and pens in the study she remembered passing and headed back to her room. There, she'd spent a couple of hours writing out everything she could think of that the Delta Team guys might need to know.

Thankfully, with her high IQ came a good memory for details, and she hoped she'd given them enough to destroy Dr. Gardner and his entire operation.

Earlier, that idea would have scared her.

Once the scientist was gone, she would be on her own. It was why she'd asked for the self-defense training in the first place. Now, even though it had been a disaster, she felt so embarrassed, so stupid, that she almost wanted it all to be over so she could be off on her own.

While she'd been writing out her notes, her gaze had kept straying to the closed door to her room. This time she'd basically locked herself in, even if there was no way to lock the door from the inside, but she couldn't help wondering if Blade was going to come and see her.

She really had to be stupid because what other reason could explain why she hoped Blade would come even as she dreaded seeing him again?

Was this what it was like to like a guy?

Did she like Blade?

She was attracted to him, yes, but she was still terrified of him, even though she'd kissed him. Honestly, Whitney was so confused she didn't even know how she felt about him. She knew he made her aroused, that overheated, tingly feeling was arousal, and she knew that when she'd kissed him she'd wanted to. Wanted him to kiss her back. Wanted him to do more than kiss her.

Maybe she was a twenty-two-year-old virgin, but she had curiosities she'd never had an opportunity to explore, and Blade stirred all of that up. If given the chance, she probably would have let him have sex with her down there in the gym, even if it wouldn't be the most romantic way to have her first time.

If he'd come up to her room to talk about what had happened, and given any indication that he was in fact attracted to her, she probably would have let him have sex with her in the bedroom as well. That would have been a little more romantic at least.

"Why are you still thinking about it?" she muttered to herself as she crept through the halls, heading for the kitchen. Whitney had no idea what time everyone ate, but it was after eight now, and she was hoping that everyone had had dinner and retired to whatever rooms they spent their evenings in.

The last thing she wanted was for anyone to spot her. Unless it was

...

"No. Bad girl. Stop thinking about him. Guaranteed he's not thinking about you right now. He had all afternoon to come and find you if he wanted to, but he didn't. Didn't even come and say thank you for all the information. Crickets. It's stupid anyway, you're being kicked out of here as soon as they know there's no danger left."

It wasn't like her little pep talk to herself did any good, but at least she was most of the way to the kitchen, and so far no one seemed to be about.

Or that's what she thought until she was two hallways away and heard footsteps.

Muting the shriek that wanted to pop out, she opened the closest doorway and darted inside the room. It was a beautiful library, and one she would have loved the chance to explore if she were there as anything other than a tool for them to use. A tool that had already outlived its usefulness. Now she was just a burden that had to be protected. Although she doubted anyone actually cared if something happened to her or not. Rose and Cassandra had been nice to her, but she wasn't sure if it was just to keep her happy so she cooperated or if it was genuine.

The footsteps got closer, and she backed further up into the dark room, wondering if she should find a place to hide.

No, that would be silly. What were the chances that with all the rooms this mansion had, whoever was walking past would be coming into this one?

Famous last words.

When it sounded like the footsteps stopped outside the door, she whimpered and backed further into the room.

*Don't be Dragon. Don't be Dragon. Don't be Dragon.*

But when the door opened it was indeed Dragon standing there. Was he going to follow through on what he'd started last night? Cassandra said he was just scared because she'd been in the explosion and they were together, and Whitney got that. But she still didn't want the terrifying man to kill her.

"You really should know better than anyone else that there's no hiding from us," he said from the doorway, not taking a step into the room.

Unsure how to respond and not wanting to say anything to anger him, Whitney just stood there. A deer in the headlights. Unsure if she should scream for help or pray that his anger had cooled enough that he wouldn't kill her.

Dragon flicked the light switch, and the room was suddenly bathed in light, making Whitney feel even more exposed. Dragon was so big, and even if they'd finished off their self-defense lesson, she wouldn't have any skills that would get her away from him. She still remembered what Blade had told her, to play it smart, catch an attacker by surprise, but she truly doubted that anything would catch a man like Dragon by surprise.

As though sensing her growing fear, Dragon stayed by the door, and she was grateful for that at least. But she did note that he was blocking her exit. Maybe she could try to get out the window if it came down to it, but she didn't doubt that Dragon would catch her before she could escape.

"Would you stop looking at me like that?" he snapped, although there was no real heat to his words. "You know I'm not going to kill you."

"Uh ... I do not know that," she said before she could catch herself.

The huge man rolled his eyes, and the sight of it was so normal, so something she had not expected to see him do, that it actually surprised her enough that she relaxed ever so slightly.

"You're a sassy one, just like Rose," he said, and there was some affection in his tone as he mentioned the other woman.

"I'm not sassy," she quickly protested. She never sassed anyone back, not even before she'd been sold to Dr. Gardner and certainly not after. He would have punished her for anything like that.

"How would you know? Have you been given a chance to find out who you are?"

Her mouth opened to answer, but Whitney couldn't think of an answer, so she snapped it closed again.

"That's what I thought." Taking a single step into the room, Dragon paused and speared his fingers through his hair. "I'm sorry about last night. I smelled those explosives on you and ... I lost my mind. Cassandra was in there, and we split up, left her and Rose in a room because we heard someone else in the building. Turned out it was one of the mercenaries out to collect the bounty on Cassandra's head. We were apart when the place blew up. I didn't know ... I feared the worst. Thought she could be dead. Then when we got to the room, she was gone, and I blamed myself. I never should have let her come with us."

"From what she told me, she *wanted* to be there," she said softly, taking a tentative step forward, wanting to soothe Dragon's guilt.

He chuckled mirthlessly. "Yeah, she did. But still, it's my job to protect her. I know you've spent the last twelve years with Dr. Gardner, he thinks we're monsters, but—"

"You're not," she quickly asserted. "I never thought you were. The drugs, they don't remove your conscience or your ability to feel emotions, just dull them a little, you know that, right?"

"We're getting there. Hard to change thinking you've had for a decade."

"It is," she agreed.

"Blade, he's got a lot running through his mind right now, battling a lot of stuff internally."

"I am too," she reminded him. Standing up for herself like this was an odd feeling. Whitney was someone who always went with the flow. But she'd built that secret identity with the intent of building a new life, becoming a new person, she didn't want to waste that even if things hadn't worked out the way she'd planned.

Dragon's unusual violet eyes gave her an assessing onceover, and then he nodded. "Then it's a good thing you just got adopted into a ready-made family who gets what you're going through and has your back. I really am sorry about last night. It won't happen again, I'm no threat to you, Whitney. None of us are."

With that, Dragon left the room, and she stood there staring after him. He'd just said that she was part of their family, but there was no way that was true. Was it? And had her kissing Blade ruined that? He didn't want her, and she couldn't imagine that he wanted her to become part of his family.

# CHAPTER

## *Fourteen*

January 14th
12:24 A.M.

He couldn't settle.

There were definitely times when Blade hated enhanced hearing that never gave him a moment of peace. Sound was a constant, he wasn't like Lion, who could close his eyes and shut off his enhanced sight, and although Dragon was also constantly able to smell things, the man seemed to have honed his skill and enjoyed having it.

It wasn't that Blade didn't like his ability to hear things in near-perfect detail, even from a distance, and there were definitely times when it had saved the lives of him and his teammates, but at times it wore on him.

Like when he heard Whitney's soliloquy as she crept through the halls after hiding out all day. He'd heard her the second she was out of her room, but he hadn't been ready to face her yet, which made hearing her words that much worse.

*Why are you still thinking about it? No. Bad girl. Stop thinking about him. Guaranteed he's not thinking about you right now. He had all after-*

*noon to come and find you if he wanted to, but he didn't. Didn't even come and say thank you for all the information. Crickets. It's stupid anyway, you're being kicked out of here as soon as they know there's no danger left.*

Blade assumed the *it* she was talking about was their kiss, and it had taken every ounce of his self-control not to storm down the stairs, shove her up against the closest wall, and crush his lips to hers. That should erase any doubts in her pretty little head about whether he was still thinking about her.

But it was the complete and utter conviction in her tone when she said she thought she was going to be kicked out that had broken his heart.

If he hadn't heard Dragon heading toward her, he probably would have shoved his fears aside and gone to her. As it turned out, he didn't have to. Dragon had told her exactly what she needed to hear, and coming from the man who had tried to kill her when the leash of control he had on his anger slipped, it would mean so much more.

After Dragon had left, he hadn't heard Whitney talking to herself again, but he'd tracked her to the kitchen, heard her prepare herself some food, eat it alone, and then retire to her bedroom. He'd listened as she showered and imagined her hands, covered in soapy suds, roaming her body as she cleaned herself. Wished it was his hands instead, trailing across that petal-soft skin.

Of course, if it were his hands on her body, he wouldn't just be washing it.

Instead, his fingers would be plucking at her nipples, kneading her perfect breasts, dipping between her legs, and teasing her bud before sinking inside her, grazing that spot that would make her see stars. He wouldn't stop until he had her panting and writing against him, begging him to let her come. When he'd drunk in the sight of her flushed skin and heavy-lidded eyes enough, then he'd let her come.

No way would he stop there, because Blade already knew that if he let himself have just one taste of her, he'd become addicted.

If he let himself become addicted to the petite blonde, what happened when she left? What Dragon had told her was true, she was part of their family now, another victim of the crazed scientist who thought he got to play God. But it didn't seem fair to make her stay there, caged all over again, when she'd been trying to break free, find her own way, her own path, and figure out who she was and how she wanted to live her life.

Staying away from her was safer for her and for him.

Because while Blade would never ever deny Whitney pleasure in the bedroom, if anything, he'd make her come over and over again until her system was thrown into overdrive and she was pleading with him to give her a break, his tastes in the bedroom were no doubt more than she could handle.

He and his team had never discussed their sex lives. He had no idea if before Rose, Steel had gone to one of the nearby towns to seek out a woman to share his bed, or if Dragon had before Cassandra. Just like he hadn't told the guys that some nights, when his need for blood got too much for him to handle, he headed into town, sought out a seedy bar, and picked up a woman he knew wouldn't mind him indulging himself.

But Whitney never was and never could be one of those women.

Her sweet, innocent little mind couldn't comprehend his need to draw blood, to see it stain the skin of the woman sharing his bed as he pounded into her, seeking a release that seemed harder and harder to find each time he tried.

In fact, chasing that release had gotten so hard that he hadn't bothered going into town for that particular purpose in over a year. There had been plenty to keep him busy with everything going down with the Charleston Holloway family, then getting the name of the doctor who ran the program, that he hadn't even had time to think about sex.

Until Whitney.

His pretty little captive, who wasn't really his captive anymore, with her wide blue eyes, so innocent and vulnerable, her pouty lips, and those blonde locks he wanted to tangle his fingers in as he guided her mouth to his. Whitney had zero idea that she was the sexiest thing he'd ever laid eyes on, and that she thought he hadn't kissed her back because he didn't want her and wasn't attracted to her made him want to howl out his frustrations.

Instead of going to her, he prowled the hall outside her room.

So close and yet so far away from where he wanted to be.

It would be so easy to just shove open her door, stalk in there, pin her to the bed as he made her take back her words, punish her for thinking that any man in their right mind wouldn't be attracted to her, make her blood run as he showed her exactly how gorgeous he thought she was, how hard she made him.

Talk about terrifying her.

As it was, she was barely tolerating being near them. Not because she thought they were monsters, he believed her when she said she knew they weren't, but because she still thought they wanted to punish her for actions she'd been given no choice in.

There was no shortcut, Whitney would have to learn to trust them as they showed her that they posed no threat to her. Hopefully, handing over her intel and seeing that nobody had kicked her out onto the street would help, as would Dragon's assertion that she'd been adopted into their family.

Could he go in there now and assure her that what Dragon said was true?

The light was on so he assumed she was awake. Although he couldn't hear her moving about, he could hear the steady and reassuring beat of her heart.

Curling his fingers into fists to stop himself from making a rash decision, one he knew when he was thinking with the right head would do more harm than good. Bursting into Whitney's room at midnight wouldn't convince her that she was safe there and they saw her as family.

Yet she'd wanted him to come to her today.

Been disappointed that he hadn't.

Thought that he hadn't even been thinking about her when it was all he'd done.

Overwhelmed with a need to show her how very wrong she'd been, Blade couldn't hold himself back any longer. Bad idea or not, he needed to see her, talk to her, taste her again. That kiss earlier had caught him by surprise, and by the time his brain caught on to what was happening, Whitney had already been pulling back.

Not going after her earlier had been a mistake, one he wasn't going to repeat now.

Shoving open the door, he came to an abrupt halt when the thin light of the lamp on the nightstand didn't show Whitney lying tucked under the covers like he'd expected.

The bed was empty.

Next, his gaze flickered to the rocking chair by the window, but that was empty too.

There was no light on in the bathroom, so he knew she wasn't in there, and he could hear her breathing, evenly like she was asleep, so she was somewhere in the room even if she wasn't in bed like she should be.

Worried, Blade spun in a circle, finally finding her curled up in a corner of the room, her forehead resting on her knees, apparently fast asleep. What the hell?

~

January 14th
1:43 A.M.

Something nudged her from sleep.

The eerie feeling of eyes on her.

Wouldn't be the first time Whitney had had someone watching her while she slept. There were two men in particular who would sneak into her room at night or would flat out refuse to leave when she retired for the night, stating she was a security risk, even though her chances of escaping had been zero.

One of those men was dead now. Mark Lucas, her handler, had been killed in the forest by Blade. She knew he was dead, had seen it happen, felt his blood splatter her clothes, there was no chance he was watching her now.

Terry Richards then?

While she was most scared of Mark, that was mostly because she just saw him every day, heard his lewd comments daily, endured his rough treatment with no way to stop it from happening, there was a coldness about Terry that said quite clearly he was someone to be feared. He was head of the entire security division, so most days he wasn't on site, moving around with Dr. Gardner, but when he was there ...

He terrified the life out of her.

More than once, she'd caught him watching her with an assessing detachment that turned her blood to ice. If he was watching her now, she was in big trouble.

"Relax, darlin'," a voice soothed. Blade somehow realized that she was afraid even though she hadn't said anything. Hadn't even opened her eyes, didn't even know he was there.

Where was there?

For a moment, she couldn't remember where she was or why Blade, one of the men from the only surviving team that had undergone the experimental drug program, would be anywhere near her. How did she even know his voice? It had been a long time since they were held captive in that glass cage, and even then, she'd never seen them in person, but she had been privy to some of the live camera feed footage to try to find workarounds for the drug's side effects.

"You can wake up properly, darlin', you're safe here," Blade's warm voice soothed again, and Whitney found that it did indeed calm her. Comfort her.

Which was crazy given that he'd tortured her.

As sleep filtered out of her mind and awareness filtered back in, she found herself no clearer on why Blade was in her bedroom than she'd been in her foggy in-between state about how she even knew what his voice sounded like.

At least it was him and not Mark or Terry.

Although given the embarrassment of the last time they'd been together, she quickly rethought that.

Blinking open her eyes, she saw that he was sprawled out on the floor beside her. He had an elbow propped up on the floorboards, and his chin was resting in his palm. Wearing nothing but a pair of gray sweatpants, she got a perfect look at his toned abs as the room was partially lit from the lamp on the nightstand she'd left on when she fell asleep.

"What are you doing down here on the floor?"

Groaning before she could catch herself, Whitney knew her cheeks would be flaming red, darn her pale skin and tendency to blush when she was embarrassed. It made it impossible to hide what she was feeling, and this wasn't something she wanted to share.

What had happened in the gym was mortifying enough, she had no intention of humiliating herself all over again and answering that question was definitely going to humiliate her. Blade wasn't interested in her, him not kissing her back was proof enough of that. The last thing she wanted to do was admit that she was attracted to him and that when she'd climbed into bed, all she could do was imagine him in the bed with her.

While of course she knew what sex was, her information was all technicalities, she had no idea how one went about making love. Still, that hadn't stopped her body from heating as she imagined hands touching her, a long, thick penis sliding inside her. There would be burning pain at first as her virgin vagina was stretched, but according to what she'd read, so long as she was with a generous lover, who was attuned to her body, and put in some effort, then she would experience her very first orgasm.

But Blade didn't want to be her lover, and she was pretty sure nobody else would either. She was a weird and inexperienced twenty-two-year-old who had nothing to offer anyone but a lifetime's worth of random facts about topics they wouldn't have any interest in.

"What are you doing in here?" she asked instead. When she'd gone to bed, then been unable to stay in the bed because the throbbing between her legs was too much and she wasn't brave enough to put her fingers there and do something about it, she hadn't been expecting a late-night visitor.

"Couldn't sleep," Blade replied, then arched a brow at her, daring her to not answer his question.

Whitney hesitated. She guessed she really couldn't embarrass herself any more than she already had in front of this man. He'd probably call her an idiot for being attracted to him, maybe tell her something was wrong with her for being attracted to him after he'd tortured her, but the truth was, he couldn't tell her anything she hadn't already said to herself. Plus, Whitney was well aware of the fact that attraction had nothing to do with logic.

"I'm sorry," Blade said, catching her by surprise.

"For what?" Apologies from a man like Blade were not at all what she was expecting. She was the one who had so much to apologize to him for, more than she could ever make up for in several lifetimes. What did he have to be sorry about?

Straightening, he shuffled backward until he was leaning against the ornate wardrobe that dominated one wall. There was a pensive look on his face, and she found herself holding her breath as she awaited his answer.

"Everything," he said, and her brow furrowed.

"Everything?"

"What I did to you at the farmhouse, not making sure you properly understood that I wasn't abandoning you in the woods, not protecting you from Dragon when we arrived here. For what happened in the gym."

Did his apology ease the sting of his rejection?

Maybe a little bit.

"Dragon apologized to me," she said, not quite ready to address the gym situation yet.

"He felt bad. We all do when we lose control of our anger like that."

"He also said ... that it's lucky I've been adopted into a family full of people who understand where I'm coming from and have my back."

"You have been," Blade rushed to agree.

"Is that how you see me? A member of the family? Like a sister?"

"Is that what you want? For me to see you like a sister?"

While Blade didn't give any outward indication of it, Whitney couldn't help but feel like this was a make-or-break moment. If she gave the wrong answer, whatever chance there might have been for something to happen between them would disappear like a puff of smoke.

A lie was on the tip of her tongue.

In the back of her mind, she knew she was no match for a dominant, powerful man like Blade, especially in the bedroom.

But ...

For some reason, she couldn't make the lie come out.

Instead, she shook her head slowly. "No," Whitney whispered, "I don't want you to see me as a sister. I don't see you as a brother."

Desire flared in the dark eyes that seemed to pin her in place, and when he slowly and deliberately began to move toward her, her breath caught, and her heart rate kicked into high gear as the throbbing between her legs returned.

"Good," he murmured, his voice low and seductive. "Because I definitely don't see you as a sister."

Stopping close enough that she could feel the warm puff of his breath against her skin, Whitney felt it stoke the fire currently burning low in her belly, and she had to squirm as the need for stimulation down there became too much.

A smirk kicked up one side of his mouth. "Do you know why I didn't kiss you back in the gym?"

Whitney shook her head.

"Because I couldn't process that someone as sweet and innocent as you would want to kiss a man like me."

She sucked in a surprised breath at the revelation. As far as she was concerned, he had things backward.

"Do you know why I didn't come and find you afterward?"

Another shake of her head.

"Because you're so vulnerable, so very innocent, that I'm afraid of hurting you, scaring you. What I like ... let's just say the name Blade doesn't just mean I prefer killing with a knife over a gun."

Was he saying that he liked to use his knife in the bedroom?

The shadows in his eyes, the self-recrimination, the longing that he was doing his best to tamp down seemed to suggest that he was. Could she handle that? The fact that the tingling between her legs had only increased indicated that she could. Maybe it even excited her.

Her entire life had been orderly, organized, neat and tidy. She worked in a lab, she ran problems through her mind, adjusted formulas, and worked to correct her mistakes. She didn't do crazy things like have sex with a man who still scared her a little and give him permission to use his knife on her, cut her skin, and make her bleed.

And yet she wanted this—wanted him—more than anything else she'd ever wanted.

Without giving her logical mind a chance to talk her out of it, for once in her life, Whitney just went with her gut and threw herself into Blade's arms, pressing her lips to his and praying he didn't reject her all over again.

# CHAPTER

## Fifteen

January 14th
1:59 A.M.

Shoving all doubts from his mind, all insecurities, all concerns about whether Whitney could handle this, handle him, Blade let himself fall headlong into the kiss.

His sweet little genius kissed tentatively, unsurely, but he didn't sense any doubts in her. Whitney might not know how to kiss, but she had jumped all in.

Grabbing hold of her hips, Blade dragged her forward, setting her on his lap with her knees on either side of his thighs. There was no way to kiss her and not want so much more, and his body hardened accordingly.

It was impossible to hide the fact that he was hard for her, and he wasn't sure how she'd react to that. Wanting to kiss him wasn't the same thing as wanting sex, especially with how he'd admitted he liked it.

But she didn't pull away, didn't pull back, instead, she did the opposite.

Letting her hips sink down further, she pressed her center against the bulge in his sweatpants. He remembered Dragon's conversation the other day about how Cassandra had reacted to him wearing a pair of them when he joined her for her morning yoga session. Apparently, they were a turn on for women, and he'd raided his friend's closet to steal a pair when he'd gone through his own to find he didn't own any. Well, none in gray, and he didn't know if the color made a difference or if any sweatpants would do.

Not that he'd known he'd wind up in there.

Maybe subconsciously he had, and when he'd found Whitney sleeping on the floor, he'd stretched out beside her, content to doze and watch over her, unable to leave in case she was sleeping on the floor because she'd been afraid.

From the way her cheeks had reddened when he asked why she wasn't in bed, he didn't think it had anything to do with fear. She was feeling things she'd never experienced before, and it was confusing her. Something he was pretty sure her genius brain wasn't used to.

"More," she whimpered, pressing harder against his thickening erection.

Happy to oblige, Blade used his grip on her hips to grind her into him, rocking her backward and forward, then circling her slightly. At the same time, he nudged the tip of his tongue against her lips, commanding her to open for him, and she quickly obliged.

Plundering her mouth like it was a trove of treasure, she moaned and thrust her chest forward, and he didn't hesitate to take advantage. Keeping one hand on her hips, moving her against him, his other hand grabbed one of her breasts, kneading it roughly as he closely monitored her reaction. Just because he liked his sex hot and bloody didn't mean he was going to force that on her. If she didn't like it, he'd find a way to give her what she wanted. In the end, she was the sexiest thing he'd ever laid eyes on, and he was coming regardless.

"More," she whimpered again.

Framing her face, he pulled her back enough that their gazes could meet. "Are you sure you know what you're asking for?"

"I kissed you," she said like that explained everything.

"Going to need more explicit consent than that, darlin'," he told her. Kissing didn't mean sex, and sex certainly didn't mean playing with his knife.

"You want to cut me," she said so pragmatically that he almost choked on a laugh.

"And how do you feel about that?" he asked as his thumbs caressed her cheekbones.

"I never thought about it before. I didn't know it was a thing, but then again, I don't know anything about sex outside of what I've read about the specifics. I know penises go in vaginas, and I know stimulation, both external and internal, can cause a woman to have an orgasm, but I don't know how to make that translate to like ... actual sex," she finished with a shrug, like she had considered herself and found herself lacking.

With uncharacteristic tenderness, he leaned in and pressed a kiss to her forehead.

"When you mentioned that you like using your knife in the bedroom, the tingling between my legs got more intense, so I'm assuming that means I like the idea. I want to do this, Blade." Lifting her hands, she pressed them to his. "I created that new identity because I wanted to be free, I wanted to be normal, I wanted to live a real life. I want to have sex with you, I don't think I'll be very good at it, but I'm always good at everything and ... I kind of like the unknown of this."

"There is no way in hell you won't be perfect, darlin'." Returning his hands to her hips, he lifted her along with him, carrying her to the bed and tossing her down onto it, making her bounce and then giggle.

The sound was stunning, and it obviously caught them both by surprise because her eyes widened, then softened and grew watery.

"Strip out of those clothes, darlin', I want you naked," he told her, and although she blushed, as he'd known she would, she hurried to strip off the fuzzy sleep pants and long-sleeve T-shirt she'd put on when she got ready for bed.

As he watched her, Blade pulled out his knife. It was always with him, even when he hadn't been planning on using it, he just couldn't seem to go anywhere without it. Now he held it, the point pressing into one of his fingers as he spun it around in circles, watching as Whitney shimmied out of her clothes.

The sight of the thin red lines on her skin from where he'd cut her before stalled his arousal.

Pain.

Not the kind that got him hard, but the kind that destroyed.

What if he hadn't scared Whitney into telling him the truth? Would he have killed her? Taken an innocent life? Deprived the world of something special?

"I understand, Blade," she said softly, running a finger over the already scabbed-over wound. "You thought I was one of them, and you aren't wrong. I *am* one of them. I understand if that means you don't want—"

With a growl, he cut her off, shoving off his sweatpants like he found them offensive, and pounced on her. "Don't want you? Is that what you were going to say, darlin'?" he demanded as he held the knife to her throat.

Although her eyes widened, he quite clearly saw the arousal dancing in them, so he didn't move the knife, and when she gave a shaky nod, a small line of blood appeared on her slender neck.

"I want you more than I want to breathe. You're so innocent. Do you have any idea how badly I want to corrupt you? But make no mistake about it, darlin', I would be corrupting you. We do this and there's no going back."

"Don't want to go back, never back, only forward."

Her bravery, her trust, handing something so special to him when he was the least deserving person to take this gift from her, had him growing almost impossibly hard. But he had to prepare her, this wasn't just sex it was her first time, and he wanted it to be everything she deserved.

Dragging the tip of his knife down her skin, he scraped it across her pebbled nipples, and her hips came flying off the bed.

"You like that, darlin'?"

"I have no idea why, it should hurt, and it does, but ... in the best way. Does that make sense?"

"Perfect sense," he assured her as he continued his exploration. His knife scraped the underside of her breasts, then dipped into her navel, before settling between her legs. The tip of his tongue followed the path the knife had made, licking up the thin trails of blood left behind.

There was a hitch in her breathing as she watched the knife between her spread legs, but her pupils were blown, and she whimpered when he hesitated. Keeping it light, he let the tip of the knife trail over her swollen bundle of nerves, and she moaned in delight. Who knew his perfect little genius virgin would be into knife play?

Never could have guessed this one.

Throwing her legs over his shoulders, Blade spread her wide open to him, blowing a breath on her bundle of nerves, making her shiver.

"Want me to taste you, darlin'?"

"Do you want to?"

Smacking her wet center with the flat side of his knife, he tutted at her. "Are you implying eating you out wouldn't turn me on?"

"Umm ... no?"

Swiping his tongue over her to ease the sting his knife would have caused, he loved every hitched breath, every moan, every rock of her hips, as he started to lick and suck at her entrance and her bud. Teasing her, working her higher, bringing her pleasure he knew she couldn't understand yet.

"Blade, it's too much ... I can't take more ... it's ... it's ..."

"You can take it, stop thinking, feel," he ordered, then closed his lips around her bundle and suckled hard, not letting up as he swept the blade of his knife up the inside of one of her thighs, and then down the other one, and she shattered for him.

With a shaky scream, she came, her body rocking beneath him, her cheeks flushed the prettiest shade of pink, her eyes falling closed as she lost herself to the sensations assaulting her body.

Without giving her time to overthink things, because he was pretty sure Whitney needed help getting out of her own head, he kept her legs over his shoulders as he shifted his position, so he could nudge her entrance.

"Watch me, darlin', watch me take you."

Her eyes opened, and her blue gaze locked onto his as he edged inside her. When she winced, his fingers found her bud, playing with it to distract her from the stretching pain. She never asked him to stop, and her hips rocked forward as he took his time burying himself inside her. She was so tight it felt like she was strangling him, and he had to cling to control so he didn't come like some adolescent who didn't know how to properly take care of his girl.

When he was completely inside her, he paused for a moment, letting her adjust to his size. Not to toot his own horn, but he was big, definitely a lot to take for a virgin.

It was only when she shot him an annoyed frown that he began to move.

No holding back. His sweet little genius wouldn't want him to do that. She was braver than he would have given her credit for, braver than she would have given herself credit for.

So he began to move, his fingers still played with her bundle of nerves, and his other hand moved his knife to her chest, above her heart, where he cut the shape of a heart above it, not deep enough to leave anything permanent behind, but he needed something on her that was his, a way to mark her.

With each thrust, he pulled almost all the way out before slamming back in. The room was filled with the sounds of Whitney's needy moans, and he could feel her internal muscles begin to flutter. Blade was holding on purely by force of will, waiting until his little genius came before he let go.

"Blade," she whimpered, and he dug his knife a little deeper into her skin, giving her what she needed to break free from the confines of her mind and explode.

Nothing was more beautiful than the sight of Whitney feeling life rather than observing it from the confines of her big, beautiful mind. Her internal muscles clenched around him, setting off his own release, and her bliss-filled cries spurred on his pleasure, until it felt like it was never going to end.

It did come to an end, though, and when he looked down and saw concern edging into Whitney's eyes, he felt his heart clench.

She regretted it.

About to pull out of her, clean her up, apologize, and go back to his room, he stopped when she spoke.

"Are you leaving now?" she asked like she already knew the answer.

Realizing her concern was because she thought he'd taken what he wanted and had no more use for her, he kept himself buried inside her as he lifted her legs down off his shoulders and lowered as much of his weight onto her as he dared.

"No, darlin', I'm not going anywhere," he promised as he swirled the tip of his tongue over the small cut on her chest, licking away the blood and easing the sting.

Offering him a shy smile, she fought a yawn. "Okay, that's good. I wasn't ready for you to leave. Is that okay to say?"

Chuckling, Blade nuzzled her neck as he rolled them slightly so she was tucked against his side. "Yeah, darlin', it's okay to say."

Better than okay. He was in too deep, and he had no idea what Whitney wanted, or what he wanted. Only right now, he didn't have it in him to care.

~

January 14th
7:13 A.M.

"You're still here," Whitney said in surprised wonder when she yawned, rolled over, and found herself staring at a naked chest.

An extremely delicious naked chest, and the urge to run her tongue along each defining ridge caught her by surprise. That wasn't her. She didn't have those thoughts, and yet ... apparently now she did.

"We're going to have to talk about those abandonment issues of yours at some point, darlin'."

That low, steady voice of his seemed to roll right over her, blanketing her with a warmth that had been lacking in her life even before she'd been sold off. Blade seemed to actually care about her, but she didn't understand it at all.

"Thank you for last night," she said shyly. There was a slight pain between her legs, but it was the most delicious kind. She felt like she was no longer a scared little girl, she was a woman now. A brave one? Maybe not yet, but at least she felt like she was getting there, taking control of her own life, making her own decisions, and it was wonderful.

Beside her, Blade's face grew troubled, and that tentative hope that had been building inside her seemed to pop like a balloon.

He regretted it.

Of course he would.

There was no way a confident man who looked like Blade wasn't experienced. She'd probably done it wrong, not been very good at it. She'd said she was okay with the knife thing, but he hadn't really cut her much, maybe she'd been a disappointment, and ...

"Whoa, don't go spiraling there, darlin'."

Although she remembered falling asleep with Blade still inside her, worn out by their lovemaking and feeling safe and content, at some point in the last few hours, he'd slipped out of her and she'd put a little distance between them. Or maybe that had been Blade. Now, though, he hooked an arm around her and hauled her up against him.

"Whatever thoughts were running through your mind just now, get rid of them. Last night was perfect, you were perfect, but, Whitney ... we didn't use protection."

It was clear Blade was troubled about this, and she relaxed at his praise. She doubted she was actually perfect, but if he cared enough to try to reassure her, that was a good thing, so she hurried to reassure him. "It's not the right time in my cycle, I just finished my period a couple of days before you found me, so I'm not ovulating. We didn't get pregnant, and since I was a virgin up until a couple of hours ago, I didn't give you anything." Before he could open his mouth, she continued, "I don't think you would have risked my health by taking me without a condom if you had something you could have passed onto me."

"I'm clean," he confirmed. "But I still should have been more careful. I won't be reckless like that again. Not when it comes to you."

Impulsively, she leaned up and kissed his cheek, touched by his sweet words. Whitney had no idea what was going to happen between her and Blade, but she wasn't going to fight against it. Worst case scenario, she made some fun memories and learned some things about her body and sex, then left once Dr. Gardner was dead. Best case scenario, maybe she really had found a family who wanted to keep her.

"We'd better get up," Blade said, although he didn't sound pleased about the idea. Something had shifted in his demeanor, though, and she tried not to panic that she'd somehow done something wrong.

"Did something happen?" It was weird remembering that Blade's superior hearing probably meant he could hear every conversation happening in the house. Because of her job she knew better than anyone exactly what these men could do, but knowing it, and being with them to see it, were very different things.

"Maybe, I'm not sure." Somewhat sheepishly he shrugged. "When I'm with you, I can dull it a little. My hearing. Maybe it's because you make me feel more so I can shut it down a little. It's nice. Peaceful."

Beaming with pride, Whitney kissed him again on the cheek before climbing out of the bed. She was halfway to the bathroom when Blade stopped her, his hand closed around her wrist. She hadn't even heard him moving, it was like he'd crossed the room in a split second.

"Where do you think you're going?" he growled, the possessiveness easy to hear in his tone.

"Umm ... to take a shower?"

"But you're ..." Blade waved a hand at her body, at the small scratches from his knife that would be healed in a day or two, and the evidence of what they'd shared still staining her legs.

"Covered in blood and your semen?" she asked, unsure if she was reading his expression correctly.

"Yes," he growled again, but it wasn't an angry growl, just one that made her blood heat and her body pulse with desire.

"You want to mark me?" That was sweet in a way she definitely hadn't been expecting.

"Does that scare you? Make you think of me as an animal?" he asked, a little defensively.

"No. Why would it? I'm not proud of it, but I was part of what was done to you, Blade. I'm the whole reason it started. I know that you're not an animal, and I wish I could undo all the horrible words Dr. Gardner said to you. I'm sorry that I didn't find a way to stop him," she said softly. It seemed impossible that Blade didn't hold it against her, that it wouldn't come between them.

"You were just a little girl."

"At first, yes. But I'm twenty-two now, I've been an adult for four years. I should have done something to stop it. Stop him." Maybe he was prepared to let her off the hook, but she wasn't as generous when it came to herself and what she'd participated in. Those marks on her back were a permanent reminder of the deaths she had caused.

With another growl, Blade snatched her off the floor, and automatically her legs hooked around his hips, her arms around his neck. "You were manipulated and all but erased from existence. You had no choice, they were keeping you a prisoner. But that didn't stop you from finding a way to get yourself out. Despite what he told you, you are not responsible for any of those deaths."

His hand swept up her back, tracing lightly over the brands on her skin. His words weren't enough to convince her even a little bit, but the sadness in his eyes, that hit her hard.

When his lips caught hers, it wasn't in a fiery, passionate kiss or a clumsy one like hers from the gym. It was soft and sweet, tender and affectionate. It was exactly what she needed.

"Go, take your shower, I'll meet you downstairs," Blade announced, pulling back and setting her on her feet, wasting the perfectly good erection that had been hardening as he kissed her. "Go," he said again when she couldn't seem to tear her eyes from it.

"Thought you didn't want me to shower."

"I don't," he snarled, making her giggle.

"I'm pretty sure they'll know what we did in here," she soothed him, secretly pleased that he wanted to mark her to show the rest of his team that she was taken. His at least for now.

"Oh, darlin'," he called as she gathered some clothes and headed to the bathroom.

"Yeah?"

"You better not do anything about that throbbing between your legs. I'm the only one who gets to make you come."

With a smirk, he left her standing there staring after him as he strode out of the room, the throbbing between her legs that much more prominent than it had been a few seconds ago.

Crazy caveman.

So possessive.

Still, she was smiling as she brushed her teeth and took her shower. And she didn't do anything about the need thudding through her system, although she desperately wanted to. After breakfast, maybe she could convince Blade that a workout in her bedroom counted as part of the training system he wanted to set her up on.

By the time she was clean, her hair twisted into two braids, dressed in jeans that hugged her legs, and a pastel pink sweater that she hoped highlighted her breasts enough to capture Blade's attention, Whitney was feeling more confident about herself, her body, and her life than she had in a long time.

In ever really.

That confidence carried her through the halls and down to the kitchen, where she could hear muted voices. But it wavered when she stepped into the room, and all eight heads turned in her direction. It wasn't that they were all looking at her, although she did hate to be the center of attention, that had her freezing, it was the worried expressions on all their faces.

"What's wrong?" she asked, already feeling the need to shrink into herself, make herself a smaller target.

Before anyone could answer, her gaze landed on the TV screen where a huge picture of her face was displayed along with a note saying she was wanted for murder.

# CHAPTER

*Sixteen*

January 14th
  8:10 A.M.

"I ... I don't understand," Whitney stammered, her gaze locked on the news stream displayed on the TV. "I'm wanted for murder? They know?" At her words, her arms twisted behind her back, and he knew that she was fingering the brands on her skin.

This was not the news he'd been expecting when he'd caught the worried tones of his teammates while still in bed with Whitney.

Not how he wanted to spend his morning either.

If she hadn't been too sore, he would definitely have taken her again, as many times as he could get her, but at the least he would have run her a hot bubble bath, let her relax, and ease any pain she had between her legs. This urge to take care of rather than just protect was new to him, but he'd liked the idea of washing every inch of her perfect body just as much as having sex with her.

But all of that had been ruined now.

"No, darlin'," he said gently as he crossed the kitchen to grasp her wrist and tug her hand away from the wounds she was forced to wear for crimes she didn't commit. "Not about those. It's the warehouse. Someone called in a tip that a former employee was disgruntled and blew the place up."

Her brows knit together in confusion. "Then who did I supposedly kill?"

"There was a mercenary there, after the bounty on Cassandra," Steel explained, and Whitney nodded.

"Yeah, she told me. Dragon did too. Apparently, she found out there was also a contract out for Rose. Both women were to be delivered alive to Dr. Gardner," Whitney said.

"Right, and when we split, the explosion occurred," Thunder added, making Whitney wince.

"I'm sorry, I really didn't know anyone was in there. I should have checked, but I was scared and desperate to get away, I'd already been there too long and—"

Crushing his lips to hers to stop her rambling, Blade kept the kiss a lot more PG than he would have if they'd been alone. "We know, and we believe you," he assured her when he pulled back. Although she nodded, she didn't look convinced

"When we found the room empty and went after them, Cassandra had been able to get away, running off into the forest. We followed, and when Dragon saw the man on top of Cassandra, he lost it and killed him," Lion explained.

"So they think I killed him?" Whitney asked.

"From what they're saying, the body was found inside and died in the explosion," Voodoo said with an eyeroll. There was no way the damage Dragon had inflicted matched that scenario.

"There were sirens coming when we left," Steel told her. "So we're assuming that Dr. Gardner has a contact at the police department. That's the only way the reports wouldn't match the scene."

"And he's saying it was me?" Whitney asked.

"You're no longer wiped out," Steel informed her. "When we got your name, you didn't show up anywhere on any database, just like you said you wouldn't. But now you do. Everything. Everywhere. You've been working for From Nature since you were sixteen, and before that, they have you down as doing a range of internships with various pharmaceutical companies."

"I never did any internships," Whitney said, voice strained. "I went straight from graduating college at ten to being sold to Dr. Gardner."

"We know that, darlin'," he soothed, sweeping a hand up and down her spine as he kept her tucked against his chest.

"They're setting me up," she whispered.

"They are," he agreed.

"But I *did* set the explosives. So I *am* guilty."

"Of blowing up a building you thought was empty," Lion reminded her. "Not of killing anyone. And don't even start in on what he told you you're responsible for," the man warned when Whitney opened her mouth. "Because not a single one of us thinks that you are responsible for a single death. From what you said, and from what Blade got out of one of the guards, the reason the drugs keep killing people is because Dr. Gardner keeps messing with them."

The words coming from someone other than him seemed to do more good, and Whitney relaxed a little against him.

While he wanted to be the one to soothe and comfort her, Blade understood that Whitney knew he had some feelings for her, even if she didn't understand the magnitude of them—he didn't either—so someone else saying it meant it had more weight.

"Why are they setting me up?" Whitney asked.

"Trying to draw you into a trap," Dragon replied. Growled would be a more appropriate word. Seemed that after almost killing her, the man had now completely accepted his role as protector and didn't like someone messing with their little genius.

"A trap?" Whitney asked.

"A warrant for your arrest means that as soon as you're found and taken into custody, whoever was paid off will hand you over to Dr. Gardner," he explained.

"And likely wipe out your existence all over again," Steel added. "You'll go back to being invisible, another news story will come along, and people will forget all about the woman who supposedly killed someone when she blew up a lab. With no one to ask questions about where you are and what happened to you, Dr. Gardner is free to do whatever he wants with you."

He didn't need enhanced hearing to hear Whitney's gulp, and she began to shiver against him.

"Do ... do you think that Dr. Gardner still ... wants to use me, or ... is he ready to just kill me and be done with it?" Whitney asked, and Blade loved that she was handling this head-on and not trying to run or hide from it.

"What do you think?" Steel countered. "You know him better than any of us, other than maybe Rose, but she had a different relationship with him."

"I ... think that deep down he knows he can't do this without me," Whitney answered. "I'm smarter than him. He hates that, but not enough to get rid of me. I don't know if he has a particular reason for it or not, but he really wants this drug to work the way he wants. The way he wants ... it's never going to completely work. I can't erase a conscience. I can't remove emotions. I can disrupt the brain connections and dull them, but that's it. The other things are easier, but it's the lack of conscience and emotions that he really wants. I think it's just to prove that he can, then use it to gain respect, power, control, and money. I think he sees this as the future of the world, and himself as the God who orchestrated it all."

"Agreed," Rose piped up. "My brother has always had delusions of grandeur. And he's smart but not a genius like Whitney. He isn't stupid. He won't get rid of her because if he does, his whole program falls apart. But ... sorry, Whitney ... he's going to punish her for the trouble she's caused him. Badly. And if he gets her back, she'll never have another chance to escape."

Fear for the woman in his arms flooded his system, trying to push his anger into overdrive. It wasn't until her small hands lifted to rest on his biceps and she squeezed gently that he realized he was basically crushing her.

"Sorry," he murmured, dropping a kiss to the top of her blonde head.

"Good news is, he's looking for you still close to the site, he has no idea you're with us," Voodoo said.

"What about all those dead bodies?" Whitney asked. "There's no way Dr. Gardner can think I killed them all."

"My guess would be that when they didn't check in, he sent out more guards. When he found the bodies he probably knew you had help, but that doesn't mean he knows it was me," he told her. "Chances he knows we were there when the building blew up are slim. Even if he does, he probably thinks we left before we could be found. That means you're safe here. He won't think to look for you with us, and if he did, he has no idea where we are. He's not getting his hands on you again, darlin', I won't allow it."

In his embrace, he felt Whitney drag in a deep breath, and he assumed she was taking his reassurances to heart, convincing herself that her tormentor wouldn't get her back and would have zero control over her future, like he'd controlled her for the last twelve years.

"Dr. Gardner wants me back. We all agree on that. We also agree that he has to be paying someone to have me framed, because he's the one who wiped out my identity, so he's the only one who would know to put it back up. He's obviously desperate enough to go to any length to try to secure me. What if we use that to our advantage?" Whitney asked.

"What do you mean?" Blade demanded, afraid he knew exactly what she was trying to say, but not willing to accept it.

"I mean, what if instead of him luring me into a trap, we lure him into a trap? We use this opportunity for you guys to get the revenge you so badly deserve, and we use me as bait to do it."

∾

January 14th
    8:21 A.M.

"Absolutely not," Blade roared.

So loudly in fact that Whitney winced and would have pulled back, only his grip on her had tightened again, to the point of being painful, even though she knew he wasn't trying to hurt her.

Everything inside her screamed to backtrack, to submit, to tell Blade what he wanted to hear. Anything to prevent getting in trouble.

But that had been the story of her life.

Avoid trouble no matter what.

Never rock the boat.

Do what's expected of you so that you won't be punished.

Where had any of that ever gotten her?

Nowhere.

It had gotten her stuck in a situation she hadn't tried hard enough to get herself out of quickly enough. It had gotten her a back seared with marks for all the people who had died because of a drug she'd created. It had gotten her almost killed by this man, who had quite rightfully been seeking revenge against the monsters who had played with his life like it wasn't important, like it didn't matter.

Now she had the opportunity to do something about it. But if she wanted to hold onto that opportunity, do something to right her own wrongs, make up for what she had caused, even if none of this had been her intention, then she couldn't be meek and mild. Meek and mild Whitney would just say okay, submit to what Blade wanted, and hide out there while he and his team eventually found another way to get to Dr. Gardner.

That Whitney would be a coward, and she didn't want to be a coward anymore.

This whole thing, setting up the fake identity, warning Delta Team, erasing all of her data, blowing up the lab, had been about finding herself. Well, she'd found herself here, with men who should hate her, had every reason to, and yet instead were offering her a place in their little family.

If she wanted that place, she had to earn it.

Blade was offering her more than a family, at least she thought he was. He was offering her a chance to be seen as a woman, a person, not just the baby genius that everyone else in her life had categorized her as.

There was no way she was letting this opportunity slip through her fingers.

Defiantly, she tilted her head back and met his eye. Fighting against the urge to cower, instead, she maintained eye contact and mostly kept her trembling to a minimum. She was scared, but she wasn't backing down.

"Yes," she said, her voice wavering just a teeny bit. "I want to do this. I am doing this. It's the best way to get to Dr. Gardner, and we all know it, including you."

"Best way to get you killed," Blade retorted, and she could quite clearly see the panic swirling in the depths of his dark eyes.

"I'm not asking for your permission. I've already made up my mind." She would love his support, though. Just because she knew she had to do this didn't mean that Whitney wasn't absolutely terrified at the idea of willingly handing herself over to the man who had controlled her life for more than half of it.

"Who says you get to make up your mind and make a unilateral decision?" Blade taunted, his voice reminding her of how he'd spoken to her when he had her hanging from that tree, but she knew this time it was harsh from fear, not anger.

The others said nothing, but she could feel their watchful eyes on her and Blade as he kept one arm banded around her, his other lifting to press against her chest, above her heart. Right where he'd cut into her skin. Now he pressed his palm against the small wound, making it sting.

"You gave me this body last night. I asked you if you were sure, gave you every opportunity to say it was too much for you, but you didn't. Do you know what that means?"

Staring up at him with wide eyes, Whitney shook her head. Maybe she hadn't fully understood what she was getting into with this powerful, dangerous man, but she did know one thing. She didn't regret what they'd shared last night.

More than that, she wanted to do it again.

And again, and again.

"It means you're mine now," he said simply, pressing again against the shallow cut and making her wince, then crushing his mouth to hers and kissing her until she couldn't breathe.

When he pulled back, they were both panting, and although she thought she should be embarrassed to have been kissed like that with an audience, Whitney couldn't find it in her to care.

But the kiss didn't change anything.

Didn't absolve her of the need to redeem herself, even if she was only doing so for her own benefit in her eyes.

"I still have to do this," she said softly. "You can't argue that it's the best way. We all know that."

Blade glared at her, then turned that glare on the others. "You agree with her?" he demanded.

"It is a solid plan," Steel said, not bothering to cater to Blade's obvious panic.

"Did you think it was a solid plan when it was Rose wanting to play bait?" Blade snarled.

Steel's jaw tightened. "That wasn't the same, and you know it."

"How was it different?" Blade shot back.

"I'm not sure it was different," Rose piped up from where she was sitting on Steel's lap, and the big man growled at her. "Sorry, Steel, but you know it wasn't. I played bait to lure in my brother and it worked. Well almost. If he hadn't gotten away, it would have. It was our best play in the moment, and while upsetting Blade isn't my goal, I think this is our best play now. Assuming Whitney really is okay to go through with it."

"I am," she quickly assured Rose, assured everyone. She was the weak link here, she wasn't even pretending otherwise, but this was something she would do no matter how scared she was.

"You're okay with this?" Blade snarled, turning his wrath on Dragon. "Didn't learn your lesson last time? Taking Cassandra with us almost turned into a disaster that we couldn't recover from."

Dragon snarled right back at Blade, baring his teeth. "It was a mistake, but this is different. Cassandra came because she no longer wanted to be a passive part of her life, but as much as you hate it, Whitney is right. This could work. Dr. Gardner is desperate to get her back. He knows he needs her, he was willing to reinstate her entire digital identity just to try to get her back. She calls up the local police department, offers to turn herself in, and we know she's going straight to him. This could be our chance."

"And you're all just prepared to sacrifice Whitney to get it?" Blade growled at his entire team like he was one step away from tearing their heads off.

But this wasn't about them. Well, not fully anyway. As much as she wanted them to get the revenge they so badly deserved, she wanted to do this for herself as well.

She *needed* to do this.

If she was going to have any chance at building a new life, she needed to find her self-respect again. It started with this. If she stayed there and hid, continued to be a coward, then she would never be able to start over, have a real life, she'd constantly be mired in the past.

Placing her hands on Blade's chest, she began to pet him gently, drawing his attention to her. "Please understand, Blade. This isn't something I *want* to do, it's something I *need* to do. I know you all say that I'm not to blame for what happened because I was just a child, and then a woman who had been controlled and manipulated for so long she didn't know what else to do. But now I know what else to do."

Beneath the fear and panic in Blade's eyes, she could see the understanding. He might hate what she was suggesting, but he got where she was coming from.

"I started this, and I can be the one to finish it. Maybe the only one who can finish it. Rose is right, her brother wants me back, enough to go to these lengths to get me. We can pretend that I want to hand myself over to the cops to clear up the misunderstanding, and then you can follow me in. Do you know why I know I can do this?"

When he gave a small shake of his head, she leaned into him, wanting him to feel, not just hear what she was saying.

"Because of you. You stayed with me. In the woods, when we spotted those cars, you could have just left me behind. I know you wanted my intel, but I don't think that's why you really stayed, killed them all, protected and saved me. I know you're not going to leave me behind now. I can do this because for the first time ever, I actually have a team. I have people on my side, people who will have my back. Together we can finally destroy the man who played God with all our lives."

# CHAPTER

## *Seventeen*

January 15<sup>th</sup>
11:35 A.M.

"Are you mad at me?"

The question, asked so softly that Blade was sure if he didn't have enhanced hearing, he would have struggled to catch it, made his heart ache. He wasn't used to feeling so much. Whitney had explained to all of them that there was nothing wrong with their conscience or their ability to feel emotion, both were still intact, but the drug had affected the way the brain processed both, dulling them but not eliminating them.

Despite that, he'd spent a decade believing he'd been turned into a monster, you didn't just get over that overnight. In the intervening years, he'd learned not to put much stock into his emotions. Other than anger, everything else felt so distant that it wasn't worth paying any attention to.

Being around Whitney changed that.

It was like his emotions had gone into overdrive, and he was having a hard time keeping up with them.

"No," he assured her. "I'm not mad at you."

Instead of pushing further, Whitney merely nodded and then shifted in her seat so she was staring out the window instead of looking at him. Although she was doing her best to fight through her own insecurities, he knew she was struggling. Just like for the last decade, he'd believed himself to be a monster, she'd learned to acquiesce and not fight back, accept her situation and not hope for more.

But now she was hoping for more.

Actively working toward it.

Unable to have this conversation in the car with the rest of his team listening in, Blade reached around Whitney, opened the car door, then unsnapped her seatbelt, scooped her into his arms, and climbed out with her. They still had almost two hours before Whitney was supposed to meet up with the cop they believed to be dirty and on Dr. Gardner's payroll, so he doubted anyone was set up watching the meeting point yet. They'd waited to call in the tip to the cops until they were already there and in position, wanting to maintain the upper hand.

Now he took advantage of that and carried his girl through the park and into a thick forested area. This was the very same park where Whitney had lain in wait for Cassandra to approach her as the other woman went for her nightly run. They'd chosen it because it was a public area, making it harder for the dirty cop to try anything, and giving them some coverage if they had to act quickly.

It also offered him privacy, and he needed it for what he had planned.

"You are mad," Whitney said when he had her alone and set her down on her feet. "You've been mad ever since I suggested doing this."

"Scared," he corrected. His ego took a dent saying the word aloud, given the enhancements to his body, his endurance, his skills, all his training and experience, and his dulled emotions, he shouldn't be afraid of anything. But he was. And what good was an ego when the woman he had fallen hard and fast for was preparing to go into battle for him?

"I'm scared, too, Blade. Terrified. I know this is the right thing to do, and I want to do it so badly. But it doesn't mean I'm not drowning in fear. You know the only thing keeping me afloat?"

"What?" he asked as he brushed a stray lock of silky, soft blonde hair off her cheek, tucking it behind her ear, and then letting his fingers trail down her neck, settling over her pulse point.

"You."

"I'm making things worse. Stressing you out," he reminded her. "You think I'm angry with you."

"Yet you're here anyway. I do think you're angry with me, but I know that it comes from a place of fear. But you didn't leave me in the woods, and you're not leaving me now. You're here, and you're supporting me and this plan, even though it's the last thing you want to do."

"If I thought I could get away with it, I'd have you locked in my room at the mansion. I'd keep you there where I know you're safe and nothing and no one can touch you forever. But." Blade sighed because it pained him to admit this. "I know if I did that, you'd hate me."

"You'd be just another person to cage me. I never got to grow my wings, but now I want to. I want to be a grown-up instead of being perpetually stuck in the baby genius persona. I want to work on my drug the way it was always supposed to be. I want to learn to be assertive, to stand up for what I want, state clearly what I'm thinking, not always be afraid, trying to be quiet, small, so no one sees me."

"And what happens when you grow your wings, darlin'? Are you going to fly away and leave me behind? Am I just a steppingstone along the way to you finding yourself? Am I good enough to be with you, or are you going to leave me in the dust?" Blade hated to sound like he was whining, and insecurity wasn't something he was used to. As a kid, he'd always been confident in his looks and his personality, knowing he was a catch. Maybe he'd been a little arrogant back then, but it had never occurred to him that he might not be good enough for someone. That they might not like him, sure, but not that he was lacking in some way.

"I thought you said I was yours? Are you throwing me away already?" Whitney asked instead of answering any of his questions.

Hating hearing those words coming out of her mouth, instead of answering, Blade spun her around, then yanked her back against his body, pinning her in place with a hand around her throat. His other hand dipped inside her jeans and panties, cupping her core with a finger poised just at her entrance without slipping inside her.

"Throwing you away, darlin'? Do you know that if I could, I would stay permanently inside you so I never have to be away from you."

Sinking two fingers into her, when Whitney cried out, he shifted his hand from her neck and placed it over her mouth. The last thing he needed was anyone, passerby or crooked cop, to find them.

"Shh, darlin'. You make a sound, I stop. Got it?"

Only when she gave a shaky nod did he start to pump his fingers in and out of her tight, wet heat. With each thrust, he brushed his finger-tips over her bud, before plunging them back in again and grazing that spot inside her that soon had her body squirming, and her breathing growing ragged, although she did her best to keep it quiet.

"Always mine," he growled in her ear as he picked up his pace. "Never throwing you away."

"Not flying away, not a steppingstone, too good for me," Whitney whispered, her hips rocking against him as he continued to work her body.

"Never," he snarled, angry at hearing her put herself down. "You're too good for me. You're perfect, and I want to watch every second of you finding your wings and flying high. Come now, darlin', want to feel you clench around my fingers, want to know I'm the only one who's ever brought you pleasure."

Like his words held power, Whitney combusted, coming with a scream, she did her best to mute it. But he didn't give her time to float down from her high. Just shoved her jeans down her hips, unzipped himself, and slammed into her in a single thrust, causing her to cry out, forgetting to mute herself this time.

"Told you not to make a sound, didn't I, darlin'?" he asked as he pulled his knife out, stroking the tip backward and forward across her neck. "You won't make that mistake again, will you?"

Frantic shaking of her head made him chuckle.

"That's right, my girl is a fast learner. You like me filling you up, don't you, darlin'?"

"Yes," she whispered, the word barely more than a breath of air.

"And you want me to move, don't you, darlin'? Make you come all over me?"

"Yes."

"Then be a good girl for me and let me remind you how ludicrous the idea of me ever growing tired of you is."

Not bothering to keep his thrusts gentle, Blade slammed into her over and over again. As he did, he circled one of her wrists, lifted her hand, then with a single slice cut open her palm. Her cry of pain quickly morphed into one of pleasure as he pulled all the way out then slammed back home.

Touching soothing kisses to the slender column of her neck, Blade released his hold on her wrist, then sliced along his own palm. Tucking his knife away, he reclaimed his hold on Whitney and pressed their bloody palms together.

"Bound by blood now, darlin'," he whispered against her soft skin.

Closing his lips over the hollow in her neck where her pulse was fluttering wildly, Blade sucked lightly at first and then harder, as he moved their joined hands to her bundle of nerves, pressing Whitney's palm against her bud as his covered hers, and moved them both.

"You'll never doubt me again, will you, darlin?" he demanded.

Tilting her head so she could look over her shoulder at him, she met his question with one of her own. "And you'll never doubt me again, either, right?"

"Right," he said on a chuckle, and she nodded.

"No doubts. This is crazy, what's happening between us, so fast, and so unexpected, but it's *our* crazy."

"Our crazy," he agreed as he banded an arm around her waist and slammed into her again and again, until he felt her internal muscles quiver, and then she bit her lip to keep her scream in as she clamped around him, her hips undulating as her orgasm tore through her.

Allowing his own release to crash down upon him, he held onto his girl, an anchor in all the storms of life, the good ones and the bad, Blade tried to accept the fact that in just a matter of minutes, he had to pull out of her and then let her walk off alone to fight their enemy without him by her side.

～

January 15<sup>th</sup>
    1:21 P.M.


She was really doing this.

Timid, scared, always hiding and doing whatever wouldn't get her in trouble, Whitney Daley was taking the biggest risk of her life.

Setting up a secret new identity had been a risk.

Going to Cassandra with a warning for Delta Team had been a risk.

Blowing up the lab had been a risk, and a little bit of getting her own revenge on the man who had held her captive for more than half her life and controlled her every move.

But this topped all of that put together.

This time, she knew exactly what the danger was, and instead of hiding from it, pretending it didn't exist, she was walking straight toward it.

There were a lot of things up in the air about this. When she'd called into the precinct with a request to meet with the lead detective on the case to clear the air, prove that she didn't kill anyone, they'd set up the park as a meeting place. The cop had agreed to the meeting, but that didn't mean he wasn't coming with an entire team of cops to put her in handcuffs and haul her down to the station. If that happened, then she had to trust that Prey would find a way to clear her name and get her out.

It wasn't what they were expecting, though.

This cop was working for Dr. Gardner, it was the only way to explain why she suddenly existed again when she'd been wiped off every digital record more than a decade ago, which meant he wanted to get her back to the man who had bought her. The best way to do that was to agree to the meeting and then whisk her away quietly and deliver her to the scientist who had ruined her life along with so many others. Then, no doubt the cop would return with fake proof exonerating her, pointing to someone else, likely the dead man, according to Blade and the others, and everyone would forget about her, and she'd be wiped out again.

Was that what would happen? She had no idea.

But she had to trust the guys, and surprisingly, that was easier than she would have expected.

People had been using her for her entire life. Blade might have started out using her, but that had shifted when he saved her life, when he brought her to his home instead of having the guys meet them somewhere neutral, when he made love to her, when he claimed her as his own.

Now Blade and the others were sitting in two vehicles, watching over her as she took this step to secure all of their freedom.

The weight of what she was doing rested heavily on her shoulders, and her gut churned with anxious nausea as she sat on the park bench and waited.

There were only nine minutes to go until the meeting time, although there was every chance that the police officer, an older man, close to retirement age, called Detective Deacon Hayes, might come early. Might already be there, staking out the meet spot to see if she came alone. Even if he didn't know it had been Blade, Dr. Gardner had to suspect that someone had been helping her, because she didn't have the skills to kill twelve armed men.

Minutes ticked down, and she wasn't sure if she was being watched. She didn't have that kind of sixth sense that the guys all seemed to have, and which she assumed was normal for special forces operators.

At exactly half past one, she saw a man walking toward her. He was dressed differently from the other people at the park. Maybe she could believe he was a businessman there on a lunchtime stroll, but he was striding toward her with purpose.

And she was pretty sure she could see the bulge under his jacket indicating he had a weapon there.

Fidgeting with the hem of her coat, Whitney fought against the urge to bolt, to get out of there, to run and hide, take the easiest route. But she didn't. She sat and watched the man approach.

When he came to a stop in front of her, she had to tilt her head way up to meet his face. It was weathered, lots of lined, wrinkly skin, and small, narrow eyes, that were now watching her with an apprehension that would have put her on edge if she wasn't already about as on edge as it was possible to be.

"Ms. Daley?" he asked after a long moment of silence.

All she had to do was pretend to want to clear her name. That was her goal. She had to act like she had never met Blade and his team, that they hadn't tortured her, hadn't taken her under their wing, weren't sitting just at the edge of the park waiting to see where the cop took her.

"Y-yes," she replied. "Are you Detective Hayes?"

A single nod was the only response she got.

"Please, you have to believe me, I didn't kill anyone, and I'm not a disgruntled employee. I'm not even an employee, I was being forced to work there against my will," she rambled, the desperation easy to fake because she really was fueled by fear right now.

"Shh," the cop hissed, looking over his shoulder like he expected someone to jump out from behind the trees.

If anyone was out there, she couldn't see them, but there had to be one of Dr. Gardner's people somewhere close by, assuming the plan was to pass her off to them.

"I just want you to understand that I didn't do anything wrong. I never killed anyone, and I only blew up the place because I was trying to escape." That was mostly true, even though she hadn't technically needed to set off those explosives to get away. She'd already broken Dr. Gardner's hold on her, she'd just wanted him to suffer for putting her through everything he had.

"Let's not talk here in the park. We wouldn't want anyone to spot you and call in the cops," he said, which he had to know made him look suspicious because he *was* the cops. If she hadn't come here to set a trap of her own, she would have known then that something was up and he wasn't there to listen to her try to clear her name.

He didn't have to listen to her, he knew she had committed no crime.

"O-okay," she agreed. "Where do you want to go? You're not taking me to the station, are you? Because I swear, I didn't hurt anybody."

"All right, all right," he said, reaching out to grab her arm. His grip was hard enough to leave behind bruises, and she had no doubt that Blade would punish the man for hurting her like that.

While her instincts told her to pull away, to run, because this man screamed danger and he wanted to deliver her to people who would take pleasure in punishing her for her dissent, Whitney didn't. She allowed the cop to lead her through the park, knowing that Blade could hear her every word.

They went to the far side of the park, crossed the street where there was a row of shops, bakeries, and cafes, gift shops, and a store that sold children's clothing. Bypassing all of them, he led her through a small alley leading between a store selling fresh fruits and vegetables, and a travel agent with bright pictures of tropical islands on its windows.

"Where are we going?" she asked, tugging slightly back against him. Not because she was going to attempt to escape, but because if she really was there to clear her name, she'd be wondering why they were walking down an alley.

"My brother owns the produce store, thought it would be a quiet place for you to show me your evidence that you claim clears your name without anyone spotting you," the cop replied, but even without training like Blade's, she could hear the lie in his voice.

Opening up a door at the back of the alley, they stepped inside a large open space lined with huge wooden boxes filled with a range of fresh produce. Whitney was glad the man had said where they were going, so she didn't have to, and knowing where they were meant the guys would be closing in, waiting to see when Dr. Gardner was going to pop up, or if he didn't, following her to wherever the scientist was holed up.

"Can I give you my proof now?" she asked.

"Sure, whatever," the cop replied, looking about nervously, obviously expecting someone.

No one appeared, but a loud crack suddenly split through the air, and the older man beside her dropped.

Whitney was scrambling backward before she even realized what she was doing. Someone had just shot Detective Hayes. Killed him. The bullet hole in the center of the man's forehead confirmed it, as did his sightless eyes now staring at nothing.

"He was annoying, right?" a voice asked, and she saw a shadowy figure step out from behind two of the pallets of fruit.

A voice she knew.

A voice she feared.

"Time to come home, baby genius," Terry Richards, Dr. Gardner's head of security, said with a smirk.

# CHAPTER

## Eighteen

January 15<sup>th</sup>
1:58 P.M.

Blade was so on edge it didn't take much to set him off.

The crack of a gunshot was more than enough.

He was out of the car and moving before he even processed what he was doing. Every fiber in his being screamed at him to get to Whitney.

Protect her.

If he hadn't failed already.

They'd been banking on the fact that Dr. Gardner wanted Whitney alive more than he wanted to punish her for betraying him. Was he going to punish her? Absolutely he was, but he still needed her, she was too smart, too valuable, he couldn't do what he wanted without her.

But it was still a gamble.

There was every chance the deranged doctor was too blinded by his rage at having someone he thought he'd molded into the perfect little scientist slave that he didn't have to worry about her loyalty, suddenly turn on him.

And not just turn on him.

Whitney had told them how she'd destroyed all her notes, all her formulas, all her calculations, all of it gone. Without her, there was no way for him to get it back. That was definitely enough to push the scientist over the edge.

"Wait," Steel ordered from behind him.

For the first time since they met and formed their team, back when they all signed up for the experimental drug program and were placed together, Blade ignored a direct order from his team leader.

No way in hell was he stopping.

Not when Whitney might have just been shot, could be dead this very second, or lying on the floor bleeding out, wondering why he wasn't there to protect her like he'd said he would be.

Failed. He'd failed the woman who had become incredibly important to him in a short space of time. He'd promised her he would be there for her, and he hadn't been. He'd let her do this when he knew it was too risky a move, and he should have locked her up at home where she could be angry with him, hate him if she had to, but be alive and safe.

All of a sudden, Thunder had bypassed him and was in front of him, blocking his path. That split second it took him to attempt to adjust his course, cut through the park to reach the row of shops and the produce store that Detective Hayes had said they were going into, was thwarted when Thunder and Steel boxed him in.

Keeping that much distance between them and Whitney had been a huge mistake. If they'd been closer, he would have heard whoever was waiting in that store to shoot Whitney when she walked in the door.

"You're not thinking," Steel said in a patronizing tone that rubbed him the wrong way.

"Damn right I'm not thinking of anything other than getting to Whitney," he growled, for the first time in his life actually considering killing one of the men he considered a brother.

"For a guy who has superhuman hearing skills, you aren't using them very well," Voodoo said.

"What do you mean?" He'd heard the gunshot and would have heard it even without Whitney wearing the comms unit.

"Listen," Dragon said quietly, his unusual violet eyes filled with an understanding that came from being in the same position before, terror for the woman you were falling for temporarily disrupting your connection to logic.

Forcing himself to shove the panic back a little, he focused.

And then he heard it.

"Y-you killed him," Whitney said, her voice weak and wavery, reminding him of how she'd sounded when she first started talking to him when he had her hanging from the tree. Since he knew that her immediate reaction to trauma was paralysis, he assumed these were the first words she'd spoken since the shooting.

Not dead.

Whitney wasn't dead.

Which meant the shot had to have killed the cop.

Given the man had turned dirty, been willing to sell out Whitney for a bag of cash, Blade didn't have it in him to summon even an ounce of empathy. The crooked cop had gotten exactly what he deserved.

"She's okay," he murmured the words on an exhale, barely able to believe them. He'd been so certain that the bullet had struck his girl, taken her from him, that he hadn't been able to think of any other possibility. This one made much more sense, though.

"He's not going to kill her," Steel said with a whole lot more confidence than Blade was currently feeling. Then again, it was easy for Steel to be confident when the woman he was in love with was safely tucked away at their home.

"Do we know who that is?" he asked, trying to cling to the control he was scrounging up. Facts would help him do that. Whitney liked facts, had shared dozens of them with him over the last few days.

"I sent a copy of his voice to Raven and Olivia. You know if anyone can identify him it's them and their teams," Lion assured him.

"You've almost caused more hassle than you're worth," the voice in his ear spoke, and he caught Whitney's whimper. Whoever this man was, she knew him, and she was terrified of him.

"I was just here to clear my name," Whitney said in a small voice. Despite how scared she obviously was, she was doing everything they could have asked of her. She was working through her fear and maintaining her cover. The last thing they needed was for her to let on that she was playing them while they thought they were the ones playing her.

"What name?" the man mocked, and he could hear footsteps crossing a concrete floor, that combined with another whimper from Whitney, and Blade knew the man was moving closer to her. "Whitney Daley doesn't exist. Gone, poof, like a puff of smoke."

"They erased her again," Thunder said, stating the obvious, and Blade threw his friend a quick glare.

"Why can't you just leave me alone?" Whitney asked, and there was a pleading quality to her voice he knew wasn't all acting. All she wanted was to be free to be her own person, make her own choices, live her own life.

"You know why," the man replied.

"But he never listens to me anyway. He fiddles with every variation of the drug I create. The reason they keep dying is *because* of Dr. Gardner. If he wants to do it himself, then let him," Whitney begged.

"Don't think you really want to be making that argument, baby genius," the man taunted. "Because if he does it all himself and doesn't need you anymore, then that makes you expendable, doesn't it? And if you're expendable, I could just put a bullet through your head right now and be done with it."

The threat—empty though he was sure it was—was all it took to snap the control he'd been clinging to, and Blade was off again.

Muttered curses sounded from behind him, but he heard feet pounding the path he had taken. As he ran, he kept listening, not letting fear make him completely useless, but as he approached the street where the produce store the cop had taken her to was located, he almost tripped over his feet when the comms unit suddenly went quiet.

What the hell?

There were too many competing sounds from the others, the vehicles on the street, the people in the park, those in the stores, and wandering down the sidewalk, for him to be able to zero in on Whitney and the man with her. At least quickly enough to figure out what was going on.

"Did everyone else lose them?" he demanded, not slowing his pace as he dodged around two women and several toddlers. Thankfully, they'd dressed to look like they blended in at the park, wearing sweat-pants, hoodies, and sneakers. Not only did they look like they were all just out for a run, but the hoodies provided some cover for their faces.

"Yeah, they're gone," Voodoo replied.

"Probably jammed the signal," Steel added.

"Right up ahead," Lion said, pointing at the store about midway down the street.

"Wouldn't have gone in the front door," Thunder said, "and there's an alley beside it, I say that's where we go."

Moving as a solid unit, they darted across the street between cars, not bothering to use the crossing and wait for the lights, and headed for the alley. There was a door toward the far end of it, and when Blade tried the lock on it, it swung open.

Not even two steps inside the back room of the store was the body. Deacon Hayes, dirty cop, lying dead in a pool of his own blood. A single bullet to the forehead was the obvious cause of death.

Besides that, the room was empty.

No Whitney. No shooter. Nothing.

Not even the sound of her voice in the comms unit.

"I can't get a read on the tracking devices," Lion announced, and it took Blade everything he had not to break down right then and there.

Whitney was gone, and he had no way to get her back.

～

January 15th
7:12 P.M.

A fiery ball of nausea burning up her esophagus ripped Whitney from unconsciousness.

Managing to turn her head before a rush of vomit came spewing out, she groaned as she sank back down as soon as she was done throwing up.

She felt like she'd been run over by a truck.

Since she knew she hadn't, she had to attribute the feeling to the drugs that Terry Richards had given her. The last part of what happened in the back room of the produce store was a little bit hazy, but she remembered the cop being shot, remembered trying her best to get away from the highly trained head of Dr. Gardner's security.

It didn't make a difference, though.

One single self-defense lesson that had ended before it even really got started when she'd kissed Blade wasn't enough to equip her to put anything into practice in a real-life experience. Especially when she was scared out of her mind.

Stupid survival instincts picking freeze instead of fight or even flight.

Not that she would have been able to flee from this situation, and realistically speaking, even if she wasn't fighting against her body's natural inclination to freeze in trauma situations, there was no way she was winning against a man like Terry Richards in a fight.

While nowhere near as big as Blake and the other members of Delta Team, he was way bigger than she was, and he actually knew how to fight and wasn't trying to convince his body not to freeze up on him the same way she had to.

Still, wasting time thinking about what had happened and what she could have done differently wasn't productive right now. Later. If she got back home, she'd make sure she and Blade worked on self-defense skills until her muscles no longer locked up on her. With enough practice, she could rewrite her body's instincts.

"No, not if, when. You have to think when or you're not going to make it until the guys find you," she rebuked herself.

She was wearing several trackers in case one or more of them were discovered, and she'd had the comms unit in. The guys would have heard the gunshot and come right away, because Blade would have been terrified she'd been the one who was shot. Even hearing her speak and knowing she was okay would have made him want to be closer.

The guys were coming, and hopefully Terry Richards had taken her straight to Dr. Gardner. Blade and the others had talked through every scenario with her, and she knew that they'd been hoping that Dr. Gardner would be there when she met with the cop, but they didn't think it was likely. Instead, it was more probable that she would be transported to a secondary location. They would be following her every move, waiting for confirmation that the doctor was there before moving in.

If Dr. Gardner never showed, they would move in anyway, extract her, and take whoever they could prisoner to try to get intel out of them on where her former boss had squirreled himself away.

It had seemed like a solid plan, one she'd been one hundred percent committed to, but now that she was there, in the middle of it, it suddenly seemed like a whole lot of things could go wrong.

No wonder Blade hadn't wanted her to do this.

"You told him you could do this, so you have to," she reminded herself. "Besides, it's not like you have a choice. You're committed now, you have to endure whatever is coming next."

She'd said she could do this, and she wasn't going to let anyone down.

Especially herself.

Okay, so she had to think about this logically. Maybe fighting wasn't her skill set, but logic was. Solving problems was. Assess her situation, weigh up all her options, and then formulate a plan.

Step one, assess.

It took Whitney a moment to figure out if the room she was in was just pitch black or if her eyes were closed. It wasn't until she blinked them several times that she concluded they were, in fact, open, and this room was so dark she couldn't tell the difference.

Fine tremors wracked her body in a constant stream, and now that she focused on it, she could tell it wasn't all fear. It was cold in there. Freezing in fact. Enough that she felt it even though she was wearing jeans, a sweater, a coat, gloves, and a scarf.

Wasn't she?

Panic chased away the cold, and she bolted upright, ignoring the still lingering nausea, and began to run her hands over her body. If someone had taken off her clothes, there was every chance that wasn't all they'd done to her.

The gloves were no longer on her hands, and she couldn't feel the scarf, but when she felt down to her chest, Whitney noted the soft cashmere of the sweater she'd put on for the meeting with the cop. No coat, but it seemed like her other clothes were in place.

Except for her shoes and socks. Because when she got to her feet, she found them bare and cold to the touch.

"At least you're not naked," she reminded herself, although it did little to calm her rising panic.

Maybe she hadn't been raped yet, and maybe it wouldn't happen, but until the guys came for her, the people holding her could do whatever they wanted to her. Dr. Gardner wanted her back, and Terry Richards had already told her that she was going to be punished for her betrayal.

What if it took too long for Blade to come?

What if by the time he got there, she'd already been hurt?

Scrambling up onto her knees, determined to find a way out, or at least something to defend herself with, Whitney swayed slightly as she pushed to her feet, but she ignored it. The drugs would soon be out of her system, and she needed to be prepared.

Blade was coming, he'd promised her, told her they were bound by blood now. Chances were, he was somewhere close by right now, every bit as anxious to get to her as she was to get to him. But he was also trusting her to have it together, stick with the plan. All the guys were, Rose and Cassandra, too. And any other victims still being held prisoner and tested on.

Beneath her bare feet, the floor was cold and hard. It didn't feel like a regular floor, not floorboards, or even concrete. It almost felt like some sort of metal. Maybe something like a shipping container?

With her hands out in front of her, Whitney walked until she touched something. A whole five steps. Five small, timid steps. Sidestepping along to her left, she made it another three before she found a corner. Ten steps made it to the other side, and then thirty along until she felt the next corner. Those dimensions could definitely fit with a shipping container, but as far as she knew, Dr. Gardner didn't have any connections with a shipping yard or dock.

Then again, what did she know about the crazed scientist other than what she saw when he was in the lab with her? Maybe he did have connections she didn't know about. After all, she was his prisoner not his friend, not a colleague, not an equal in any way.

The sound of clunking had her scrambling backward away from

what she was sure was the door to the shipping container that she was far too close to. In her hurry, she tripped over her feet and went down hard, pain spiking up her spine and her hands, which had taken the brunt of the fall.

Blinding light suddenly flooded inside her dark cage, and she had no choice but to squeeze her eyes shut, even knowing it made her that much more vulnerable.

"Ah, the baby genius is awake," Terry Richards' voice rang out, and she curled in on herself.

The man terrified her, and even knowing that Blade was coming for her didn't erase the fear of what would happen to her before he arrived.

"We've always had a special connection, haven't we, little one?" Terry asked.

"What?" Her eyes snapped open at the ridiculous statement. They'd had no connection whatsoever as far as she was concerned. She was forced to work for their boss, and he seemed to be there by choice. He was old enough to be her father, and she'd been scared of him from the beginning.

"Don't pretend otherwise, little one," Terry warned, stalking closer to where she was huddled on the floor. "You always flirt with me, have since you first arrived."

"I was ten," she reminded him. She'd never seen the man look like this. He was always cold and indifferent, always calm and in control. Now he looked almost manic, and the lecherous grin he was giving her meant she needed zero imagination to figure out what he wanted from her. "I didn't even know what flirting was back then, and even if I did, I never would have flirted with you. You were one of the people keeping me prisoner."

Terry just laughed. "Pretend all you want, little one, but we both know you wanted me even back then. Dr. Gardner didn't want anyone messing with his precious little baby genius, but since you've proven yourself to be a nuisance, that's changed. You're mine now, little one. Mine to play with, mine to use however I want, mine to break so you never consider running ever again."

# CHAPTER

## *Nineteen*

January 15th
8:39 P.M.

Too many hours had passed since Whitney had disappeared, and Blade was dangerously close to losing his mind.

Or maybe he'd already lost it.

Ever since he'd realized that their plan had been derailed, and the tracking devices on Whitney had either been found and destroyed or their transmission was being blocked, he'd felt like his skin was too tight on his body. His anger felt trapped inside him. Wanting to let it out, to rage at something or someone, but not having an available target, made him turn that anger on himself.

When it boiled down to it, he was the one to blame.

He'd gone against his better judgment in letting Whitney play bait. Hadn't learned his lesson from the disaster things had turned into when they'd gone this route before with Rose. Steel had almost lost her, and they hadn't even got their hands on the doctor.

At least they'd gotten Rose back alive, but whether they'd find Whitney before it was too late was still up in the air.

As much as he didn't want to lose hope, and he would never give up, the chances of them finding her were slim. Whitney had been their best source of intel, and she hadn't been able to lead them directly to the insane scientist. Without her, he couldn't help but feel that they had nothing.

They'd never had anything.

They'd been chasing their tails for seven years now, always playing defense. Even when they'd finally learned the name of the man they'd known only as doctor during their time in the program and while held captive, their one attempt at gaining the upper hand had only led to them to take a step toward becoming the monsters Dr. Gardner had always told them they were. Rose had easily flipped to being on their side, she had even more reason to hate her brother than they did, but she didn't know anything about her brother's evil plans. Prey had been doing everything they could, but even they hadn't been able to pinpoint anything that would give them the doctor's location.

Why should he believe that would change now that the life of the woman whose big innocent eyes, and sweet timidity had pierced his heart was on the line?

"If you keep doing that, there's not going to be any of you left when we find her," Dragon said quietly from beside him.

Glancing down at the skin on his forearm he'd been absently peeling off with the blade of his knife, Blade just shrugged. The pain was the only thing keeping him marginally sane. A way to work out his anger and keep the panic at bay enough that he didn't go off on a screaming rampage. A rampage that would do no good. By the time they'd gotten to the produce store, Whitney and whoever had killed the cop were gone, and they hadn't been able to pick up a trail.

The kidnapper had come prepared to throw off their enhanced skills, and it had worked.

"We have a name," Steel suddenly announced, and Blade's gaze jerked up from his bloody skin.

"Of him?" he asked, wanting clarification before he let himself light even a glimmer of hope. After they'd searched the entire area without coming up with a single angle to pursue where Whitney had been taken, they'd gone back to their cars, called Prey to get Cyber Team going through CCTV footage, and then checked into a nearby hotel.

The plan had never been to hang around there. If they were lucky and Dr. Gardner had come to the meet up with the cop, they would have moved in and taken the scientist with them. Otherwise, the plan had been to follow the trackers and let Whitney lead them right to the man they all wanted to destroy.

"Yep," Steel agreed, shooting him what Blade was sure was supposed to be an encouraging smile. "His name is Terry Richards. Served a single tour for the Marines before being honorably discharged. He's forty-three years old. Grew up in the foster system after he was taken from his parents before his first birthday, due to drug use and abuse in the home. No siblings. Not married, never has been, and no kids. He's done security work ever since leaving the Marines. Started small, working at a mall, then moved up to a bank. Before taking on a new job about thirteen years ago, working as the head of security for a pharmaceutical company called Nature Plus."

"As in From Nature, dressed up under a new name, when it was taken over by Dr. Gardner," Thunder muttered.

"That's my guess," Steel agreed.

Backstory for the man who had been in that room when the cop was shot, who had taken Whitney from him, and who had quite obviously terrified her, was the last thing Blade was interested in right now. "Address?" he barked out.

"Raven said that the address listed for Terry Richards is actually an empty plot of land," Steel replied.

If Raven Oswald, the second oldest of the six Oswald siblings, and a computer genius who led Cyber Team, said it then he believed it. He also knew her team had been running every CCTV camera in the area they could get, but all they'd been able to pick up was a man all in black pushing out a trolley with pallets of fruit and vegetables to a van that delivered to a local charity right around the time he and his team had arrived at the store.

There was no doubt the man in black was Terry Richards, and that Whitney's unconscious body had been hidden beneath the produce, but the van had disappeared along the way, and Cyber Team was yet to pick it up anywhere.

"Address on the business?" Blade asked. If they couldn't find Terry Richards through his home address, they'd just get to the man through his work one.

"Only address listed for it is the same building where Whitney used to work, the one she blew up," Steel answered.

"Damn," Blade swore, his knife moving automatically back to peel away at his skin. It seemed only fitting that he keep punishing himself because who knew what kind of hell Whitney was going through at this moment.

"Stop doing that," Dragon snapped, reaching for the knife, but Blade swung it out of reach.

"We were supposed to be following her, but we lost her. I promised her she'd be okay, and we all know she's not," he snarled. His gaze fell on the small cut in his palm. His promise to his girl, broken already.

"Even if they found the trackers on her, she still has the one Teresa invented, that doesn't get turned on until it's activated," Voodoo reminded him, like that was any comfort. In theory, the device created by Cyber Team member Teresa Dash was a workaround for most situations, but if someone was using a jammer, then it was useless.

"Problem is, we shouldn't have assumed she'd be taken straight to Dr. Gardner," he said. Whitney had told them that the only other person who worked for the scientist who might want to get his hands on her was her former handler, who was the man Blade had killed last in the forest that day. There didn't seem to be any reason to suspect that having her taken straight to the man who bought her wouldn't happen.

What had just hours ago seemed like a perfectly logical plan, let Whitney play bait, follow at a distance, be led straight to the source of all their suffering, now seemed like it was so full of holes that a kindergartener could have come up with something better.

"We don't know that she hasn't been taken straight to Dr. Gardner," Lion reminded him.

"Well, we sure as hell know that we have no way to track her regardless of where she is," he snapped back. In the end, it didn't matter if she was still with Terry Richards. If she was with Dr. Gardner, or if she was with someone else, or hell, even dumped alone somewhere. She wasn't with him and that was all he cared about.

"Your girl is smart," Steel said, his expression and his voice fierce. "She survived these people for twelve years, and she was only a child back then. She knows we're coming for her, she knows she's not facing this alone, and she knows her brain is too valuable to Dr. Gardner for him to risk hurting her too badly. She will survive, and we will find her. We have a name and a company, and there will be something linking them to actionable intel that will lead us to them. None of us is giving up on Whitney, which means you can't either."

"Rather be dead than give up on her," he said simply, and the gravity of his own words hit him hard. Sitting there, peeling off his own skin was wasting time. Time Whitney might not have.

~

January 16th
   4:52 A.M.

So many hours had passed since she was taken.

Too many.

Was Blade still out there? Somewhere close by, just waiting for a glimpse of Dr. Gardner before he came swooping in on his white horse to save her?

Or ...

Had he left? Maybe not even followed her to begin with? Maybe when he'd found the dead cop and her gone, he'd just decided this was too much hassle and he and his team had headed back home to come up with a new way to go after the man they despised.

"No," she said aloud, her voice loud and strong, if slightly panicked, and she traced a fingertip around the gash on her palm almost convulsively, like she'd been doing most of the time since Terry had left her alone. "That's just your fear talking."

There was no way Blade would just leave her there.

Bound by blood. That's what he'd promised her.

"He wasn't lying to you when he said you were his, that he wanted you," she assured herself, annoyed that doubt remained. Whitney was ninety-nine percent sure that Blade hadn't been playing her, that he'd been serious, that he knew she would help regardless, so he didn't have to lead her on to gain her cooperation.

Yet ...

There was a teeny, tiny, little piece of lingering doubt. She hated it, but it was there nonetheless, and no amount of reminding herself of Blade's words, his touches, his kisses, could seem to eliminate it.

A fingertip lingered over the small tracking device that had been placed under her skin right beside the wounds from the ropes. It was created by one of the people who worked for Prey Security's Cyber Team, and Whitney thought it was a brilliant idea. Apparently, it remained inactive so it wouldn't be picked up by a scanner and then was turned on by the fingerprint of the person it had been programmed for.

When Terry Richards had been in there earlier, he'd taken great pleasure not only in describing in vivid detail what he planned on doing to her body, but also in letting her know that her little plot, as he'd called it, had failed. The man had scanned her after drugging her and taking her there, and he'd found all eight of the trackers that had been hidden on and under her skin.

Eight trackers was the number that had been planted on her by Blade minus one.

The one only she could access.

As they'd been planning this op, they'd discussed this being like the failsafe, her option if anything went wrong. Of course, they'd hoped that some of the other trackers wouldn't be discovered because they were an easier way for her to be followed by Blade and the others. But Terry had said he'd found the trackers *after* he already had her there, so she still believed that the guys had been able to follow her to this location and were waiting nearby.

But if they weren't ... then this tracker could be the only thing that would save her life.

And since Terry had been in a very chatty mood earlier, she knew that Dr. Gardner wouldn't be going there. The plan was for Terry to break her, then when she was once again the obedient, meek, terrified little lab soldier, she would be taken to a new lab where she would continue working.

So if the guys were out there, they were waiting for the arrival of a man who wasn't coming.

Only they didn't know that.

It was time to activate this tracker so they would know to come and get her. If they made it in there before Terry Richards made it back, they could lie in wait for the man, and if not, then they could still get him the second they opened those doors. Her position in the hierarchy had been at the bottom of the pile, but Terry was on top, second only to Dr. Gardner himself, which meant the man would have a lot more information to share than she had. She was sure that the guys were persuasive enough to get him talking.

Touching her finger to the spot where the tracker wasn't even noticeable, she let out a breath as her tense body marginally relaxed. Blade was coming now.

Any minute, he'd be there, and this would all be over.

Whitney knew she was lucky that Terry had been called away earlier before he got his filthy hands on her. For the last few hours, she'd debated with herself whether to activate the tracker or if she should give it a bit longer just in case Terry was wrong and Dr. Gardner decided to make an appearance just to scream at her and tell her she deserved to suffer for betraying him.

Although she had no idea how you could betray someone who had literally bought you and kept you prisoner since you were a child, forcing you to work on something you didn't believe in, and making you carry marks on your body for each person that died because of something outside your control.

Still, it didn't matter, Blade was coming. He and the others would get Terry and take him back home with them so they could interrogate him. Soon, Dr. Gardner would be dead and all of them free to live their lives without having to hide.

"Soon," she whispered aloud, because she needed the sound of her own voice to break through the deafening silence.

Who knew silence could be deafening?

It seemed to pound in her ears, echoing inside her head almost to the point of pain. Or maybe that was the beginning of dehydration, giving her a headache. Terry hadn't brought anything for her to eat and drink, and the drugs she'd been given had contributed to dehydrating her body.

But Blade was coming.

Probably in just a few minutes, he'd come bursting through that door, and the first thing she was going to do when she saw him was throw herself into his arms and kiss him. Then she was going to tell him she never wanted him to leave her again.

Surprise had her straightening from where she'd been huddled in one of the corners of what she knew now was indeed a shipping container. That was true. She didn't want him to leave her ever again. It made absolutely zero sense that the man who had tortured her had become the man who made her feel safe and seen. But it was true. Crazy but true.

Sounds outside the shipping container had her pushing to her feet.

Someone was out there.

Blade.

Relief almost made her lightheaded as she hurried toward the door. She'd been hiding out at the far end, wanting a tiny bit of distance between her and her captor, but now she needed to be close to Blade. Seeking out his comfort had become easier than she would have guessed. Even before she was sold to Dr. Gardner, there hadn't been much warmth in her life. Her parents didn't understand her, she didn't have extended family, and she had no friends. Blade and his team had offered her more care and acceptance than anyone else ever had, and like the love-starved girl she was, she was soaking it up.

Now she was bouncing on her toes, excitement and relief bubbling inside her.

It wasn't just that she wanted out of this shipping container, although she absolutely did, it was that she was itching to see Blade again. How quickly she'd grown so attached should scare her, but it didn't. Who you developed feelings for was the one thing in the universe she believed you couldn't explain. When it happened, it happened, and given that she'd been sure it was never going to happen to her and then it had, she wasn't going to waste time trying to figure out the whys and hows.

As the door creaked as it swung open, Whitney was already moving.

It never occurred to her that it would be anyone other than Blade on the other side. His promises that he wouldn't let anything happen to her had been real, and it wasn't a coincidence that just after she'd set off the tracker alerting him that she needed him, someone had come to her.

But then a single shadowy figure filled the open doorway.

Because it was dark outside, it didn't take her eyes long to adjust to the slight light now filtering into her prison.

Enough to see that it wasn't Blade standing there.

Either he and his team were too far away to get to her quickly, or they didn't even know that she'd turned on her tracker, because they weren't there.

Terry Richards was, though.

"Morning, little one, I've cleared my schedule, so for the foreseeable future it's just going to be me and you."

# CHAPTER

*Twenty*

January 16th
9:04 A.M.

Another twelve hours gone.

No closer to finding Whitney than they'd been before.

With each passing second, it felt like she was slipping further out of his reach.

How was he supposed to find her and bring her home when they couldn't get a single actionable piece of intel?

Knowing she was out there, alone and scared, most likely hurt, wondering why he hadn't come for her was killing him.

Slowly but surely.

Blade had already peeled off the top layer of skin on both his forearms. They were the easiest to access, but he was going to move on to his legs now, start peeling skin from his thighs, making his way down toward his feet. It was only fitting that he suffer right along with Whitney.

For failing her, he deserved a whole lot worse.

If he got her back alive and in one piece, he would offer her his heart on a platter if that was what it took to earn her forgiveness, even if he wouldn't be there to enjoy it.

"Cut that out," Dragon's voice ordered, and there was an accompanying slap to the back of his head that made him growl.

"No," he snapped, knowing that he sounded like a petulant child and not caring in the least. Dragon had gotten Cassandra back mostly unharmed after he'd thought he lost her in the explosion, and Steel had gotten Rose back after their plan to lure her brother into a trap failed.

They didn't understand.

They didn't know what this cloying fear felt like.

When it had been Rose in danger, she'd been alone with her brother only long enough for them to drive off and then crash. And Cassandra hadn't been alone with the bounty hunter for more than thirty minutes or so at the most.

It had been almost twenty hours since Whitney walked away from them to go to the park bench, and he'd been forced to let her. Before he knew it, it would be twenty-four hours, a whole day since she'd disappeared. One day would quickly become two, and then it would be a week. A week would turn into a month in the blink of an eye, and then she could be gone for good.

How she'd managed to make such an impact on him in just a matter of days should be impossible, but it wasn't, and he would be eternally grateful for those days he'd had her as his, even if he would never forgive himself for losing her.

"That isn't going to bring her back," Dragon said, setting food down on the small table in their hotel suite.

"Neither is anything else we've been doing," he shot back.

They had a list now of every one of the men who had been in the forest the day he and Whitney had left the farmhouse. Snapping pictures of each of the dead men before they left had let Prey identify all of them. They had the name of the man who had abducted Whitney and shot the cop, and they had all the intel she'd given them. Names, dates, locations, you'd think enough to dismantle the entire operation.

But Whitney had been right when she said that Dr. Gardner moved labs regularly. Prey had sent out other teams to the locations on the list and found them all either abandoned or sold and now run by other companies. One had even been turned into a pet store selling a huge range of products for everything from dogs and cats to reptiles and exotic fish.

"We're building a lot of evidence against these people," Thunder reminded him as the rest of the guys began to trail into the room.

"Don't care about convicting them, that was never our plan. We wanted Dr. Gardner dead, and as badly as I still want that, I would spare his life if it meant getting Whitney back alive," Blade said, never more sure of anything in his life.

For the last decade, all he'd cared about was revenge. It had fueled him, got him through the dark days when anger and suicidal thoughts seemed to consume him. It had been all he'd wanted, and he'd believed that once they had it, they would finally be free.

Only he'd already found freedom.

A different kind than he'd been expecting. This freedom brought with it peace that had been so desperately lacking, a quietness that, after ten years of hearing every single little sound, was refreshing. It brought hope for the future and a desire to be something more than a man who had been genetically altered to have enhanced skills and stamina.

If he had a chance to give up revenge for hope, he'd do it in a heartbeat.

"None of us wants Dr. Gardner in a jail cell," Steel told him. "And none of us is giving up on either one of them. Priority is Whitney, though."

Maybe it shouldn't come as a surprise that Steel was willing to put Whitney above their revenge, given that he'd prioritized Rose over her brother. But that was different. Steel had been obsessed with Rose from the moment they realized she wasn't what they'd been expecting and that breaking her wasn't going to happen. Add in that Whitney had unintentionally started the program that ruined their lives, and asking anyone other than himself to put her above everything they'd wanted for a decade seemed like a pipedream.

"Stop acting surprised," Voodoo muttered, flopping down into the seat beside his. "And give me that knife."

No one was more shocked than Blade himself when he handed over his favorite knife to his friend without hesitation. Maybe it was because he was spiraling. Already in the last twelve hours, he'd promised himself a dozen times that he would stop wallowing in fear and panic and focus on finding Whitney. Each time he'd broken that promise to himself.

To think clearly, he needed to let go of the past.

That knife represented everything about his past that he'd held onto for ten long years. The people he loved and had left behind to protect them, the family that had once meant everything to him.

But he had a new family now. A future where he could be happy again, and that future was all wrapped up in a five-foot-three, blonde-haired, blue-eyed package that was currently counting on him. He'd already let her down once, he couldn't allow it to happen again.

"Whoa, didn't think Blade would really give up his blade," Voodoo teased, and since he knew it was said in an effort to help him pull it together, he offered up a weak smile.

"We've been going through all of these people for hours now, and don't have anything. We need a new angle," he said.

"Their prior work histories," Lion said without hesitation, causing all of them to turn to look at the man who had been hammering away at his keyboard during their entire exchange.

"Work histories?" Blade asked.

Glancing up, Lion gave a quick nod, then continued working while he spoke. "Between the dead bodies and the intel from Whitney, we have a pretty comprehensive list. Different ages, different ethnicities, different socio-economic groups, some military, some scientists, there is nothing cohesive enough amongst them to say that's how they're being recruited. Until we start looking at their work histories."

"You found some links?" Steel asked.

"A couple," Lion replied. "Since we know Terry Richards, Dr. Gardner's head of security, is the one who abducted Whitney, I've been focusing more on the security side of things than the science side. My guess is there's a chance some of the other scientists working for the doctor were also recruited under false pretenses, although I doubt anyone was strictly there as a prisoner like Whitney was. When I started looking more closely into the dead men, I found that three of them had previously worked for a trucking company before being hired, and four of them had worked for a shipping company."

"Names for both?" Blade asked, and Lion rattled off two.

"Been looking into both businesses, and they both seem like they're a little shady. The trucking company is legitimate, they take contracts from a range of different companies that I can verify are above board. But there have been a few investigations into them. Products going missing. Some fraud and tax evasion. Some rumors that they might be hiding drugs inside their trucks and running them for a few gangs. Definitely something we need to look into closer."

"And the shipping company?" Blade asked.

"Again, there were some insinuations that they might be shipping drugs and weapons, but investigations failed to turn up any proof. There was a murder at the shipping yard about two years ago that remains unsolved, but guess who the lead detective on the case was?" Lion asked.

"Detective Deacon Hayes," Blade guessed.

"Bingo. My guess is that the cop found something that linked Dr. Gardner to the murder. They offered him money in exchange for his silence, and then they either offered him more or blackmailed him to get him to promote Whitney as a suspect and then hand her over."

Both options sounded like viable ones, and for the first time since he heard that gunshot, Blade felt like things weren't completely hopeless.

∼

January 16th
   11:23 P.M.

For whatever reason, they weren't coming.

It was becoming increasingly clear of that.

As badly as Whitney's fear was urging her to believe that it was because Blade was just like her parents and had decided to abandon her, she was doing her best to push through that and ignore those feelings.

Because they weren't true.

The cut on her palm and Blade's vow assured her he wouldn't do that to her. If he hadn't come when she turned on the tracker embedded in the outskirts of her wounds, then it was because he couldn't. Maybe Terry was using a jammer to block any signals. It would be a smart thing to do since he knew how smart she was and that she might want to protect herself if anything happened to her by giving access to the trackers to someone.

Although, who he thought she would give them to she had no idea.

As far as Terry Richards knew, she'd been on her own. They hadn't discussed how all those men had wound up dead in the forest, he hadn't seemed to notice the scratches on her skin and bruising on her neck, and she had never mentioned that she was no longer on her own. That the very men Dr. Gardner wanted back almost as much as he wanted her back were almost within Terry's grasp. That they'd found her, hurt her, saved her, and were trying to get back to her, ready to dismantle the doctor's entire operation.

So far, all Terry seemed to care about was her. It seemed he'd been waiting a long time to get permission to do whatever he wanted to her, and that was all he could think about.

The things he'd done to her in this shipping container ...

Whitney wasn't ready to address them yet. If she tried, she was pretty sure it would shatter whatever slim control she still had on her panic. If it slipped, then she'd shatter into a thousand pieces, pieces she wouldn't be able to put back together in time to save herself.

And there was no doubt that she had to save herself if she didn't want to wind up in Dr. Gardner's clutches again.

No one was coming for her, and if she didn't find a way out, she had no doubt that Terry would do exactly what he said he would and break her.

Already, she was crumbling.

It didn't matter that when the shipping container door had closed behind Terry, and he'd switched on a lantern he'd brought with him and began unzipping himself, that she had promised herself she wouldn't cry, wouldn't scream, wouldn't beg.

All three of those had happened.

The truth was, she wasn't strong, she wasn't going to be able to survive. If she was feeling this broken after just one day with the man who seemed to think she belonged to him now, then she wasn't going to endure much longer.

Once he broke her, he'd take her back to Dr. Gardner, and Whitney was under no illusion that things would be different this time around. While she might be made to work long hours in the lab, instead of going back to her own room at night for a few hours respite, she'd be spending those hours as Terry's plaything.

Unless she found a way to save herself.

Could she do that?

Did she have it in her?

If she was going to try, now would be the perfect time. After unzipping himself, Terry had spent the day playing with her. He'd made her take him in her mouth and her hands. He'd stripped her of her sweater and bra and got himself off by thrusting between her breasts. There was no doubt in her mind that he was on something because he seemed to be able to get hard almost immediately after already coming, and there was no way a penis behaved that way unless its owner was using a stimulant of some sort.

It seemed to go on for hours, but trapped there with no way to mark the passage of time, maybe it wasn't as long as it felt. Regardless, it didn't really matter. Finally, Terry had fallen asleep on the floor, whatever drug he'd been using likely out of his system now.

She would have guessed that when he finished using her as his personal toy, he would have left to go home. But he must have been more exhausted than he realized, because when his eyelids began to droop, he'd mumbled something incoherent and then grabbed her and lay down with her on the unforgiving floor.

Almost immediately, Terry had gone to sleep, but exhausted as she was, sleep wouldn't come for her.

Not when his arm pinned her to his body.

Not when she could feel his length—still partially erect—pressed into her backside.

Not when she was covered in his semen, dried in places, still sticky in others, coating her chest, her hands, arms, face, and neck.

Trying to escape was her only chance. If she stayed, she knew sooner rather than later, he would be putting that disgusting penis of his inside her. Maybe not just in her vagina. He wanted to degrade and humiliate her, wanted to break her, and what better way than to take her backside.

As far as Terry knew, she was still a virgin. He knew no one had touched her while she was still with Dr. Gardner, and she'd only been gone a couple of weeks. There was no way he could have figured out that she'd managed to fall hard and fast for a fierce warrior, who would do anything for the people he cared about.

She was one of those people now.

Blade was out there somewhere, and she wanted to get back to him.

So she was doing this. When Terry woke up, he might be ready to take her for what he believed was her first time. No doubt he loved the idea of tearing her virginity away from her, knowing she had no say in the matter, and Whitney was infinitely glad that even if she didn't make it out of there that was something he could never take from her.

Because it already belonged to Blade.

Entire body trembling, she did her best not to let her fear take over and wrapped her hand around Terry's wrist. The man wasn't as big and muscled as Blade, wirier than anything else, but her fingers still couldn't circle his wrist.

Still, she was able to lift his arm, heavy though it was, enough that she could wriggle out of his hold.

Each movement was nerve-racking.

At any second, he could wake up.

If he found her trying to escape, she had no doubt she'd be punished. He might not be able to kill her, but there were plenty of things he could do to make her wish she were dead.

Once she was out of his hold, Whitney carefully laid his arm back down again.

As she did so, he huffed, shifted slightly, and she froze.

Was he waking up?

Did he realize she was no longer pressed up against him?

Holding her breath, she waited, counting the seconds in her mind, praying that he wasn't going to open his eyes and see that she was making a move.

If worst came to worst and he woke, she could always lie and say she had to pee. Chances were, he wouldn't believe it because he hadn't given her anything to eat or drink since he brought her there, and she'd already been forced to pee in the corner a couple of times. Now, though, there was nothing left in her system to come out, and she was already feeling the effects of dehydration.

After counting to one hundred without him opening his eyes, Whitney determined that it was safe to move. Staying low, she scrambled on her hands and knees a couple of feet away from Terry before stopping again. Even though she wanted to just get up and run, she also wanted to do this carefully, minimizing the risk of Terry waking up.

Since he had no weapon on him, and she couldn't beat him in a hand-to-hand fight, her only option was to flee, but this time she was determined there would be no freeze.

Scrambling another few feet away, she paused again. As badly as she wanted to try to find her top, she wanted out of here and away from this man more, so when he still didn't wake, she crawled the rest of the way to the door.

This might be the hardest part because the door creaked slightly as it opened. Thankfully, Terry hadn't locked it behind him. It was closed, but it wasn't latched in, so all she had to do was ease it open enough to squeeze through.

As her hands touched the cold metal, Whitney had never been more grateful in her life for her small size.

Glancing over her shoulder, she confirmed that Terry Richards was still fast asleep, then she dragged in a deep breath and went for it. The more she hesitated, the greater the chances of getting caught.

Pushing against the door, it was heavier than she had been anticipating, and she had to shove it with every drop of strength she had left in her weakening body.

It moved, and she let out a sigh of relief.

Just one more push should get it open enough for her to fit through.

Another check to confirm that Terry was still passed out from the drugs he'd taken, and then she pushed again.

This time her luck didn't hold.

The door squeaked.

Behind her, she heard Terry stirring.

Without looking back, Whitney scrambled through the small opening and tried to close the door behind her. When she found it was too heavy for her to move, she gave up, and instead took off at a dead run, her bare feet pounding the ground as she heard Terry swear as he obviously realized she was gone.

# CHAPTER
## Twenty-One

January 17th
    12:12 A.M.

"Is that what I think it is?" Blade demanded when he heard a small beep go off on the tablet Lion was scrolling through.

Hope blasted his chest before he could stop it.

It had been a long day. They'd scoured every corner of the internet for intel on both the shipping company and the trucking company linked to Dr. Gardner's men. Hours of grueling work, sitting staring at a screen when what he wanted to do was tear apart the world to find his missing little genius.

While it about killed him, he'd agreed to lie down for a few hours while they waited for the sun to set and the moon to rise. Sleep was the last thing he wanted, and he'd only agreed because the guys were right. Whitney's life was hanging on the line, and if he messed something up because he hadn't slept in days, he would never forgive himself. The enhancements done to his system and those of his teammates meant they could go longer without sleep, but his body still needed it and would function better even with a couple of hours.

The trucking company had been a bust. They'd found some illegal drugs in a few of the vehicles, but there was no sign of Whitney. Of course, they'd let Prey know what they'd found, and he had no doubt that the cops would be making a visit to the company in the morning, but Blade couldn't care less about some drugs in comparison to the life of the woman who had swept into his life like a breath of fresh air.

Now they were on their way to the shipping yard. It would be harder to search, even with their enhanced skills, because it was a whole lot bigger than the yard where the trucking company was based. Not that Blade cared, it felt good to be out actually doing something, and now he'd heard the sound he'd been praying for.

"Got her," Lion exclaimed in response, and Blade felt relief rush through his body, easing the tension that had been there ever since Whitney saw her face on the news and decided to use this opportunity to play bait.

"Which tracker?" he asked. Their theory was that Terry Richards had been using a jammer to prevent any trackers Whitney might have on her from being useful. A jammer would still mess with the tracker that was lying dormant under her skin until she set it off, but if she'd set off that tracker, it meant she was in trouble and couldn't wait for them any longer.

After all, Whitney didn't know that they hadn't been able to track her. As far as she'd probably been aware, they were sitting somewhere close by waiting for a glimpse of Dr. Gardner before swooping in to rescue her.

"The one she has to activate herself," Lion replied.

"Think Dr. Gardner made an appearance?" Voodoo asked.

"Possibly," Blade answered. "That, or they're moving her, and she's now outside the range of the jammer."

"If she just set it off now, she might have been out of the range of the jammer for a while and only just decided she needed to let us know to come to her. Maybe Dr. Gardner arrived, or maybe ..." Blade couldn't even finish that sentence.

There were too many maybes.

Maybe she'd been tied up this entire time and only just been able to get her hand to her wrist to set off the tracker.

Maybe she'd been unconscious the entire time, drugged up and unable to get herself help.

Maybe Dr. Gardner had been there all along, but she hadn't been able to set off her tracker for whatever reason.

Maybe the threat to her had increased to the point where she could no longer wait for the doctor to arrive because she was in danger now.

Maybe they were about to move her, and she knew she'd be spirited away someplace where she'd never be found.

Maybe the tracker had been active for hours, and she'd been waiting all this time for him to come, and he hadn't.

"Drive faster," he told Thunder, who was sitting in the driver's seat, already driving their large SUV above the speed limit.

"Going as fast as I can," Thunder assured him, their eyes meeting briefly in the rear-view mirror.

"Not fast enough," he shot back. Hope and relief were wonderful things. Now he knew that Whitney was alive and cognizant enough to set off her tracker, hopefully, that meant she wasn't badly injured. They also had a way to find her now. All they had to do was follow the little dot on Lion's tablet, and it would lead them right to her.

"I go any faster, and we're not going to be making it anywhere because we're going to be crashing into something," Thunder said.

"You never crash," Blade muttered. Somehow it was true. Thunder was almost always their driver, and while there should be no reason his enhanced speed would help him to drive faster, somehow he managed to maintain perfect control of a vehicle no matter how fast he was going.

"And I want to keep it that way," Thunder told him. "What are the coordinates for Whitney's position, Lion? So I can input them into the GPS."

"No need. She's at the docks," Lion replied.

After spending a day and a half searching for Whitney, to find that they'd already gotten their own lead on her location was the first bit of good news he'd had. The reason they'd checked out the trucking company first was because it was closer. The docks were in the next state over, but since they were close enough to the border to drive, they'd gone with that rather than wasting time going to the airport, readying the plane, and finding a private airfield close to the docks to fly into.

Now they were already heading for the docks, less than thirty minutes out.

Thirty minutes.

A lot could still happen in that time.

Especially if Whitney had activated the tracker because she was about to be moved. So long as the tracker stayed on, they'd still be able to find her, but as soon as she was near a jammer again, they'd lose her, and a jammer was the only way Terry Richards would have been able to get Whitney out of the produce store as quickly as he could.

The tension in the car grew as Thunder sped along the roads. Thankfully, it was the middle of the night, and the roads were quiet. They made good time, and just over twenty minutes later, they were pulling up at the docks.

While the tracker still beeping quietly on Lion's tablet told them they weren't too late and Whitney was still here, it wasn't going to lead them to her exact location. Thankfully, they didn't need a tracker to do that. Between the six of them, there was no way they wouldn't find her, and whoever was with her didn't know they were enjoying their last minutes on this earth.

Climbing out of the car, Blade cocked his head and listened.

Two distinct sets of footsteps could be heard. Running.

Had Whitney escaped? Was that why they'd just gotten the alert of her location, because she'd gotten herself out of the jammer's zone?

"I smell them. Two of them," Dragon said from beside him. "It's him, Terry Richards. I recognize the scent from the store. Definitely her too."

"We should split up," Steel announced. "Blade and Dragon will have the best chances of pinning them down, it's too hard for Lion to see much with all the containers stacked up like this. Thunder and Voodoo with Blade, Lion and I will go with Dragon."

There was no need to discuss it, this time Blade didn't intend to argue with his team leader. The sound of Whitney's ragged breathing echoed loudly in his ears, and he could tell from the way it hitched that she was crying while she ran.

Following the sound, Blade took off, Thunder and Voodoo on his heels. This whole place was like one giant maze. Stacks of shipping containers rose up to the sky at every turn, and it made trying to find the right path to take to get to Whitney almost impossible.

Not that he was giving up. Blade would go to the ends of the earth for Whitney Daley, burn the entire planet to the ground if that was what it took to save her life.

"We're getting close," he told the others as he stopped to get his bearings. Whitney was just up ahead, but he had to make sure he chose the right direction, otherwise, they'd find themselves blocked again by these damn shipping containers. "This way."

Neither Voodoo nor Thunder argued, and the three of them dodged around a corner, then another.

"Found where he was keeping her," Steel's voice came through to him from wherever the others were. "Open shipping container, her sweater is in here, and her bra." There was a pause, and then Steel sighed, his voice tight when he spoke again. "Dragon says it smells like sex in here."

Rage more powerful than anything he'd experienced before clouded his vision, attached itself to every drop of blood pumping through his body, and when Blade turned the next corner, he spotted her.

Whitney, on top of a stack of three containers, and she wasn't alone.

Terry Richards was running right at her.

≈

January 17th
12:50 A.M.

Running wasn't going to work indefinitely.

There had been barely a head start, she'd made it around a corner when she heard the door to the shipping container flung open hard enough that it slammed into the side of it, if the bang echoing through the quiet night was anything to go by.

Whitney hadn't been sure where the shipping container was, because she'd never gotten a good look outside the door the couple of times it had been opened, and she hadn't been sure if she was being held at a shipping yard at a dock somewhere, or if the shipping container had been set up someplace else.

As soon as she'd stepped through its door, she got her answer. They were at a dock, and there were stacks of other shipping containers everywhere. It was like being trapped in a maze. She was trying to find her way out, find her way to a road, an office with a phone, something, anything that could get her to safety.

So far, all she'd found were more shipping containers.

And more, and more, and more.

They were everywhere, and it was starting to feel like she was never going to find her way out of them.

Didn't help that she had to keep darting in different directions to try to evade the man after her.

Terry Richards was bigger and stronger and faster, but she was smaller, and she used that to be able to squeeze herself into small spaces to hide.

Twice now Terry had gone right past her, close enough for her to see, close enough that if he just turned his head, he'd be able to see her too.

Thankfully, he never did. He thought he was going to use the things he had over her to his advantage, but big and strong didn't always win, Whitney was starting to realize that.

Still, she also knew her luck couldn't last indefinitely.

Sooner or later, he was going to turn his head at the wrong moment —or right moment for him—and spot her.

What she needed was a proper plan. One that didn't just involve running in circles, crossing her fingers, and hoping for the best. That wasn't going to save her life, and that's what she was playing for. Terry might want her back because he was obsessed with her, but she wanted to live. For the first time ever, a chance at a real life, at autonomy, at happiness, at independence, at love, was within her grasp and she wasn't giving it up.

Not for Terry Richards, and not for Dr. Gardner.

"You can't outrun me forever, little one," Terry called out, far too close for her liking. But at least he sounded winded, so she wasn't the only one exhausted from running through the shipping yard.

Weak as she'd already been before she snuck out of that shipping container, now she was teetering on the edge of utter exhaustion. Changing direction once again, Whitney eyed the stack of containers beside her.

What if she could climb up them?

Not only would Terry not be looking for her up there, instead assuming she was still running, but it would also give her a better view of the yard. Maybe then she'd be able to find a way out, because if she kept trying to outrun Terry, she was going to wind up collapsing from exhaustion.

Once that happened, it would all be over.

She'd be found, he'd take her away someplace else, or put her back in that shipping container, but wherever he put her, she knew he would never allow her another opportunity to escape.

If she wanted to live, find her way back to Blade, then she had to try this.

Taking another couple of turns, the sounds of Terry's heavy breathing and pounding footsteps dulling a little as she put a bit of distance between them, she stopped. It felt wrong not to be moving, even as her shaking body thanked her for the reprieve, but Whitney knew she had to play this smart.

So she reached up for the shipping container before her and started to climb. It wasn't easy, it felt like working her way up the side of a mountain. There weren't many places to grab onto, and she had no experience with rock climbing, any sort of climbing, or even something as simple as hiking. As a kid, she'd been made to study all the time, extracurricular activities like dance, t-ball, or soccer weren't on the table, so her muscles were weak, and she had been shaky to begin with.

Somehow, determination proved to be what she needed, and an excruciating however many minutes later, she pulled herself up onto the roof of the top container.

For several minutes, all she could do was lie there, panting, tears burning her eyes and spilling down her cheeks, leaving icy trails in their wake. Shaking from cold, fear, and exhaustion, Whitney knew she still needed to keep moving, she was far from safe even if she'd bought herself a little bit of time.

When she knew she couldn't afford to waste another second, she rolled over onto her front, planted her palms against the cold metal, and pushed up onto her hands and knees. The world swirled around her, and she had to pause before shoving up to her feet.

Again, the world did a sickening spin, and she threw out a hand to catch herself on something, only there was nothing to catch herself on, and she staggered sideways, coming precariously close to the edge.

The last thing she needed was to fall.

She was twenty-five odd feet high on top of the three container stack. While she could survive that fall, even with the concrete ground below, she wouldn't be surviving it intact. Broken bones, internal injuries, spinal cord damage, brain damage, any or all of those could occur, and since she and Terry were the only ones out there, he'd be the one to find her. He'd either finish her off, or if Dr. Gardner was determined to keep her, she'd be taken to a doctor first, then returned to work when she was healed enough.

Righting herself, Whitney looked around, trying to make sense of the maze of containers to find a way out.

Something caught her eye.

Movement.

But not one person, it looked like several, three at least, moving together, closing in on her location.

Had Terry called in help?

Heart hammering in her chest, she tried to breathe through the panic threatening to render her useless.

The figures started moving faster. Heading right for her.

Had they spotted her?

A small whimper escaped even though she did her best to hold it inside. It had been stupid to think she stood a chance at escaping. Of course she didn't.

"Whitney!"

That voice. It was Blade's.

Snapping her gaze back to the three figures she could see approaching her, she tried to look closer, see if she recognized them. It was Blade's voice, so he had to be one of them. Maybe they really had been there all this time, trying to find her.

Hope soared until she heard Blade call out again.

"Behind you!"

Spinning around, she saw her worst nightmare coming to life right before her very eyes, and she was powerless to do anything to stop it from happening. Terry Richards was running toward her. There was a manic glint in his eyes that she could see even in the thin moonlight.

A glint she could easily read.

He knew the two of them were no longer alone, and he knew that if he was caught by Blade and his team, they'd torture him for information before killing him. He also had to know he was going to lose her. Even if he hadn't known before that she had joined up with the team Dr. Gardner was hunting, Blade had just called out her name so now Terry knew that the Delta Team guys knew who she was.

There was no way he was letting her go. He was definitely an "if I can't have her, no one can" kind of guy.

This was it.

This was how she was going to die.

Moments away from rescue.

Ironically enough, if she'd just stayed in that shipping container, she would have lived. The guys would have found her, they would have captured Terry Richards or at least killed him before he could take her out with him. In attempting to save herself, she'd signed her own death warrant.

"Touch her, and you die the most agonizingly painful and excruciating slow death I can give you, Richards," Blade's voice screamed.

She could hear everything she needed in it. His fury at the man who had abducted her, his fear for her, his panic at not being able to stop her death from happening, and his growing feelings for her.

At least if she was about to die, she'd gotten this, the love of another person, someone who didn't judge her for what she'd done, and just accepted her for her. She could take her final breath knowing that she mattered to someone and that she'd be missed.

# CHAPTER

## Twenty-Two

January 17th
1:01 A.M.

"He's going to take her down," Blade roared to no one in particular as he watched Terry Richards rush toward Whitney.

She'd heard him call her name, and she'd turned when he issued a warning, now she was standing there, frozen in fright and he could only imagine what was running through her mind.

He knew what was running through his.

He was too far away.

There was no way he could get to her in time if she went over the edge. He was fast, but he wasn't that fast. Nobody was. Well, nobody except Thunder.

Apparently, Thunder had the same thought he did because his friend suddenly took off at his superhuman speed. There was a chance he could reach her before she hit the ground.

Voodoo also dashed off after Thunder. His near-magic ability to heal might come in handy if the worst happened.

But Blade stopped.

Raised his weapon.

Aimed it at the lunatic preparing to take Whitney over the edge, crashing down onto the concrete below. Taking her to what could be her death. It was a survivable fall. Potentially. But with the weight of Terry Richards' much larger body following her down, likely landing on top of her, there was every chance she might not survive.

So he forced himself to slow down the beating of his heart, focused on his target, drew in a single, long, slow breath, then on the exhale, he pulled the trigger.

Blade heard the bullet whizz through the air, heard it connect with his target, heard the sound of breaking bone as it tore through the man's skull, decimating his brain, and ending his life. As much as he'd like to keep Terry Richards alive long enough to exact revenge for everything the man had put Whitney through, and to extract whatever intel they could to find Dr. Gardner, right now the man was a threat to Whitney's life, one that had to be eliminated quickly and efficiently.

The body went down, hitting the top of the shipping container with a satisfying thud, but Blade's joy and relief were short-lived, because Terry must have been close enough to Whitney to jostle her as his dead body dropped.

From where he was, Blade heard her gasp, watched in horror as her arms windmilled as she tried to regain her balance, but it was too late to stop gravity.

For a moment, it was like she hung in midair, not fully falling, but without steady footing on the shipping container.

But then she was falling.

Fast.

She screamed.

Or maybe he screamed.

Perhaps it was both of them.

He started running again, but he felt so far away from them, and when her body disappeared behind the rows of containers between his position and hers, Blade kept waiting for the sickening sound of her body hitting the concrete.

Instead, he heard Thunder's oomph as he must have gotten to her in time to catch her before she could slam into the ground.

"We got her, Blade." He heard Voodoo's reassuring words, but nothing was going to make him believe that she was alive and in one piece until he could get eyes on her.

Seconds later, he rounded the corner, just in time to watch Thunder kneel, setting Whitney down as Voodoo knelt on her other side. She wasn't moving, but he didn't think she could have injured herself in the fall, although there was, of course, a chance that she'd struck her head or another body part on the containers as she dropped. Just because he hadn't heard it didn't mean it hadn't happened, because he'd been too busy focusing on each beat of her heart to process anything else.

Skidding to his knees at her side, he dragged Whitney into his lap, cradling her like she was the most precious thing in the world.

Because she was.

"She's breathing right?" he asked as Voodoo pressed fingertips to her neck.

"You can hear her breath," his friend reminded him.

"No. I can't. What the hell?" The only thing Blade could hear right now was his own pulse rushing in his ears like a waterfall.

"You don't need to hear, all you need to do is feel," Voodoo said gently, reaching out to pick up his hand and place it on Whitney's chest right above her heart.

Where he could feel each steady beat.

Each bump against his palm calmed him a little more until his own breathing slowed, and his hearing returned. Then he could hear her measured breaths. Slow and even. She wasn't dead, and she wasn't breathing like she was injured. She'd just passed out. Her overloaded system was probably checking out as she plummeted toward the ground, likely with no idea that Thunder was there to catch her.

"Thank you," he said, voice rough as he looked up at Thunder, who had stood and was standing, weapon aimed, at attention, just in case there was another threat out there. If it hadn't been for his friend using his enhanced speed, Whitney would have hit the concrete. Could be dead right now instead of just unconscious.

"Course, man, she's family," Thunder said like it was no big deal, but it was a big deal.

The biggest.

"She injured?" he asked, shifting his gaze to Voodoo, whose hands were skimming across Whitney's too still body.

"Dehydrated, hypothermic, bruising, but she's going to be okay," Voodoo assured him, and as Blade let out a breath of relief, his fingertips brushing across petal-soft skin, it registered.

Whitney was half-naked.

All he'd been focused on when he first saw her and then spotted her abductor rushing toward her was the fact that she was in danger. Then all he'd cared about was whether he was still going to lose her, even though he'd eliminated the threat. But now he realized that she wasn't wearing a top, and he remembered what Dragon had smelled.

Sex.

With Whitney in his arms, he could see that bruises weren't the only thing covering her skin. There was dried semen all over her, and a roar rumbled through his chest, bursting out into the night like a living, breathing creature.

How dare Terry Richards put his hands on her.

If he could, he'd climb up there, bring the man back to life, and then kill him all over again. The kind of death he deserved this time around. In fact, he had half a mind to ask Voodoo if he could revive Richards, even though he was pretty sure his friend's amazing skills didn't go that far.

"Relax, B, you're scaring her," Voodoo said gently, empathy in his eyes as he rested one hand on Blade's shoulder, the other smoothed down Whitney's hair.

Blinking away as much of the rage as he could, he focused instead on his girl, who was whimpering, shifting in his hold, her eyelashes fluttering on her cheeks as she slowly swam back to consciousness.

"It's okay, darlin'," he crooned, forcing himself to relax because it was obvious Whitney was feeding off his emotions.

"Blade?" she whispered, eyes still closed, but her body drifted closer to his, curling in against his warmth.

"Right here, darlin'," he assured her.

"I-I'm scared."

"He's dead, darlin'. Can't hurt you again."

"S-scared this is a d-dream. That y-you're not r-real," she stammered, her voice catching, and a couple of tears leaked out, trailing down her temples.

"No dream, my sweet little genius. I'm right here. Terry Richards is dead. He's never going to touch you again. We're going to get you cleaned up, get some fluids in you, warm you up, and take you home."

"You came," she whispered.

"Nowhere on earth you could be that I wouldn't come after you, darlin'. So let that be a warning for you if you're planning on ditching me after we get you back home. Bound by blood."

"Bound by blood," she echoed, then slowly her eyelids lifted, obviously still worried that when she opened them, he wasn't going to be there. The relief in those wide blue eyes of hers when they met his gaze was something he would never forget.

Running his knuckles down her cheek, he then palmed it and leaned in, feathering his lips across hers. He'd come so close to losing her, yet she was here, alive, mostly unharmed, physically at least, although she was going to have some major trauma to work through on top of what she was already attempting to handle.

"Never letting you go again," he whispered against her lips, meaning it sincerely. She was his, she'd said she was, and he wasn't going to let her take it back.

"Okay," she agreed, snuggling into him, exhaustion weighing her down as she let him take all of her weight.

"I'm serious, darlin'," he warned her as he tucked her closer.

"I know."

"And you're really good with that?"

"Already told you that I was."

Chuckling, he shifted his hold on her as he stood, keeping her pressed against him, both to share his body warmth and to shield her half-naked body from the others. "Rest now, darlin', I'm here to take care of you."

There was no better feeling in the world than his girl acquiescing, allowing herself to drift off to sleep content in the knowledge that she was safe in his arms.

～

January 17th
    10:49 P.M.


"This isn't necessary," Whitney told Blade, even as she curled instinctively into him. It felt like the most natural thing in the world to turn to him to seek comfort, and in his arms already felt like the safest place to be.

Maybe she'd been a little clingier than she should have been these last several hours, but after spending over a day with Terry Richards, the wealth of emotions she'd experienced, the fear and terror, her determination to remember that Blade wouldn't abandon her, then him saving her life all over again, she couldn't seem to help it. At Blade's side was the only place where that storm of emotions stilled enough that she could breathe.

But she was worried about becoming a bother. A burden.

Would he grow tired of her if she didn't find a way to pull it together quickly?

Blade had lived through three years of captivity. Held in a bullet-proof glass cage, experimented on, forced to kill who he was told when he was told to do it, she hadn't even been kept by Terry Richards for two days, and she felt like she was handling things worse than he had.

"Absolutely is, darlin'," Blade returned, touching a kiss to her temple.

The kiss made her heart melt, even as her anxiety grew and tears seeped out, rolling down her cheeks in sad little trails. She didn't want to cry again, it felt like she'd been doing it all day when she wasn't sleeping, but she couldn't seem to stop.

"Darlin," Blade said, his voice pained, like if he could he would take her suffering and make it his own, but that wasn't what she wanted. He had more than enough of his own to shoulder.

"Sorry," she hiccuped, doing her best to rein in her emotions.

"Don't be sorry, darlin'. It's normal to be a mess after being abducted and assaulted, you have to know that in that big, beautiful brain of yours."

"I'll do better," she promised. Losing Blade wasn't an option.

Losing the rest of Delta Team wasn't either. If she had to pretend to be okay, she'd find a way to do it. There wasn't any other choice.

"No one expects you to."

"I expect me to."

Kicking open the door to his room, he carried her inside and set her down on the bed. Without speaking another word, he slipped off the fuzzy slippers she'd been wearing, then lifted her enough to tug her leggings down over her hips, pulling them down her legs. Taking her hands as though she was a child, he slipped her arms out of the sleeves of her sweater and then pulled it over her head, leaving her in just her panties. Taking her clothes, he carried them into his bathroom, and she assumed set them in the hamper before returning, minus his own clothes, tucking her under the covers, and sliding in beside her.

"Your arms." She gasped when she saw the torn and bloody skin on his forearms. Had he been hurt and not told her? "What happened?"

"It's nothing," he said, brushing off her concerns as he climbed into bed beside her and settled her against him.

"It's not. Tell me."

He sighed, and she was sure he was going to refuse to answer, but then his hand began to stroke down the length of her spine. "Couldn't handle losing you, darlin'."

"You did this to yourself?" Trailing a fingertip along the smooth skin along the edge of the torn skin, her heart ached at the thought.

Blade shrugged. "Don't want to live without you, darlin'."

"I don't want to live without you either," she told him, pressing closer, determined to make sure her trauma didn't cost her this man.

"Your expectations for yourself are too high, darlin'," he whispered as though he knew exactly where her thoughts had headed.

"They're not," she argued. "He only had me for a day. I should be able to hold it together." Only she couldn't, and proof of that was that her words ended on a choked sob.

Grabbing her under the armpits, Blade hauled her over so she was draped across him, her knees on either side of his thighs, his huge length, contained only by a pair of boxers, nestled against her center. Maybe it should have terrified her, given what Terry had done to her, but it didn't. The opposite, in fact. It reassured her, made her feel safe, because

Blade had only given her pleasure, and he'd saved her from giving Terry Richards her first sexual experiences.

"It wasn't one day, darlin'. You've been held captive for more than half of your life. Dr. Gardner had me and my team for three years, and it messed us up. All of us. We all have nightmares about it, all struggle with anger. It's why we've been pushing so hard for revenge. He had you four times as long as he had us. Four times, darlin'. I don't think you've had any time yet to even begin to process the trauma you endured. There is no timeline to recover from trauma. I think deep down you know that."

Those dark eyes of his seemed to see right down deep into her soul, and more tears welled in her eyes as she was unable to break away from the hold they seemed to have on her.

"I'm scared," she whispered.

"Of what?" When she hesitated, the hands on her hips tightened. "Need you to be honest with me here, darlin'. It's the only way we can get you the help you need to begin healing."

"That if I don't pull it together quickly enough, you're going to get tired of me because you're so strong and I'm so ... not."

A growl rumbled through the chest her hands were planted against, and then Blade's hands were framing her face, and his lips crushed against hers, his tongue demanding entrance. Yielding to the kiss, Whitney let thought fly from her mind and instead focused only on the feel of Blade's lips, his tongue, the fierce way he kissed her. So full of possession, and even though she'd basically been owned for over half her life, this ownership didn't feel stifling, it felt freeing.

"Do you honestly think most people could survive twelve years of being held prisoner? Spent some of their childhood, their entire adolescence, and into adulthood under someone else's rule, and still have the ability to love and care about other people? Even after what I did to you." Blade paused, drew in a deep, somewhat shaky breath, as he ran a finger along the healing wounds on her wrists. "You still gave me and my team everything you had to help us. You trusted me with your body, and you didn't give up on the knowledge that I would come for you."

"I don't know how to be a real person," she admitted. "I don't know how to get over what he did. I don't know how to live freely. I don't know how to believe that I'm not responsible for so many deaths when I am the one who originally created the drug."

With another growl, Blade reclaimed his grip on her hips and spun her around, moving her body like it was nothing. Then his mouth was on her back, his lips and tongue worshiping every single mark branded into her skin.

Tears flowed freely, and this time Whitney didn't allow them to make her feel guilty or weak. Her tears were a real expression of all the years of pent-up pain that had been festering inside her.

"Make me come, Blade, please," she whispered. After what had been done to her in that shipping container she probably should be terrified of the idea of anything to do with sex, but it was different with Blade. She needed him to cover her in his semen, wipe away the feel of that other man's emissions on her skin.

Expecting him to protest, or at least confirm if she was sure, Blade just ripped her panties right off her body, leaving stinging marks behind on her skin. Whitney relished them, they made her feel alive and gave her an outlet for her mixed-up feelings.

He pushed inside her with a single thrust, and again she clung to the burning pain as her body stretched to accommodate him, letting it remind her that she was alive, in charge of her own destiny, and that she was choosing this.

Never again would anyone else control her life.

Fingers found her bud, playing with it, pushing her toward an orgasm. Blade's thrusts became faster, harder, and she met him thrust for thrust. Pleasure built inside her, growing too big to contain, and then it burst into a fiery ball of white-hot liquid pleasure that consumed her.

Then she felt spurts of warmth squirt across her back and knew that even without her saying it out loud, Blade had somehow known that she needed to feel *his* semen on her skin, and he'd chosen to put it on the marks that covered her back, a physical symbol of everything she'd suffered.

"Mine now, darlin', not his," he said, his breath hot against her skin as he nuzzled her neck. "You have all the time in the world to find out who you are, who you want to be, what you want to do with the rest of your life. You have a family now, people who will have your back, who will go to the ends of the earth for you. And you have me. I might not ever be good enough for you, but I will give you every single piece of myself, dedicate my life to making you smile."

Giving a growl of her own, it sounded like a kitten's in comparison to Blade's, she scrambled around to face him again. "Don't say that again. The way we met can never be erased, but everything since then, you've been exactly what I didn't even hope to want. Everything I needed. You're mine and I'm yours. Together we can both find the peace that has eluded us for so long. Bound by blood," she reminded him as she found his hand and pressed her palm to his.

There was tenderness on Blade's face as he guided her down to kiss her, and Whitney allowed herself to free-fall into the kiss, knowing that Blade would always be there to catch her, no matter what.

# CHAPTER
## Twenty-Three

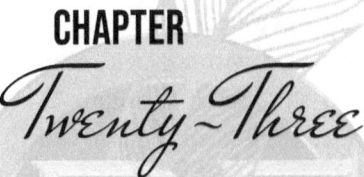

January 18<sup>th</sup>
2:45 P.M.

"Did you know that a group of butterflies is called a kaleidoscope?" Whitney asked.

There was excitement in her voice as she used one of her self-soothing techniques to help her keep her emotions under control after a rough night of nightmares, and a panic attack earlier this morning when she hadn't heard one of the guys come up behind her in the kitchen.

"Nope, didn't know that one, darlin'," Blade replied, happy to see a little color in her cheeks, and the haunted look in her eyes pushed to the background. At least for now. But he knew that Whitney had a long road ahead of her as she rebuilt her life and figured out what it would look like.

He had a lot to work through himself. Blade was trying his best to learn to ignore the sounds he heard so clearly. What he wanted for his future with Whitney was to focus on feelings, not on using his enhanced skill as a crutch for everything, and an excuse to shut himself away from the others to at least attempt to get some peace and quiet.

"And did you know that a group of cats is called a clowder?"

"Didn't know that one either," he told her as they walked into the kitchen, where the other two couples were sitting around the table drinking coffee and eating homemade cupcakes with cookie dough frosting that Whitney had made with Cassandra earlier.

"What's a group of frogs called?" Rose asked.

"An army," Whitney said with a giggle, and it felt so wonderful to hear her laugh after all she'd been through. "Maybe we should start calling you guys frogs, cos you're a little army. Or Navy, I guess. Aren't SEALs called frogmen?"

"Think that's funny, do you, darlin'?" he asked, tugging on the end of her ponytail as he pulled out a chair, sat down in it, and tugged her into his lap.

"Yep," she agreed, shooting him a warm smile.

The bruises on her skin were darker today, and the shadows in her eyes, while receded a little, were still present. When they got home yesterday afternoon, he'd helped her wash up properly in the bath, although he'd cleaned her up in the car on the way to the airport. He knew from the way she constantly rubbed at her chest and face, that she still felt the phantom feel of Terry Richards' semen on her skin.

But she was doing the best she could, and that was all he could ask of her.

Honestly, he was so proud of her, he was practically bursting with pride.

"What's a group of ladybugs called?" Steel asked, obviously noting that defaulting to random facts was helping Whitney remain calm and in control and playing along, something for which Blade was infinitely grateful. It helped Whitney to know she didn't just have him, but also his entire team as part of her new family.

"A loveliness," she said with another giggle.

"Aww." Rose smiled, snuggling into Steel's embrace. "I'm glad you came up with the nickname ladybug for me, even if it was annoying at first."

"Better than your nickname for me." Steel smirked. "Mr. Bedroom Man doesn't have quite the same ring to it."

Rose shrugged. "Then maybe don't break into people's bedrooms in the middle of the night to kidnap them if you don't want to wind up with a stupid nickname," she sassed, making them all laugh, and Steel grabbed her chin and took her mouth in a fiery kiss.

"And a bunny?" Cassandra asked.

"Well, there are a few, like all of these, but my favorite one is a fluffle," Whitney replied.

"Aww, adorable," Cassandra cooed.

"I am not getting you an entire fluffle of stuffed bunnies to keep in our room." Dragon huffed, although Blade was pretty sure the man would do anything, including fill his room with stuffed bunnies if it made Cassandra happy.

Whitney giggled again. "Did you know there are several names for a group of dragons?" she asked, and when they all shook their heads, she continued. "Flight is one, that's used for a group of flying dragons. Then weyr is used for a group of non-airborne dragons. Clutch for hatchling dragons, and brood for young dragons with their parents. A wing is three to six adult dragons and their riders, and then there's thunder for a group of large dragons flying."

"What's a thunder?" Thunder asked as he strolled into the room, Voodoo and Lion trailing after him. "Other than the obvious thunder and lightning."

"It's a group of large flying dragons," Whitney replied.

"There seems to be an awful lot of names for an animal that doesn't even exist," Blade said to Whitney as he reached for a cupcake, pulled off the paper, and pressed it into her hand.

"Dragons exist," Cassandra contradicted, tilting her head up to touch a kiss to Dragon's jaw.

"One of them, maybe," Blade agreed.

"Or more than one, one day in the future," Cassandra said, and Dragon's eyes widened in shock, before softening as they moved from her face to her stomach.

"One day," Dragon agreed.

"One day we might have a whole gathering of tadpoles," Steel added.

"A school," Whitney corrected.

"Sorry to break up what seems to be a little school lesson," Voodoo teased as he took a seat at the table and grabbed a cupcake. "But we heard from Prey."

"Yeah?" Steel asked, his expression immediately snapping into business mode.

"Heard from Prey?" Whitney asked uncertainly, looking up at him for more information.

She'd been unconscious again by the time they got back in the car to drive to the airfield, and she'd been clingy and emotional on the flight home, so none of them had updated her on anything. This morning, Blade had been aiming for normalcy, or at least figuring out what their normal was going to look like going forward, rather than catching her up on everything.

Not that he had any problem sharing intel with her. She was an equal part of this now, in this fight together with him and his team, Rose, Cassandra, and Prey.

"We found two links to Terry Richards and some of the men who I killed in the forest. One was to a trucking company that's trafficking drugs. We checked them out, but you weren't there. We were already heading to the shipping yard when your tracker came online. Before that, we didn't know where you were. Richards must have had a jammer, anticipating you might have tagged yourself. We lost you that day before we even got to the produce store."

Blade had to pause to take a breath. Whitney's hand smoothed up and down his arm before she tangled their fingers together, pressing her cut palm against his. The reminder of their promise grounded him.

"Before taking you to the docks, he must have found and removed all the other trackers, but also kept the jammer on. When you escaped and ran, you must have moved outside the circle it could block, and that's when you popped up. We were about thirty minutes out by that point."

"So you were coming anyway. If I hadn't run, you might have been able to take Terry Richards alive," Whitney whispered, sounding like she was ridiculing herself.

"Never doubt your decision to fight to live, darlin'," he told her. That she had fought for her freedom and escaped made him so proud.

"No certainty it would have changed anything anyway," Lion told her. "Even if we'd eventually found you in the shipping container, we might have had to kill Richards to save you."

"Saving you was always number one," Blade assured Whitney. "When we got there, we split up. We spotted you first, but the others found the shipping container. Richards had left his phone behind when he chased you. We handed it off to Prey's Cyber Team because it was locked, and they'd have a better chance at accessing the data on it." Blade turned to Thunder, Voodoo, and Lion now. They'd come into the room with intel the rest of them didn't have. "I take it they found something."

"Message and call logs confirm that Terry Richards was corresponding with someone during the time he had Whitney about the setup of a new lab," Thunder explained.

"He left for a while," Whitney piped up. "Said he had something important he couldn't avoid, and that when he came back, we were going to play." When she shuddered, Blade tightened his hold on her, showing her with his body that she was safe now, protected, and no one would ever hurt her again.

"That's likely where he went," Lion said. "As head of security, he had to make sure the new lab was secure. We were in luck. The GPS in his phone tracked where he went."

"So we have the location of this new lab?" Steel asked.

"We do," Voodoo replied with a grin.

"Dr. Gardner usually worked out of the main lab, but since that's destroyed, he might be working out of the mobile lab," Whitney told them.

"I think it's time we go hunting," Blade said with renewed vigor. Now he had a whole new reason to want the scientist who had destroyed his life to suffer and die, and she was sitting in his lap.

For Whitney, for him and his team, for Rose, for each mark on Whitney's back that represented a person who hadn't survived Dr. Gardner's experimental drugs, the man deserved every bit and more of what was coming to him, and they might just have taken a step closer to making their revenge a reality.

. . .

**Voodoo will risk everything to save the only other living recipient of the drug that changed him and his teammates in the fourth book in the action packed and emotionally charged Prey Security: Delta Team series!**

Cunning Revenge (Prey Security: Delta Team #4)

# Also by Jane Blythe

Detective Parker Bell Series

A SECRET TO THE GRAVE

WINTER WONDERLAND

DEAD OR ALIVE

LITTLE GIRL LOST

FORGOTTEN

Count to Ten Series

ONE

TWO

THREE

FOUR

FIVE

SIX

BURNING SECRETS

SEVEN

EIGHT

NINE

TEN

Broken Gems Series

CRACKED SAPPHIRE

CRUSHED RUBY

FRACTURED DIAMOND

SHATTERED AMETHYST

SPLINTERED EMERALD

SALVAGING MARIGOLD

River's End Rescues Series

SOME SAVIORS CAN BREAK YOU

SOME REGRETS ARE FOREVER

SOME FEARS CAN CONTROL YOU

SOME LIES WILL HAUNT YOU

SOME QUESTIONS HAVE NO ANSWERS

SOME TRUTH CAN BE DISTORTED

SOME TRUST CAN BE REBUILT

SOME MISTAKES ARE UNFORGIVABLE

Candella Sisters' Heroes Series

LITTLE DOLLS

LITTLE HEARTS

LITTLE BALLERINA

Storybook Murders Series

NURSERY RHYME KILLER

FAIRYTALE KILLER

FABLE KILLER

Saving SEALs Series

SAVING RYDER

SAVING ERIC

SAVING OWEN

SAVING LOGAN

SAVING GRAYSON

SAVING CHARLIE

Prey Security Series

PROTECTING EAGLE

PROTECTING RAVEN

PROTECTING FALCON

PROTECTING SPARROW

PROTECTING HAWK

PROTECTING DOVE

Prey Security: Alpha Team Series

DEADLY RISK

LETHAL RISK

EXTREME RISK

FATAL RISK

COVERT RISK

SAVAGE RISK

Prey Security: Artemis Team Series

IVORY'S FIGHT

PEARL'S FIGHT

LACEY'S FIGHT

OPAL'S FIGHT


Prey Security: Bravo Team Series


VICIOUS SCARS

RUTHLESS SCARS

BRUTAL SCARS

CRUEL SCARS

BURIED SCARS

WICKED SCARS


Prey Security: Athena Team Series

FIGHTING FOR SCARLETT

FIGHTING FOR LUCY

FIGHTING FOR CASSIDY

FIGHTING FOR ELLA

Prey Security: Charlie Team Series


DECEPTIVE LIES

SHADOWED LIES

TACTICAL LIES

VENGEFUL LIES

CORRUPTED LIES

TRAITOROUS LIES


Prey Security: Cyber Team Series

RESCUING NATHANIEL

RESCUING TOBIAS

RESCUING MICAH

RESCUING JOSIAH

Prey Security: Delta Team Series

PERFECT REVENGE

FATEFUL REVENGE

SINFUL REVENGE

CUNNING REVENGE

Christmas Romantic Suspense Series

THE DIAMOND STAR

CHRISTMAS HOSTAGE

CHRISTMAS CAPTIVE

CHRISTMAS VICTIM

YULETIDE PROTECTOR

YULETIDE GUARD

YULETIDE HERO

HOLIDAY GRIEF

HOLIDAY LOSS

HOLIDAY SORROW

Conquering Fear Series (Co-written with Amanda Siegrist)

DROWNING IN YOU

OUT OF THE DARKNESS

CLOSING IN

# About the Author

USA Today bestselling author Jane Blythe writes action-packed romantic suspense and military romance featuring protective heroes and heroines who are survivors. One of Jane's most popular series includes Prey Security, part of Susan Stoker's OPERATION ALPHA world! Writing in that world alongside authors such as Janie Crouch and Riley Edwards has been a blast, and she looks forward to bringing more books to this genre, both within and outside of Stoker's world. When Jane isn't binge-reading she's counting down to Christmas and adding to her 200+ teddy bear collection!

To connect and keep up to date please visit any of the following

www.ingramcontent.com/pod-product-compliance
Lightning Source LLC
Chambersburg PA
CBHW050419260626

47156CB00003B/1075